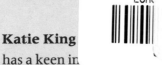

Katie King [London] [. She]
has a keen in[terest] [novel]
was inspired by a period spent living in south-east London.
The Evacuee War is the third in the Evacuee series.

Also by Katie King

The Evacuee Summer
The Evacuee Christmas

The Evacuee War

Katie King

ONE PLACE. MANY STORIES

HQ
An imprint of HarperCollins*Publishers* Ltd
1 London Bridge Street
London SE1 9GF

www.harpercollins.co.uk

HarperCollins*Publishers*
1st Floor, Watermarque Building, Ringsend Road
Dublin 4, Ireland

This paperback edition 2021

1
First published in Great Britain by
HQ, an imprint of HarperCollins*Publishers* Ltd 2021

ISBN: 9780008257606

MIX
Paper from
responsible sources
FSC™ C007454

This book is produced from independently certified FSC™ paper
to ensure responsible forest management.

For more information visit: www.harpercollins.co.uk/green

This book is set in 10.4/15.5 pt. Meridien by Type-it AS, Norway

Printed and bound in Great Britain by
CPI Group (UK) Ltd, Croydon, CR0 4YY

For Josie and Louis, always

Chapter One

Husbands were a lottery, thought a grumpy Peggy quite early in the morning. Hers – Bill – had seemed a very good one for quite a few years. Then, suddenly, he wasn't.

Of course it was easy to blame wartime, and rationing, and horrible news in the papers for Bill's disgraceful behaviour.

But Peggy wasn't having any of that.

She still could hardly believe that it had only taken a few short months of Bill being on his own at a military training camp near the East coast, where he worked as instructor, for him to forget his wedding vows.

While he was busy impregnating a NAAFI worker called Maureen, Peggy was heavily pregnant with their own much longed-for baby, Holly – a baby they'd had to wait a very long time for. At the same time Peggy had been trying, and not always succeeding, in getting used to new surroundings after being evacuated.

It had felt very strange leaving the familiar squashed-together terraces of the dark brick two-up two-downs in Bermondsey, with the oily River Thames and the busy docks only a stone's throw away, and moving to the more sedate and genteel Harrogate, where they were, at first, awed by the spacious and very comfy rectory Tall Trees, with its solid stone walls and huge windows and lofty rooms.

For it was there that she and her ten-year-old twin nephew and niece, Jessie and Connie, had been billeted within days of war being declared in September 1939. Peggy had accompanied the twins and their class on the train northwards along with her other evacuated teacher colleagues, although once in Harrogate she had decided to find something else to do as she sat out the duration.

When Peggy went into labour a few months later it had been touch and go for a while, scaring everyone. But Peggy dug deep and, to the relief of all, baby Holly had been safely delivered on Christmas Eve, and since then Peggy had done the very best she could to carve out a new life for herself and her daughter.

A life that no longer involved Bill Delbert, or at least as much as that was feasible.

The problem was that Bill didn't seem to want to take on board that *everything* had changed between him and his wife in the year since war had been declared with Germany, and that as far as Peggy was concerned, their marriage was kaput. There'd been begging telephone calls and letters, but Peggy was impervious to his silky words she'd once found seductive.

Of course, the months since Holly's arrival had proved to be a rollercoaster of emotions for Peggy, although the handsome doctor, James, who'd saved her and Holly's lives as the snow fell when Peggy went into unexpected labour, had certainly eased a little of the pain Bill's behaviour had caused.

So now it was a bitter pill to swallow that, following many

weeks of careful circling – neither sure if their obvious attraction was mutual and each too scared to lay their cards on the table – on the very night that Peggy and James shared their first proper kiss months after they met, Bill had done his very best to spoil the magic moment.

And he had bloody well succeeded!

Drunk and spoiling for a fight, even though he was supposed to be many miles away, Bill chose *that* moment to try and reclaim Peggy as his own.

What cheek. And what disastrous timing.

Peggy shuddered at the memory from the previous night of the sound of her husband's boots pounding across the back yard to the rectory where Peggy and Holly and the twins lived with the kindly rector Roger and his wife Mabel.

But although this was difficult to think about, Bill and the fight didn't have the power to diminish the exquisite sensation of the kiss and its lingering memory. Peggy couldn't resist tracing a finger along her lips to help her relive the moment.

Then she recalled how Bill's clothes were ragged and filthy, and he stank of alcohol; he had clearly been dosing himself with Dutch courage. Peggy felt ashamed at the very sight of him, shame that bubbled to fury as Bill turned on James. And then – even worse – James had given Bill as good as he got as the pair tussled each other to the ground, with Peggy screaming at them to stop, all too aware that James's hands mustn't be hurt. These were hands that saved people's *lives*, Peggy thought in distress and fury as she heard the dull pounding of fist hitting flesh, and saw a splatter of blood spraying upwards. The snarl on James's face told her that although he'd never met this man, he knew exactly who he was, and he wasn't going to step aside in the face of Bill's unwarranted aggression.

Poor Milburn, the chubby chestnut pony in the stall right beside the fight, had been so panicked as the men grunted with the effort of landing blows on each other, their feet flailing noisily against the stable door, that somehow the little gelding had wriggled over the top of his half-door, and careened out to the road, causing a traffic accident. Now, the following morning, Milburn was still bleeding from his wounds and clearly in shock, a feeling that Peggy felt she shared.

The police had carted Bill away as was only to be expected.

James meanwhile had shot Peggy a daggered look she hoped never to see again. It shouted all too clearly that whatever had been on the cusp of happening between them was now Very Much Over.

Wife of a violent drunkard and mother of his child. James's furrowed brow, unblinking gaze and total silence, insisted to Peggy as he stalked out of the yard that as far he was concerned, she simply wasn't worth the trouble. Peggy had always accepted that, even in a perfect world, James's job running a temporary recuperation hospital in Harrogate for wounded servicemen, meant he had other priorities brought about by the war effort that must be put before her; that was what saving lives meant, and it was one of the reasons she so admired the young doctor. But now he was washing his hands of her.

She'd felt in the past that as mother of Holly, she was never going to be a good option for a man like James, although then events had conspired to make her doubt this assumption.

4

But she had been right all along, Peggy thought sadly, and Bill's behaviour had just driven that point home to James sooner rather than later.

It was heartbreaking. Absolutely heartbreaking.

And, now, just when Peggy didn't think she could feel any worse, it turned out that Bill, still at the police station, had demanded that he see Peggy and Holly.

Peggy could have screamed in temper. She felt in a real bind. The sheer neck of her husband!

Once more she raised a hand to her lips, remembering the softness of James's single kiss. A kiss that would never be repeated. There was a part of her that wanted to make Bill pay for taking that away from her.

Right at that moment, Peggy hated Bill with a passion, an absolute passion.

And then, with a deep sigh, she gathered her thoughts together and told herself that she must do the right thing. She didn't want to, but if she didn't, then she would feel worse in all likelihood. Peggy couldn't ignore the fact that, like it or not, Bill was Holly's father and in wartime when life and death lived side by side, did she really have the right to deny him a few minutes with his daughter?

Bill was a wretched sight when he shuffled into the interview room at the police station where Peggy and Holly were waiting, and while she hadn't expected him to be the man she had fallen for, the decidedly forlorn sight of him quite took Peggy aback.

He had two black eyes, and his knuckles were split and weeping, although some of the smaller grazes looked to have scabbed over already. The skin all over his face looked dry and greyish, with the lines around his mouth and nose running very deep, while the flesh on his neck was wrinkled and as if it belonged to a much older man.

He kept cupping his jaw in his hand as he gingerly moved his chin from side to side, and Peggy fancied she could hear a quiet clicking noise as he did this. She guessed that at least one, if not more of James's thumps had really hit home when he had socked Bill on the chin, and perhaps Bill's jaw had been a whisker away from dislocation.

Bill's shirt was frayed and ripped, and there was a hole in one knee of his trousers. His shoes were dusty and scuffed, and the raggedy laces were knotted and unevenly frayed at the ends, rather than tied in the neat bows that Peggy remembered the once dapper Bill favouring before the war.

He appeared thoroughly unkempt, almost like a homeless man without two pennies to rub together. Perhaps worst of all was that he looked demeaned and shamed to his very bones and a far cry from the smartly suited and booted man that Peggy had been proud to walk down the aisle towards almost a decade earlier.

While she wanted him to feel bad about his behaviour since her evacuation from Bermondsey, the depressing sight before her now looked humiliating for Bill, and this was a step too far for Peggy to be comfortable with.

The detestation she'd felt for him not long before dwindled to something worse: pity.

Bill shuffled tentatively across the room and then took a while to sit down, and to judge by the careful way he lowered himself onto the wooden seat, Peggy assumed that her husband had tender bruises all over his body she couldn't see.

'I'll be right outside, madam, and so just you call me if you need to and I'll be there in a jiffy.' The policeman who'd escorted Bill to her spoke in a reassuring manner as he left the room, as if Bill were a dangerous criminal.

Peggy wasn't remotely scared at the thought of her and Holly being left alone with Bill – it was clear that all her husband's fight of the previous evening had evaporated, along with his drunkenness – but she could see that plenty of wives would be brimming with trepidation in her position and so she was grateful for the bobby's words as she knew that not all men in the policeman's position would have been so considerate of making her feel safe.

A chastened Bill ignored the retreating policeman, and instead he reached for Peggy's hand, which she quickly snatched out of his reach.

'I didn't think you'd come, Peg, to be honest,' he said.

'I so nearly didn't,' Peggy replied. 'But you put me in an impossible situation, Bill, as then I reminded myself that Holly is your daughter, and that if the worst were to happen and that you were to die at Jerry's hands, I knew I couldn't live with myself if I'd deprived my daughter of a final meeting with her father. It's not *her* fault you're a total dead loss, is it?'

Bill didn't say anything, and Peggy watched him as he looked sadly down at Holly. Holly had taken two steps that morning – her very first steps, no less! – but Peggy didn't tell Bill that. Instead she let the silence swirl between them, uncomfortable and loaded with angst.

Bill smelled still, an unpleasant mixture of sweat, grubby clothing and too much alcohol the previous day, and as Peggy shuffled her bottom back a little in the chair to bring some more space between them, she tried not to recoil too obviously. She didn't want to make the meeting more awkward between them than it already was.

Holly was sitting on Peggy's lap, and the puzzled frown on the little girl's face as she beheld her father and then swung her head around to glance up at her mother said it all.

Holly very obviously had no idea who Bill was, and the fact that she didn't much like what she could see before her was all too evident in her quizzical and clearly dumbfounded expression, and the way she angled her little body away from his.

Peggy could tell by the downcast expression in Bill's eyes that he'd seen this too and had understood his daughter wasn't impressed with the man in front of her.

'May I hold her?' he said to Peggy all the same.

It wasn't going to help anyone if Holly started to scream the place down, which Peggy thought would be the likely outcome if she handed Holly across to him.

'Let her get a bit more used to you, Bill,' she said in what she hoped was a non-committal way.

They both looked at Holly again.

'Peg, I'm sorry. Sorry about it *all*,' Bill muttered after a while. He looked earnest, and so contrite that Peggy believed him. His voice was stronger as he continued, 'I went too far last night, I understand that, my chicken, and I'll always have to live with what a blighter I was. You and I both know that, but my blood boiled when I saw you and *that* man standing so close to you, when you were looking so pretty and as if you were my true love.'

Peggy frowned to let Bill know this was a sensitive subject that she didn't want to discuss further, and the silly

8

sentimentality he was spouting absolutely wasn't the way to win her over. On top of that she had never liked it when he'd called her chicken, and it irritated her that he'd forgotten this, as she thought that at that moment he was genuinely too remorseful to be trying to rile her.

Bill took the hint that there were some areas he shouldn't stray into, and so he changed the subject slightly, saying in a confessional tone, 'It's obvious I've not been a good husband, nor a good father to our little Holly. She deserves better, and so do you. I should never have went with Maureen. Everything is my fault.'

Peggy had to try very hard not to snort in derision at the sound of Maureen's name.

Bill didn't notice, and instead he tried another smile towards his daughter, who promptly gave a whine and hid her face against Peggy's chest, as Peggy realised that she herself felt rather surprised at Bill's honesty.

He stared at his daughter shrinking away from him, and then added so quietly that Peggy had to strain to hear him, 'She does you proud though, Peg.'

Peggy knew the 'she' was referring to their daughter.

'Holly doesn't recognise you, Bill. She has no idea who you are, and so you mustn't hold that against her. I'm sure you know this already, but it bears saying again, and so just remember that from Holly's point of view you are a stranger. Still, putting last night aside for the moment, I suppose that a lot of fathers are finding the same when they see their children these days. It's not the kiddies' fault their fathers can't – or won't – be with them. Any of the kiddies in your case ...' Peggy said. She knew that was a cheap shot, but it felt good all the same.

She saw a brief flash of something that could be ire flare in Bill's eyes as he took Peggy's words for the criticism they were meant to be in view of his childbearing peccadillo, but then her husband seemed to deflate somehow, his body folding in on itself, and Peggy could see that any final vestige of temper he might have had left in him had briefly blazed and, just as quickly, dissipated.

There was a moment of stillness and quiet in the depressing room that had already smelled faintly of a men's lavatory even before Bill's malodourous arrival, as Peggy cast around for something to say to her husband about Holly that wouldn't be contentious.

This was harder than she expected, and eventually she settled for, 'Holly took her first steps this morning.'

To Peggy's ears, her voice sounded tight, and she recognised that behind her words pulsated the overwhelming desire to say something further that would be cross and hurtful to Bill.

She wanted so very much to remind him about how he'd not thought of her and Holly when he'd made Maureen pregnant, and how his infidelity had wounded her right down to her very quick. And, she thought, even when his worst had been done, how hideous it was that he'd gone out of his way to rob her of a chance of happiness with James, who perhaps in time could have made the little girl a wonderful father. A father who would have been kind and considerate … and faithful.

But Peggy found that she couldn't bring herself to speak in such a spiteful manner, not with Holly perched on her knee.

Bill seemed to understand some of the struggle Peggy was having within herself and although he sighed in a pained manner, he didn't try to defend himself further, even though

Peggy noted his eyes were shiny with tears as he regarded Holly.

After a while he waved a grimy finger at her but curled it back into his palm once more when his daughter shrank even further away from him, pressing her body more tightly against her mother's.

It was abundantly clear to all three of them that Holly didn't want to be any closer to this strange man.

Then, somehow, Peggy found to her surprise that she felt sorry for Bill, a slightly different feeling than the pity of her first sight of him a few minutes previously.

He hadn't much going for him, she realised, what with being the father of two children but not really being in the life of either of them. Or at least that was her assumption about him and Maureen, for if it were otherwise, what was he doing in Harrogate and why had he made such a fuss about her and James?

Whatever Bill's precise romantic situation was – and actually Peggy realised that now she had cast aside her emotional ties to her husband, she didn't much care what it was – he had well and truly made a hash of his life in the year since they had all left Bermondsey in September 1939. Peggy didn't think anyone would deny that.

'Bill, what is it exactly that you want to happen?' Peggy asked, and she realised then that she was actually quite interested in what he had to say on this.

'I want you an' me an' Holly to be happy together – a family like we always wanted,' Bill answered quickly and unequivocally.

Peggy sighed. Oh dear. She knew he wouldn't like her

reiterating to him what he already knew deep down, she was sure, to be the case. She had – very forcibly – told him all of this before, months ago when it had all first come out about Maureen expecting his baby, but she felt that she had to say it to him again right away so there could be no chance of muddled expectations between them.

'Look, Bill, a lot has happened in the past year. And the very instant you climbed into that other woman's bed was the moment *our* family life and promises to each other ended, and you made your wish of us all being together quite impossible. You do understand that, don't you?' said Peggy, and she backed up her words with a fierce look on her face.

There was a pause in the conversation when it looked as if Bill was struggling with his own inner conflict, but then, under the tough scrutiny of Peggy's unflinching gaze, at last he nodded and so Peggy took it that he knew what she was saying and wasn't going to try to insist that she was wrong or that she had made a mistake.

Still, Peggy drove her point home. 'Look, I suspect that you don't quite love Maureen and you never wanted to be with her long-term, but it was more a case that she was there and you were there and, well, we all know the rest. But it's 1940 now, and I'm not the woman I was a year ago. I can't forgive you, and that just isn't going to change for me, Bill. Ever. Since Holly has been born I've had sole responsibility for her, and so to go on doing that won't be a problem for me. As I've told you already, I want a divorce, and it's making me cross that you refuse to acknowledge what *I* want, or what is the best thing for Holly, when for you it's only about what *you* want. And what I want is – I'll say it again – a proper divorce, and a final formal ending of our marriage, as our solemn vows to one another have turned out to be worth less than the paper they are written on as far as you are concerned, and I can't live with that.

'I know it's unusual and probably everyone will advise me against this, thinking that to be a divorcee is going to leave me full of shame and bitterness. I don't see it like that though, as for me the shame and bitterness would lie in admitting you back into our family again. And so, although undoubtedly some people will look down on me, I can live with that. Holly and I need a proper and unequivocal end to your and my relationship – it really will be better for us all, and your various children.

'And for your information, nothing has happened with James beyond what you saw, but deep in my heart I had already given up on the idea of myself as the faithful wife to *you*; the spectre of Maureen and her pregnancy well and truly put paid to that long ago. I think we all need a clean start from here – me and Holly, and you – and frankly I just don't want to be associated in any way with you from now on. And I hope in time you will understand the value of what I'm saying.'

Bill scuffled his feet around on the floor as he sunk down in his chair, looking most unhappy as he dragged a filthy hand through his hair that Peggy could now see was thinning on top, with a mumble of 'You're wrong, Peg, very wrong, I promise'.

Peggy ignored this as she glanced with deliberate obviousness at Holly, who was now waving her rattle in the air.

Then Bill pulled himself together and sat up straighter as Peggy heard him swallow down a mumble of 'over my dead body, you and that man, there'll be no divorce while I have breath left in my body'.

She sighed and then very firmly but in a quiet voice said, 'Just listen to yourself, Bill! I want you to understand a divorce is going to happen sooner or later, whether you agree to it or not – make no mistake about that. I'm sure you can understand all the reasons from my point of view why that has to be. But in turn I promise you that I wouldn't ever keep you from seeing Holly, you do know that, don't you? You are her father, and she is your daughter.'

She wasn't finished giving Bill things to think about that she knew he would feel most uncomfortable about. 'And, while we're on the subject, I think Holly and Maureen's child should know about each other, considering they will be related to each other, after all. I expect Holly, therefore, to find you a good father to her, *and* to this other child when he or she arrives. I don't want my daughter growing up knowing her father isn't a good man who deserves her respect and love, and that he has neglected one of his offspring. Nobody benefits by that, and I don't ever want Holly for a moment to think that she might not be worthy of being a princess in the eyes of whoever falls in love with *her* when she is a grown woman, or that she should put up with being treated in the way you have dealt with both Maureen and me. You need to make Holly feel special, and she needs to see you taking responsibility for any other children you may have. That's not too much to ask, is it?'

Bill and Peggy stared at each other for a very long minute, and for a moment Peggy felt she could almost see curls of animosity between them gathering at the outermost edges of her vision.

Then Bill said, 'I doubt Maureen will be happy with having it driven home yet again that there's another child I've fathered, an' that you think the children should know about each other. She knows about you an' Holly, but it's not going to be exactly happy families for any o' us, is it?'

'Probably not at the moment. And maybe Maureen would do well to recall that it was she who leapt into the bed of a married man, no? And that she didn't seem to care an iota about that at the time? Anyway, you forget that Maureen and I have met, and she has *seen* Holly, or near enough when Maureen came to Tall Trees. Then again, you haven't treated Maureen and her child very well either, have you, Bill? I expect she will be feeling very peeved with you for quite a long while yet.' Peggy couldn't resist that little dig.

She went on, 'But there may come a time when Maureen is glad of anyone she thinks is even halfway on her side, even if that anyone is me. The passing months might alter how she feels, as that is what I've found. And while I can't make up Maureen's mind as to what she should do about her own affairs or her own child, I need to put Holly first, and that means me being honest with our daughter. And this means that as Holly and this other bastard child are related and there is nothing that any of us can do to alter that fact, it seems to me that it's only fair that they know about each other. Blood is thicker than water, as they say, and these children might want to be in touch one day, and perhaps when they are older even to spend time together.'

Bill winced when Peggy said 'bastard', and although he didn't say anything, he didn't look happy.

Peggy kept up the pressure. 'And I want you to pay what you should for both Holly's financial upkeep, and for Maureen's child too. You must treat both of your children well, you must see that, surely? And I want you to give me Maureen's address so that I can write to her.'

'Are you out of your mind, woman?' Bill sounded panicky at Peggy's suggestion. 'Maureen's not a woman to take things lying down.'

Peggy knew this already, but she almost wanted to laugh out loud at the quiver of fear in his voice.

Maureen had a famously short fuse, they both knew – Peggy because Maureen had slapped her extremely hard during that one very angry visit she had made to Harrogate to meet with Peggy back in the heat of high summer when Maureen had been visibly pregnant – and Bill was clearly thinking about Maureen's temper for his own reasons, reasons that Peggy didn't care to know about. Still, Bill's horrified expression made Peggy suspect that he and Maureen almost definitely had uncomfortable history concerning Maureen's forthright behaviour. This gave her a tiny wiggle of pleasure deep inside.

'No, I'm not, as you put it, "out of my mind", Bill. In fact, I don't think I've ever been more of sound mind. I don't take to or approve of Maureen in the slightest, but like it or not, she and that baby are now part of your own daughter's life – and therefore part of mine, as we are in hers, and so it's no good for any of us to pretend it's any other way.' Peggy heard her snippy tone, and she reminded herself once again that she shouldn't be unnecessarily mean to Bill in front of Holly. But even with her good intentions – and even though she knew her words were uncharacteristically coarse – the sight of the continuing anguish in his eyes meant she couldn't resist adding, 'For goodness sake, get a grip, man. I don't know why you are looking so put upon, Bill – it wasn't me who couldn't keep his flies buttoned! You have done this to us all, and so it's no good you now crying over spilt milk. It's time for the reckoning you must have known was coming.'

Bill remained looking hangdog though, and then Peggy saw his attitude alter when he decided that attack might deflect this awkward conversation towards something less challenging for him. Instantly, Peggy was determined that it wouldn't.

'Well, you – *you*! – you've got your own fancy man, and so you are on dodgy ground coming over whiter than white, Peg. I ask you, what am I to do about hi—' Bill sounded het up as he tried to score a point.

'Seriously, Bill, *seriously*?!' Peggy retorted. 'You made another woman pregnant, while I was always totally faithful to you – and remained so for long after I heard about Maureen's pregnancy. And in fact I have never been unfaithful to you. I've had a single proper kiss. One kiss, and that's it! You don't have a leg to stand on in the throwing-blame-around stakes, and so it's now of no consequence to you whether I have, as you put it, a fancy man, or not.

'You're to steer clear of me and not interfere with or even have an opinion on how I decide to live my life, or whom I choose to spend my time with, although I expect you to contribute to Holly's upkeep and to be a good and reliable father to her. Your and my only dealings with each other will from now on be over our daughter, and as far as I am concerned, I have no interest in the choices you make, as long as you fulfil your duties to Holly, and hopefully Maureen's child too. Have I made myself crystal clear, Bill?'

To her irritation, Peggy was never to find out whether Bill had understood fully, because the bobby stuck his head around the door again, with a 'lift's here' and a thumb jerked in her husband's direction, and Peggy knew it was time for Bill to be escorted back to the base where he worked training military personnel as drivers of all sorts of vehicles, from large lorries and haulage vehicles to small jeeps and motorcycles.

Always a petrol head; Peggy had no doubt that Bill was very good at his job. It was just as a husband that he'd come a cropper.

Bill shook his head in what might have been anger, or was it disappointment? Peggy couldn't tell.

He gathered himself, and then he kissed two fingers and gently placed them on top of Holly's head, much to the little girl's dislike to judge by the protesting squirm and irritable squeal she made. Peggy supposed he had been hoping for a tender moment between father and child as he said goodbye, but if that was the case, it was if Holly had sided with her mother.

He withdrew his hand very quickly and then, with a breathy 'ouf' of pain as he forced himself up from the chair, Bill hobbled out of the room without a word or backwards glance at either his daughter or his wife.

Peggy listened to the retreating uneven footsteps of his hobnail boots, and the clang of the door at the end of the corridor as it was closed behind him and the lock turned as he went through the entrance to where the holding cells were.

She felt unutterably sad, and although she didn't openly cry as she had done first thing that morning when she had remembered the furious look James had fired at her after the fight, a single tear dribbled slowly down her cheek as she pulled a surprised Holly to her breast for a comforting cuddle.

Chapter Two

After she got back from the police station, Peggy sat alongside her sister Barbara on a wooden bench in a patch of sunlight in the back yard. They had cups of tea perched beside them.

Barbara and her husband Ted had been on a short visit to Harrogate to see Jessie and Connie, catching the train up from London. But they had to be on the early afternoon one back later that day as Ted, who now worked on the river ambulances, knew he would be needed.

Barbara was on the waiting list to train in Air Raid Precautions, probably as an enemy plane spotter and possibly even making sure the air-raid sirens rang out, and so she would be needed back in London too.

Following the endless Phoney War, where it had been very quiet on home soil, Jerry had started to ramp things up. The Battle of Britain had been raging all summer over the English Channel, and only the previous evening at last there had been the long-awaited move of aggression inland with a barrage of German bombers flying overhead that Peggy had seen. What a momentous night, for all sorts of reasons.

As Peggy had sobbed in the darkening murk of the back yard to Tall Trees following the fight, she'd heard a strange droning noise. She looked around but it was only when she glanced upwards that the sound made sense, as she bore witness to a large stream of enemy planes flying in formation across the moonlit sky high above Yorkshire.

Everyone at Tall Trees had been up early listening to the news reports of the multiple bombings of the previous night across the capital, and the news hadn't been good.

All the same, this wasn't what Peggy or Barbara were thinking of right at this moment. They were waiting for the vet to arrive to check over Milburn, and Barbara was keen to grab this moment of quiet to hear from Peggy how it had gone with Bill.

The two sisters had lived in nearby streets, and Bill and Barbara's husband Ted had been best friends, and so they all knew each other very well. In fact, Peggy assumed that Bill and Ted would remain close; she hoped so anyway, as although she wasn't happy right at the minute she didn't want Ted to feel awkward or that he should take sides.

Meanwhile, Barbara's now eleven-year-old twins Connie and Jessie had been in and out of the back yard since first thing, trying to tempt Milburn with a variety of food they'd scavenged from the vegetable plots. But the normally greedy pony steadfastly refused to eat, and so to distract the children, who were clearly upset, Barbara had suggested that the twins pop Holly in the perambulator and walk her around the block in order that she could have a quick word with Peggy.

'Oh Barbara, what a mess,' said Peggy as the sounds of the twins' chatter dwindled when they pushed Holly into the street from the front garden path, Peggy's elbows dejectedly on her knees as she stared sadly down at the lichen-sprigged yard paving stones under their feet. 'Mabel was very kind this morning about Bill and James having a set-to, but I think Roger is avoiding me.'

'I'm not sure that's true, Peggy, so don't read too much into it. I know for certain that Roger had to go out first thing on parish calls as I heard him take two really early telephone calls,' said Barbara briskly. 'Mabel didn't say anything along those lines to me at any rate, although she did concede last night had been a "right pickle". I know they're upstanding members of the community, but they are very tolerant of human nature, you know.'

'A "right pickle" is certainly one way of putting it.' Peggy nodded, and smiled weakly at her sister. 'My first thought today was that I should make a bolt for it with Holly back to Bermondsey. I just feel so embarrassed at being the cause of a dead loss like Bill causing such a rumpus, and then James getting involved when he absolutely didn't deserve to. I can hardly bear to look anyone in the face today, that's how bad I feel about it all.

'In fact, I almost got as far as packing the moment I woke, and then I remembered the twins. I realised then, like it or not, I have responsibilities in Harrogate with Jessie and Connie as you're not here to look after them. And the more I thought about Jerry's bombers and what this really means, the more I understood it would be silly to take Holly *towards* danger as it should be reasonably safe here, and London is sure to be in for the main trouncing – which in turn makes me worry about you and Ted, and what you both might be in for. I know Ted not having to be called up as he's a docker seemed good a while back, but now I'm not so sure …' Peggy's voice was close to a wail at this point.

Barbara had clearly thought about and accepted this already, and so she remained calm in the onslaught of Peggy's anxiety. She reached for her sister's hand and said, 'If I were you, Peg, I think

I'd concentrate just on Holly and you, and let everyone else take care of themselves for the minute. You're not a bolter, that's for certain, and nobody would think that about you. Not for a minute, I promise! You know that you always try and make everyone else happy. But there are times when you need to put what *you* want first. Bill is a blithering idiot, and if I'm honest, last night James didn't cover himself in glory either.'

Peggy took a deep breath and almost made as if she was going to defend James, but Barbara gave her hand a firm squeeze to indicate she hadn't finished speaking. 'Really, what all of it adds up to is that if you don't want to stay here, Peggy, then you mustn't. The twins are used to it now in Harrogate, and while they would miss you of course, and Holly too, the truth of it is that they would be able to manage without you both, I promise. Certainly neither Ted and I would expect the both of you to stay in Yorkshire if you're not happy, and lots of evacuees have returned to London.' Barbara tried to gauge Peggy's expression.

Unhelpfully Peggy was leaning forward once again, concentrating on the flagstones with a ferocity they didn't merit, and so Barbara had to guess what her sister was thinking.

'Mabel also advised that I put Holly at the top of the list when I saw her just now,' Peggy said at last. 'And I don't doubt the twins would get on perfectly well without me to keep an eye on them, as they really are quite grown-up now, and more so every day. And while they miss you and Ted, they know they'd only cause you both more worry if they were in Bermondsey with you, and so I think they're reconciled to being here. But I don't *know* what it is that I really want to do, or what it is that I want to happen, and so what on earth is the point of me running away? What would you do in my situation, Barbara?'

There was a silence, and it was quite a long one as Barbara thought carefully about the question and the best way of answering it.

Peggy gave up waiting for her sister's reply and added, 'I'd be less than true to myself if I didn't admit that the thought of James being here in Harrogate hasn't entered my thoughts too, although know I'm the last person he'll want to see. But the thought that he's not too far away does seem *something*, even though I feel pathetic even thinking this.'

'If it were me, and I were having to consider all the things that you are thinking about,' said Barbara, 'then I don't think I'd do *anything* for a day or two, actually. I'd let the dust settle and I'd try to remember that none of us can change what has already happened. I do know that I'd hold my head up high regardless, Peggy, and not for a moment allow myself to think that I wasn't a catch and worthy of being treated well. You are not in any way to blame for Bill being drunk, or James losing his temper, remember.'

Peggy didn't say anything, but she let out a big sigh. She hadn't realised she had been holding her breath, but she had.

Barbara looked at Peggy and then she nudged her arm. When there was no response, Barbara gently elbowed Peggy again. But it was only on the third attempt that Peggy smiled and she bumped her sister's elbow back with her own.

And just then the vet arrived, and so Peggy stood up, saying softly to her sister as she laid a hand on her shoulder and squeezed quite hard, 'Thank you, Barbara, I don't know where I'd be without you.'

*

Roger had telephoned the vet before he had left Tall Trees on some parish visits, and as Barbara went to pack, Peggy introduced herself and then told the vet that she would be paying for her visit and whatever needed doing to help the pony, and that the vet absolutely wasn't under any circumstances to give the bill to Roger.

They peered over the door, and silently inspected the normally bonny pony.

Now, Milburn was anything but bonny. Although it was a sunny September day he looked cold, even though he had two tatty wool bed-blankets slung across his back, with some straw heaped underneath the wool. He was standing with his head low and his weepy eyes half closed, a small pile of untouched chopped apples from the orchard on the brick floor in front of him. The sort of pony who ate like a trooper, Peggy knew it was serious if he was off his tucker. The skin on his legs and belly was shiny pink and hairless in parts where he had scrambled over the door, with some cuts still oozing, and one of his front hooves looked painfully split where his metal shoe had been ripped off in the collision with the police car.

'Let's get him out where I can see him properly,' said the vet, tipping her head this way and that as she inspected the pony once Peggy had slipped a rope halter onto Milburn and coaxed him into the yard. He seemed reluctant to leave his stable, moving only very stiffly and slowly, and he gave a complaining groan as he went through the doorway. The vet added, 'Tell me a bit about him and then what's happened to him? He looks as if he's been through the wars.'

Quickly Peggy described the panicked pony's bid for freedom to escape from what she described as 'a fracas in the yard', adding, 'He seems to have been in deep shock since he was involved with the car, and I don't think he's eaten or drunk anything, or been to the toilet since then. The children would be devastated if Milburn had to be, um, er, um, destroyed.'

The vet took Milburn's temperature, inserting the thermometer as she pulled his tail up, and then looked closely at his eyes and mouth. The normal salmon colour inside his eyelids and on his gumline was the palest pink and even to Peggy's inexperienced eye it was clearly far too pale. The vet ran her hands all over his body, Milburn flinching now and then, after which she inspected the skin scrapes where Peggy and Roger had bathed them the previous night.

'Those external injuries will heal best if we can let the air get to them to dry them out. We can drench him to up his liquid intake, but let's see what a little walk in the sun will do for him first, as I don't want to upset him more than we need to,' said the vet as gently she pulled on Milburn's little tufted ears to comfort him. He pressed the front of his face against the vet and held it there, and Peggy's heart went out to him as he looked both terribly scared and dejected. The vet told him he was a good boy, and then added for Peggy's benefit, 'I'll take off all his shoes and trim that split hoof first though to see if that will help.'

Aiden, the most sensible of the disparate group of children who now lived at Tall Trees, had come out to see what the vet had to say, and so Peggy passed the halter's lead rope over to him, explaining to the vet that if she wasn't desperately needed for a few minutes, she should probably go inside to see if Mabel or Barbara needed her, and then Aiden could come and get her when the vet wanted to go.

Inside the rectory, Peggy found that Barbara had stripped

25

the bed she and Ted had slept in, and so while Mabel got the wooden washtub ready for the linen to be dunked into, Peggy nipped around taking everyone else's linen off; it would be criminal to waste the hot water by not doing a linen wash across the house, especially as soap of any description was so hard to get these days, and as much use needed to be made of the tub as possible once washing was going to be done.

It wasn't too long before the vet poked her head round the back door with the good news that after a gentle walk a couple of times around the large garden, Milburn had munched on some grass and taken a long drink. He was now lying down in a patch of sunlight with his eyes closed as Aiden sat quietly beside him.

A little while later Mabel and Roger's son Tommy pushed evacuee Angela's wheelchair along the garden path, followed by Larry, who'd also been in Jessie and Connie's class back in Bermondsey, to where Aiden was sitting gently stroking Milburn's velvety muzzle as the small chestnut rested.

'Do you think if we sing, it will help him have sweet dreams?' wondered Angela, who was very fond of the pony as when she had learned to drive him in the trap it had given her a much longed-for sense of freedom, as she found being confined to her wheelchair very frustrating a lot of the time.

Tommy, Larry and Aiden exchanged looks. They thought it a sissy idea, frankly, but nobody liked to disagree too much with Angela because of her being stuck in the wheelchair, and so they kept schtum.

As far as Tommy was concerned, in large part his reticence in disagreeing with Angela was because he was very taken with her, and so he always tried to keep on her good side.

'Maybe,' muttered Aiden cautiously, after it became obvious

the others weren't going to venture the first opinion on whether they should sing, or not.

'If you start us off, Angela,' added Tommy.

Angela began to croon 'Somewhere Over the Rainbow' quietly, and after a while the boys succumbed to the inevitable under Angela's eager nods that they should join in, and they began to hum along.

Milburn gave what some might say should be described as a deep sigh of horror, although Tommy insisted it was a noise that merely indicated how much the pony was enjoying their serenade.

On the other side of the greenhouse, Barbara and Peggy were gathering some greens for lunch from one of the vegetable plots, and they listened to the children. Their song wasn't at all tuneful, and it was punctuated by snuffly rooting noises from Porky, the pig the children had been looking after since he was a piglet. Now that there were stout fences around the vegetable patches to keep him out, Porky had the run of the garden, and he had sidled up to the children to see what was going on.

Jessie and Connie joined their friends, leaving a snoozing Holly in her pram in a shady spot in the back yard, and the song took on more gusto, although unfortunately not musicality. Jessie wasn't able to sing in tune, and Connie wasn't much better.

'Poor Milburn,' said Peggy to Barbara. 'As if he's not had enough to put up with already.'

Milburn whinnied as if in agreement, and lurched to his feet, turning his back end towards the children.

Chapter Three

Understandably, Jessie and Connie were very subdued after they had been to the train station to wave goodbye to their parents as Barbara and Ted made their way back to London.

Peggy wasn't a lot of help either, as with a wave of exhaustion threatening to engulf her after lunch, she'd begged Gracie, the young single mother who was also living at Tall Trees, to look after Holly for a while so that she could climb into bed for an hour. Gracie happily plonked Holly on the rug on the lawn in front of Tall Trees beside Jack, her own little boy, and then watched as the two babies crawled about on the grass, getting quite dirty but finding it huge fun if their giggles were anything to go by.

Luckily Roger was back at Tall Trees, and he stepped into the breach when he noticed Connie and Jessie were down in the mouth about their parents leaving, while all the children were still shaken by what had happened to Milburn.

'Right-o. While Milburn enjoys the sun, what say you all if we give his stable a proper spring clean as a bit of a treat?' Roger said. 'If we each do a little bit, then it won't take long and don't you think Milburn would like it?'

Milburn was once more lying flat out on the grass, only now with Porky nestled close beside the pony as the pig's fulsome snores vibrated in the air, and the pair didn't look like they were going to be moving any time soon. Bucky, the family's battle-scarred black and white tomcat who resolutely refused to answer to his official name of Nebuchadnezzar, was curled tight against Milburn's back. It was an adorable sight.

The children agreed that Roger's plan was just the ticket.

An hour later they were tired and wet from sloshing water around, and no longer convinced that Roger had had a good idea.

While he showed the other children how to make up a bran mash for Milburn – 'to get things moving' – Jessie clomped up the wooden stairs to the bedroom that Peggy and Holly shared.

'Aunt Peggy,' he called softly, as he tapped gently on the door, which was in stark contrast to the noisy ascent. 'Are you awake?'

Peggy was rousing from a heavy sleep, as Jessie's boots on the stairs had been hard to ignore.

'Jessie, is that you?' she said, her voice faintly croaky with tiredness. 'Is there something wrong with Holly?'

Her nephew gave her a shy smile as he edged into the room, shaking his head to let Peggy know that she needn't worry about Holly.

She shuffled up the bed and leaned back against the wall. She patted a spot beside her, so that Jessie knew it was all right for him to come close for a snuggle.

Peggy put an arm around his bony shoulders, thinking he was still very small for his age. 'Did Barbara and Ted get off all right, Jessie?' she asked.

'They nearly missed the train as Mabel was making them sandwiches and a flask, and that took forever, and so we all had to run the last bit.'

'I bet Barbara was cross about that.'

'She was, and she got very out of puff, but the station master with the whistle who was closing all the doors let Connie and me have a last hug,' said Jessie.

'That was nice of him.'

'Mabel was just reminding us that we have to go back to school this week,' said Jessie then, really quietly.

He was a very clever boy, and usually was top of the class – unlike his sister, who was always right down at the bottom.

It was most unusual for Jessie not to be buoyed up at the thought of his lessons and a new term, Peggy knew.

Jessie and the other children were now done and dusted with primary school; even though in other areas of the country 'primary' school could continue to teach children older than they were, the particular school they had been to previously in Harrogate didn't cater for pupils after they reached eleven, and so they were now going to be attending 'big school'.

Back when the summer holidays had begun, Jessie had seemed very excited at this prospect. But no longer was this the case, Peggy could see.

Peggy looked at her nephew, and his unhappy face told her that he definitely wasn't relishing the prospect of what the next week would bring.

'Is there a reason you don't fancy going to your new school very much?' she asked.

He shook his head, but when Peggy said very quietly, 'Are you sure, Jessie?' he stared at the eiderdown for a while.

'It's those Hull lads,' Jessie confessed at last in little more than a whisper. 'I don't think Connie saw them, and I beg you, really beg you, Peggy, not to say anything. But when we were coming back from the station today there was one of them hanging about near the dairy, and when he saw me looking at him, he did this.' Jessie looked up at his aunt as he drew a forefinger across his throat, miming what a knife could do.

Its meaning was all too clear.

Peggy could see that to a serious and sometimes timid child such as Jessie, such a gesture would be very frightening indeed. And of course it was only a few short weeks since the boys from Hull, who had also been evacuated to Harrogate but who were a little older as well as much rougher round the edges than Jessie and his pals, had beaten Jessie up very seriously, knocking him unconscious, with the result that he had had to spend a spell in hospital being looked after by James. Any child would feel wary after an experience like that.

Peggy pulled him close.

'Try not to take on so, Jessie,' said Peggy. 'I'm sure that it won't come to anything, and things rarely turn out as one might expect they will, remember. Really, you mustn't worry, I promise.'

Jessie was still tense despite her reassuring words, and it was a while before Peggy felt him relax.

Peggy felt a little bad about what she'd just said. As a former schoolteacher herself, she knew that bullying was nearly always a complicated issue, and one that could be very hard to stop. And to judge by her own recent experiences, things often turned out a lot worse than one expected them to. But Jessie certainly didn't need reminding of this.

She hugged Jessie even more tightly, taking as much comfort in holding him as he was in being held. He was only eleven and was naturally very shy, plus his head injury had been an extremely salutary experience for everyone at Tall Trees, and her heart swelled with emotion.

Peggy wished she could make it all better for Jessie, but she knew life wasn't that simple and he might well face some unpleasant times ahead.

Chapter Four

O n their first day, Connie decided that she rather approved of their new school.

She had seen it before of course, quite often in fact, when she and the other Tall Trees children had been out and about with Milburn in the trap over the summer when they had been doing their bit for the war effort by collecting scrap paper. But now Connie realised she had never really looked properly beyond the newly painted, sturdy wooden gates to what might be on the other side.

She narrowed her eyes as she inspected the school's impressive frontage as they headed down the street towards it, the children's gas masks bumping annoyingly against their hips in their cardboard boxes as they dangled on long twine loops.

Before the school gate they'd all came to a halt as if by agreement, and the children bent down to hoick their socks up as far as they would go, and then they gave each other a scrutinising once-over to make sure everyone was presentable, with tidy hair and no smuts on their faces.

Nobody had to wear uniform these days if they didn't have it, although many schools encouraged the wearing of uniforms if possible. The relaxing of the rules was a government edict designed to help the poorer families, and because there were rumours clothes would be rationed at some point in the next year, in the eyes of many clothes just for school felt an extravagance too far. But as a lot of children had been evacuated in their previous school uniforms, Connie wasn't surprised that the boys were all wearing neatly ironed white cotton shirts, and grey short-legged trousers. And she knew that Mabel had organised for donations of clothing to help many of the most disadvantaged children in the parish.

The children all going to 'big school' had been treated with a lot less excitement by the grown-ups at Tall Trees than when the evacuees had had to join their new primary school a year earlier, when the getting-ready-for-school on the first day had felt a real production the whole household was involved in.

In comparison, earlier this morning Mabel, Roger and Peggy had waved them off and had shouted repeated 'good luck's as they made their way down the road, and Mabel had packed their lunches for them. But that was about all the fuss that was made.

'I suppose it's because they think that if we're old enough to be here, we're old enough to sort ourselves out,' Connie had replied when Jessie said as much. He knew what Connie meant, and he thought there was some truth in it. But it felt a big step to him, all the same.

After everyone except Angela rubbed the top of their shoe on the back calf of the opposite leg to dust away any motes before swapping legs, Tommy had been told that his collar was standing up on one side, and Larry that his shoelaces were coming undone and he should tie the bows with a double knot, they decided everything was as it should be. They didn't want to let Roger and Mabel, or Peggy down. At least not on their very first day.

Tommy had been pushing Angela's wheelchair, but now she looked up at him in a way that let him know she wanted to wheel herself the last bit, and so with only a little reluctance – as he wanted to show any new pupils whom he and Angela were about to meet that she was spoken for – Tommy stepped back and stood beside Larry.

All the other Tall Trees children understood, but nobody wanted to draw attention to Angela and Tommy's silent dialogue.

As one, they all looked up and down the road, and they could see there were other children heading towards the school too, some looking very nervous.

The Tall Trees lot were proud they didn't seem as scaredy-cat as these others, although privately each had a little pit of apprehension churning away in their stomachs now they were so close to entering the school grounds for the first time.

Well, all of them except for Connie, but then that was to be expected with her. Nothing seemed to bother her overmuch.

Jessie realised it helped a little in their stiff-upper-lip stakes that just before they'd left Tall Trees Peggy had doled out gobstoppers to each of them in individual twists of brown paper bag for the children to suck 'on the way home', with a casual aside as she made sure that each child had one that if it all felt a bit much during the day, then they could touch the gobstopper in their pockets to remember they were all clever and that the school was very lucky indeed that they were going to be its pupils for the foreseeable future, and that they were all very loved by herself and Roger and Mabel.

It was such a treat to have sweets as they were hardly ever available anymore (or if they were, Mabel and Peggy rarely saw to it that the children had them). And Peggy had been very insistent that the children weren't to eat the gobstoppers until they headed back to Tall Trees at the end of the school day, and so the children had already made a pact that they would all pop the sweets into their mouths at the same time once the bell had rung for going home time.

Still, it all felt like something of a new beginning.

Jessie sneaked a look at Connie. Her head was high, and her shoulders back. Jessie envied his sister's bright eyes and the determined set of her mouth, and he felt a little feeble in comparison. He sighed; it had been ever thus, he supposed.

Over the previous few days, the children had agreed that the new school was a signal for a new, more grown-up phase of their lives.

And so, with reluctance, they decided it was time to mothball the TT Muskets (short, naturally, for the Tall Tree Musketeers). Although it had been fun to come up with japes over the summer designed to irritate the Hull boys under the aegis of being in a gang, all of this felt a bit babyish now that they were about to spend time with children older than themselves, although Jessie couldn't help but wonder if the Hull boys would say goodbye to their equivalent gang with the same ease that the Tall Trees children had.

Then Jessie had an even more sobering thought. He'd tried very hard not to think about them for a while, but after seeing the Hull boy near the dairy Jessie knew they were coming back into his life. And although these lads were older than the Tall Trees lot, they had clearly been in a gang in the summer.

Presumably they *didn't* see their rivalry with the TT Muskets as something babyish to be put away. What if those rowdy lads were planning some truly awful things that were still in store for Jessie and his friends? What was just as concerning was that the Hull boys attended the school that the Tall Trees children were standing in front of. It hardly bore thinking about.

Jessie heard himself swallow with apprehension. He hoped the others hadn't caught this.

As the children made their way through their new school's gates, Connie decided that the imposing stone buildings stood tribute to the fact that in all sorts of ways it was bolder and bigger – much bigger, in fact – than what they were used to. Clearly, this establishment was going to offer them a very different experience than what they had known up until then.

This school felt decidedly grown-up. It even had some tar-macked tennis courts; the droopy cast to the nets suggested the games resources were in some disrepair, although there was what Connie thought might be a netball court marked out alongside. Connie had never played tennis before, or indeed netball, but she rather fancied herself swinging a racket or shooting a ball at the netball hoop.

'Have you noticed what's over there, Aiden?' she said, nodding her head in the direction of the courts. 'What are our chances of being able to play on those, do you think?'

'Lordy, I suppose it will depend on whether there's a games master who can coach tennis,' he said.

'Or games *mistress*,' Connie said pointedly, and Aiden had the grace to look as if he had been caught out and that he knew he shouldn't have jumped to such an assumption.

Connie let him stew for a second or two, and then she added, 'Looks interesting though. And at least we'll have left the days of country dancing behind with all the rubbishy gypsy and daisy chain palaver. Don't you think it looks much too grand here for something so, um, er …'

'Parochial,' Aiden finished for her as he knew Connie was still talking about the country dancing, and he and Connie laughed. Neither had ever enjoyed this activity, which their previous teacher at primary school had been much too fond of.

In fact those country dance lessons had nearly always degenerated into something of a melee when, during a progression, the boys would try to roughhouse the girls, and swing them around incredibly fast in the hope that they might fall over, at which point, inevitably, Connie would have to give the boys back as good as she could.

The resulting bumps and grazes had indeed got so out of hand the previous term that after Tommy came home with a spectacular swelling on his brow, Roger had had to go in to have a 'little word' with the teacher, much to Tommy's chagrin.

After Roger's visit, the teacher threatened the class sternly that unless everybody was *gentlemanly* and *lady-like* (she looked piercingly at Connie as she said 'lady-like') to each other *at all times* when dancing, then she'd have no option but to insist the girls danced with girls, and – horror! – the boys with boys.

This was taken to heart by all concerned and there hadn't been a single unbidden bruise or scraped knee after that. It hadn't made any of the children enjoy country dancing the more though.

Once they'd crossed the open space inside the gates and were near to the school buildings, the children were immediately shepherded through the entrance by an older pupil wearing a 'prefect' pin, and down a wide passage towards a large hall.

They peeped into classrooms aligning the walkway through their open doors as they made their way to the hall, and it was clear that the school's buildings were designed to be daunting, with tremendously high ceilings in each classroom, and huge windows that faced both to the outside and to the internal school corridors and that had sills so lofty that pupils sitting at their desks couldn't look out and distract themselves by watching what was going on elsewhere.

The corridors were echoey, and the wooden bricks in the parquet flooring had been laid in an intricate herringbone design and had slight dips in them occasionally from having so many pupils and teachers walk on them.

At the front of each classroom was the teacher's desk on a low dais, and beside this a big blackboard propped on three wooden legs.

The school was much, much grander than the primary school in Bermondsey that Jessie and Connie had attended with Larry and Angela – and Peggy had worked as a school teacher, a profession she knew she would have to give up once Holly was born – and Jessie felt awed by its grandeur and size. However, it still shared the whiff of boiled cabbage their primary school had always had too, and so although it did feel strange, it also was slightly familiar as well.

This school was unusual though, as it was loosely modelled on a grammar school, although without perhaps quite the emphasis on a grammar school's academic achievement, having instead a bias towards technical skills such as wood- and metalwork.

Its youngest pupils were eleven years old and the eldest eighteen, although few stayed on that late, with the poorer children leaving at fourteen as their families needed the extra wage they could provide; nearly everyone else left at either fifteen or sixteen.

This latest intake of first-formers, as Connie and her pals were, had been requested to attend a day before the other years returned in order to register and learn their way about. This took a very long time indeed, the twins agreed.

It was livelier in the afternoon, as the head of year, a Latin master called Mr Sprout (no one dared giggle when his name was announced), told everyone that now the pupils were to be allocated their classes, called forms, the allocation based on each pupil's previous year's schooling.

Once they knew which class they were in, the pupils would then go to their tutor room where they would meet their tutor.

As names were read out, there was a lot of twisting and turning as everyone tried to get a glimpse of who else they were going to be taught with.

'Aiden, just look at the size of each form, each one is going to be *huge!*' hissed Jessie in an awed voice as he and Aiden waited to see where they would be sent.

Quickly Aiden totted up the numbers in all the various groups, and of those still to be called, and then he whispered out of the corner of his mouth in Jessie's direction, 'Looks like there's goin' t' be no more than forty in each class. That's good. My brother Kelvin said we might 'ave as many as fifty per teacher, but I don't think that'll be rightly so fer us.'

Jessie gulped. Ordinarily he enjoyed, quietly, being an active member of a class as learning was, generally, fun as far as he was concerned. But he didn't much fancy the idea of putting his hand up to answer a question if there were going to be forty-nine people watching him, especially if he were then to slip up when giving an answer. This, coupled with the unspoken threat of the Hull boys, made him feel very circumspect.

Connie's name was the first of the Tall Trees entourage to be called. To her horror, she was sent to the line for the lowest stream, 1E.

Immediately Aiden and Jessie were told that they should line up with the others in the top class, 1A, which they felt bad about as the timing seemed to rub Connie's nose in it; they knew she would hate her 1E status being in such immediate contrast to their own academic proficiency.

It wasn't long before Tommy and Angela were sent to the line for 1D, and then, after a long pause, so was Larry. 1D was the lower middling group, although Angela was informed almost immediately that because of her wheelchair she wouldn't be able to attend any classes on the upper levels of the school because of the stairs. This meant that at these times the teachers would set her work and she would have to go to the library to study for a period quietly on her own. Angela shook her head sadly at this as she obviously didn't want to spend what might be a large proportion of her lessons by herself.

Jessie looked anxiously over to Connie again to see how she was taking the news that she was in the lowest stream, now she had had several minutes to get used to it.

He found her staring back at him intently with over-bright eyes, and this made Jessie wonder if perhaps she might be

41

teetering on the edge of tears, or whether they might be tears of temper as Connie often had a very short fuse.

Jessie knew his twin wouldn't appreciate being so publicly shown up for having problems in the classroom. He'd always tried very hard never to draw attention to this, which wasn't easy as, being twins, they were often compared to one another, and of course Jessie had the advantage that he found schoolwork came very naturally. He'd always felt intensely uncomfortable if anybody asked Connie why she wasn't more like her brother in this respect. And if it all got a bit too much and his sister should succumb in public to a teary moment, Jessie knew that Connie would feel it to be a terrible loss of face. It was all terribly concerning and actually, the more he thought about it, the more Jessie couldn't remember the last time he had seen Connie cry, whether it be in public or not. He really hoped that today wasn't the time she broke her resolve never to sob.

As the children were sent away to meet their form tutors in their new classrooms, Jessie risked slipping briefly across the room to Connie's side, where he said in what he hoped was as reassuring a way as possible, 'They'll have just made a silly mistake, Con, you wait and see. You'll be back with the rest of us in no time. No time at all, you mark my words.'

Connie didn't say anything although she blinked several times, and then she muttered in the smallest and softest voice that Jessie had ever heard her use, a voice that clutched at something to do with them being inextricably linked as twins, 'I don't think they have made a mistake, Jess. I'm sure of it. They've seen me for the stupid nitwit that I am.'

'Well, you get first ride on Milburn then,' said Jessie. He felt put on the spot and this was the best he could come up with.

Connie's sceptical gaze made him add, 'When Milburn's got his shoes on once more and we can ride him again, of course. And if you're a nitwit, then I'm a, er, a *nincompoop*.'

Connie didn't respond with even the tiniest smile.

Even Aiden, normally so good at saying the right thing at the most apposite time and being Connie's special buddy at Tall Trees, seemed at a complete loss of how to deal with the situation now that he had crept close too. Eventually he told her in a very low voice, 'You know, don't you, Connie, that if I could change places with you, I would?'

Connie flashed the pair of them a fleeting but distinctly wobbly smile, and then she said with a dimpling of her chin and a downward tilt of her moth, 'At least I won't have to do Latin in my dunderheads group. I don't think me and Latin are made to be best friends ...'

And with that she trotted away to catch up with the rest of 1E as its last stragglers made their way to their classroom.

Jessie felt very strange as the sight of Connie's straight and resolutely proud back was swallowed up by her new classmates.

He knew he passed at being taken for a bright boy, and so Jessie wasn't particularly impressed at being chosen for the top stream as to his mind all this showed was an ability to regurgitate what teachers had said.

In day-to-day life, Jessie had always found Connie to be braver than him, and much smarter too when it came to playing memory games (or indeed any sort of games, especially ones that involved lots of racing around and practical problem-solving), or counting cards for matchsticks (which Ted always told her she wasn't to do, especially if she were ever playing cards in public, as this aptitude wasn't going to win her any favours as some would take umbrage to her counting skills), or a nail-biting round of truth or dare, or indeed in any sort of problem-solving that required quick wits rather than bookish learning, and Jessie deemed it very odd that others didn't see her similarly. In his opinion Connie was as sharp as a whip, although he was at a loss how to demonstrate this to anyone who didn't know Connie well.

But the more he thought about it now, the more Jessie realised that he simply couldn't understand why it was that Connie found her school lessons so difficult. He knew it wasn't a case of her messing around and that she could achieve higher marks if she just put her mind to it.

The fact of it was though that Connie had never impressed any of her teachers, while he had been praised to the nines unnecessarily. And this just wasn't fair to either of them.

As he took his seat in his new form room, Jessie felt like a minnow in a fast-flowing river that was threatening to send him tumbling out to sea, and he certainly wished he had a bit more of Connie's bluff and bluster about him.

There were a lot of strange faces here, many of which didn't look friendly in the slightest as the pupils banged the wooden tops of their desks closed after they'd put their possessions inside.

Right then, in Jessie's eyes, bluff and bluster certainly seemed the best qualities for helping one get on in the world. He hoped nobody had seen him jump nervously when the first desk lid had been dropped with a bang.

But poor Connie, he thought next. She'd be feeling worse than he was right at that minute. It had been a very public slating, and Jessie racked his brains to think of something he could do about it.

Chapter Five

As the children made their way to school that morning, back at Tall Trees Peggy was getting Holly ready for them both to head over to June Blenkinsop's café, where Peggy worked now, although after she glimpsed herself in the hall mirror just before she left, she let out a small groan of frustration as she looked a proper sight.

She nipped back to her bedroom and quickly wrapped her favourite silk scarf around her hair and tied it in a jaunty bow on the top of her head.

The scarf had been a present from Bill on their first wedding anniversary, back when they were thrilled, at long last, to be able to rent their first tiny home in Bermondsey, a minute end-of-terrace. Their anniversary was spent arranging their meagre possessions and telling each other that now they were living on their own for the first time, they might be poor but they were going to be 'as snug as a bug in a rug' in their new home. Back then they hadn't felt they were missing out on anything, not for a second.

A hard lump of regret of all the wrongs that had happened since rose in Peggy's throat for a moment, but then she told herself not to think about those more pleasant times.

She gave a little shake and a shrug, and then hoped she passed muster as she pulled and fussed at the scarf and tried to decide whether her ears should be covered or not. She was doubtful though; it was all very 'lick and polish', but what could she do? All the hot water had been used up the previous evening on the children having their weekly bath night, and so Peggy had had to make do first thing that morning with a strip wash in what would at best be described as lukewarm water, with only the tiniest sliver of hand soap.

Holly gave her mother a 'hurry up' sound, and Peggy knew it was time to push her over to the tea shop.

Actually the words 'tea shop' rather undersold June's establishment these days. It had been a rather quaint, old-fashioned establishment decked out in swathes of chintz and serving scones or barm cakes with pretty china tea services when Peggy had discovered it soon after her arrival in Harrogate.

Now, the floral tablecloths and napkins had long since disappeared and a more utilitarian look adopted, with bare wooden tables and cushionless chairs that felt more appropriate for the current times and, best of all, were easier to keep spick and span with the increased turnover of customers. These days the café was open long hours, serving early breakfasts, lunches and late suppers to many sorts of grateful workers, both white- and blue-collar, all at the pre-ordained government-set prices. It was now definitely a workers' café first, and a tea shop second, exactly as it should be.

June and Peggy were a strong team, Peggy felt.

June knew the food side of the business inside out and she was a very talented cook who seemed able to make a very little go an extremely long way, plus she was good at organising rotas of reliable staff. And Peggy was skilled at bookkeeping and negotiating advantageous terms with their suppliers, and she enjoyed writing out the customers' bills and giving them their change as she always took the money over the busiest periods.

In fact the tea shop was a very convivial place to work, as it was warm and full of good-natured banter between staff and customers, most of whom were regulars. There had been several fundraising schemes hatched there for the war effort, and Peggy knew that June was very proud of the gusto her patrons threw into this, whether it was a charity whist drive or collecting jumble for a sale.

When the reports in the newspapers were bleak, Peggy liked the way the customers would discuss the news with one another and then try to find something positive to say in order to gee each other up and keep morale as high as possible.

There was a fly in the ointment though.

Up until now Peggy had been able to take Holly in to work with her as June was very fond of babies, but now that Holly was on the cusp of proper toddling, Peggy knew she should make alternative arrangements for minding her daughter sooner rather than later. This was likely to be easier said than done.

As usual, everything looked very organised as Peggy manoeuvred the perambulator through the door and then into the back of June's establishment.

June smiled at Peggy as she passed, indicating 'tea?' by lifting a teacup.

'Gasping,' replied Peggy.

She felt used up after the emotional tensions of the past few days and she could really do with a short sit-down and chinwag.

This was a ritual that June and she enjoyed most mornings, when they chatted about this and that between the early breakfasts being served and the inevitable flurry to get all the lunches ready.

'Oh June, I have got such a lot to tell you!' said Peggy, as Holly played with her rattle (a hand-me-down of Tommy's) while sitting on her lap. 'Of the "you won't believe it" variety, I'm afraid.' Peggy's voice had a tense twang to it, and although she tried to smile her mouth wasn't quite playing ball.

June said, 'In that case, I'd best bring a pot over then rather than just pour us a cup each from the urn.'

And, sure enough, fifteen minutes later the two women were already on to their second cup of tea, their heads close together as they spoke in quiet monotones so that the customers couldn't overhear their conversation.

They needn't have worried in this respect as most of those in the café were otherwise engaged, studying the newspapers with shocked expressions as everyone tried to take in the grim headlines and graphic photographs of damage caused by the initial wave of German bombers.

Peggy described what had happened over the past few days back at Tall Trees, dwelling for a little longer than was strictly necessary on what a lovely time she and James had shared, and how they had drunk some champagne that James has squirrelled away pre-war, and then in the dusk had enjoyed the heady sensation of their first proper kiss outside Milburn's stable. Peggy relived the dizzy moment when she'd not been able to distinguish if the delicious light-headed feeling was because of the champagne bubbles, or because, finally, James and she were at long last in each other's arms.

Then June's eyes grew round as Peggy described how it had all degenerated into mayhem and the embarrassing fight between Bill and James.

'If anyone would have told me even last week that Bill could behave like such a pig-ignorant boor, I'd have said absolutely not and that he simply didn't have it in him. And I'm saying that as a wife who's been wronged by her husband with another woman,' said Peggy. 'But he's made me look a fool. He was a thug that night – there's just no other word for it, June, I'm ashamed to say – and a bully. In fact, I felt mortified that he was anything to do with me, and of course it all unfolded with Mabel and Roger watching on too. I didn't know this until later but they had seen the fight from the window on the stairs. I can't describe how humiliating it all is.'

Peggy flushed deeply, although whether it was from the memory of the kiss or the shame of having two men fight over her, neither Peggy nor June could say.

June nodded then as if she could picture how it must have been.

Peggy went on, 'James was livid, just furious. And poor Milburn was terrified and he managed to get out of his box and scoot in panic onto the road and he hurt himself by running into a car. He's still very sorry for himself, which has really upset the children, and it's landed me with a vet's bill I hadn't expected. And the absolute giddy limit was the next morning Bill demanded that I take Holly to see him over in the police station.'

'Really?' said June.

'Yes, really,' said Peggy. 'And I felt as if me *not* doing what he wanted was worse than me doing it, even though in some ways it stuck in my craw. I mean, I never saw myself as the sort of wife who would ever have to come down to jumping obediently at Bill's beck and call when he's treated Holly and me in such a cavalier manner.'

There was a silence as Peggy mournfully sent the tea leaves in the bottom of her teacup swirling.

'Have you talked to James yet?' June asked.

Peggy shook her head as she tried to blink away the glisten now in her eyes.

'Oh June, it's all such a disaster – the look James gave me as he left the back yard made me want to slink under a stone, hanging my head. I think I'm the last person he is ever going to want to speak to. In fact I was this close—' Peggy held up her thumb and first finger of her right hand so that the digits were almost touching '—the following morning to making a run for it and upping sticks to leave Harrogate with Holly before I stood any chance of seeing him, I felt so bad. I don't think I'll ever be able to talk to him. It feels impossible, and in any case I can't get around the fact I have Holly and an awful husband. And I know James needs to concentrate on other things as he is so busy at the hospital. What hurts too is that in the years to come when I think back to the day that Holly took her first couple of steps, it will be the day that I had to visit my husband in a police station.'

Peggy made a noise that was somewhere between a moan and a sigh, and a couple of customers seated nearby glanced in her direction, although they quickly looked away again when they noticed her furrowed brow and the corresponding concerned expression on June's face. June laid a comforting hand on Peggy's arm to reassure her.

The gesture bolstered Peggy, and she added with a little crack in her voice, 'And I was all too aware that it would have been bad form of me – very bad form – if I had shot off and left *you* in the lurch, and so I feel bad for even considering that I might make a dash for it. And now I've got a huge mountain to climb, whatever way I look at things. Aside from the mess with James, I know I should think seriously about whether I should speak to Maureen, as like it or not Bill's made her and the baby part of the equation. I asked Bill for Maureen's address, and later a card was pushed through the door with it – I think Bill must have asked one of the policemen to bring it over, but of course now that I've got it, I'm uncertain whether to get in touch with the dratted woman or not.

'Then there's the question of whether Bill starts contributing to Holly's upkeep, which he hasn't yet, and I want seriously to contemplate getting a divorce ...'

The shocked look on June's face stopped Peggy in her tracks momentarily.

If June, a youngish, forward-looking widow as well as a resourceful and independently minded businesswoman, was perturbed by the notion of Peggy instigating divorce proceedings against Bill, Peggy realised she needed to think carefully through all her options before doing anything rash, as although she knew it was a big step, perhaps it was even bigger than she currently assumed. Certainly few wives did anything about it in the legal sense, no matter how appalling their lousy, cheating spouses had been, and so perhaps Peggy would be biting off more than she could chew.

Peggy felt so pent up with emotion that her voice shrank almost to a whisper, 'The unfairness of it all ... Divorce is a much bigger step for a woman than a man, and I'd need to check how it would work as one does hear of the most terribly lurid stories of having to have quite sordid evidence, although in the case of Bill, maybe the fact there is a baby already from his liaison will sway things in my favour.' June nodded as if a judge probably would take that into account.

And then Peggy added, 'But probably the most pressing thought is that I'm also all too aware that I need to sort out a better arrangement for Holly while I'm here at yours, now that she'll be trotting around properly under her own steam within days.'

'Yes, I think you'll have to do that,' June sounded truly sorry. 'It's sad that then I won't see Holly as much as I do right now, as I love having her here. But there are far too many sharp knives and pans full of boiling water here, and hot kettles and teapots, and we're just not going to be able to keep a proper eye on her all the time once she's mobile. And I couldn't bear it if something nasty happened to Holly just because we didn't have time to watch what she's up to. Aside from that, maybe you could write a word or two to James? It sounds as if it's unlikely you could make the situation worse between you.'

Peggy knew June was right. 'Yes, I'll think about all of this. I guess that if I don't let James know how sorry I am about the fight, then that would be pretty bad form too. And if I do go on to contact Maureen, what on earth do I say to *her*? And that's not all – poor Jessie is convinced those Hull lads are still out to get him as one of them made a silly gesture, and we simply *can't* have another incident that ends up with a hospital stay again, as that would be dreadful for Jessie … and I'm ashamed even to think this, but it would definitely add to the awkwardness for me with James if he had to treat Jessie *again*.'

Peggy paused, and then added, 'And somewhere along the way, I'd like to have a bath in something that is hot and at least a whole two inches deep, with enough soap to do the job properly, and perhaps even wash my hair. Honestly, today feels like a day that's not worth putting on lipstick for, as my mother used to say. If I had any lipstick left, that would be!'

June laughed.

Peggy gave Holly a jiggle to show she wasn't forgotten.

'Thanks for letting me get all of that off my chest, June,' she added, realising she had probably just sounded incredibly self-indulgent, a quality Peggy normally abhorred.

But having June's presence beside her had been a huge comfort, although almost certainly not much fun for June.

Still, there was a lot to be said for somebody listening quietly and sympathetically, thought Peggy as June went to get them a couple of teacakes. She must remember to do that the next time somebody came to her for help, she told herself.

And by the time she had her next break – which was after the lunchtime rush, even though her mind was still a maelstrom of feelings, Peggy had made up her mind on two things.

She was going to have a decent bath that night, come hell or high water.

And she was going to consider seriously whether to write a note to James.

Just the mere thought of even getting out her pen and paper made her feel queasy, but Peggy suspected that as June had intimated, if she didn't take the bull by the horns and do *something*, then she was likely to feel even queasier.

By the time Peggy gratefully sank into the bath quite late that evening, her letter was finished and in her handbag waiting to be dropped off the following morning.

Dear James,

I shall get to the point straight away. What happened the other night was a shocking state of affairs, and completely unfair on you. Please, please accept my heartfelt apology for being the cause of the unpleasant situation you found yourself in.

I had no idea Bill was even in Harrogate. His intolerable behaviour towards you was such that there is simply no excuse that can be made for him. I hope you were not badly injured in that horrid scuffle.

Of course what happened irrevocably alters the situation between you and me, as Bill has reminded us both so unpleasantly that I am a married woman.

I shall always think of you as a valued friend. But if I put myself in your position, I know I can expect nothing further from what has already passed between you and me.

You are a good man, James, and any woman would be proud to be on your arm, and so I very much hope that you find a woman worthy of your attention.

For myself, I shall think fondly of the time we have known each other, and I want to thank you for the kindness you have shown both myself and Holly. Neither she nor myself would be here today if we hadn't been lucky enough to have had you bring her into the world, and so I will remain forever in your debt, a debt that I can never repay.

Please do not feel obliged to reply to this letter.

With best regards,
Peggy

Chapter Six

The next morning Peggy took a long time to get ready.

As the weather was still warm, even though the nights had started to edge into occasional autumnal crispness, once she had given Holly her breakfast, Peggy put on the summer dress that she knew showed off her figure to best advantage, and a clean cardie that complemented the dress's gaily-coloured floral cotton. As she polished her sandals Holly crawled around on the bedroom floor, throwing Peggy's ancient slippers this way and that. Peggy left her to it as it was keeping her daughter amused.

She spent some time taking the grips out of the pin curls she had slept in. She tipped her head forward and ran her open fingers through the curls once, shaking her head as she then stood up straight.

Peggy looked in the mirror and decided that although she had had better days, she would have to do.

She felt foolish about the effort she was making, but even after what had happened, just the mere thought of James made her heart skip and there was something about this that compelled her to do what she could to make herself as pretty as possible.

Peggy couldn't analyse what it was about him that had caught her attention so, especially as they had only talked a handful of times and really had spent very little time together, with practically none of this being just him and her.

But right from the beginning she'd found herself wanting to hear what he had to say, and then enjoying the warm way in which James would reply to anything she said, even though quite often they were a little tongue-tied around each other. They'd never declared themselves romantically, but Peggy thrilled anew as she thought of the electricity that had fizzed through her whole body as their lips met.

Wetting a flannel in the large china washbowl in her bedroom, she gave Holly's face and hands a quick rub, and then she popped her into a clean outfit.

A few minutes later, Mabel found Peggy in the kitchen shaking out the blanket from the perambulator while Holly banged a wooden building brick onto the tray of her high chair, where Peggy had plonked her for five minutes.

'You're lookin' very best bib an' tucker,' Mabel said. Clearly it had not gone unnoticed that Peggy had put a little more effort into her appearance than was usual before she set off for June's tea shop.

Peggy went a bit pink. 'Do I look too much? I've written James a note of apology, but I don't want to look silly if I were to run into him. Not that I'm expecting to, of course. Um, but, er, you know what I mean …'

Peggy realised that what she had just said to Mabel was a fib.

In fact she knew all too well that James should be arriving at the hospital about the time that she herself would be there too, provided that she didn't dilly-dally too much longer at

Tall Trees, and while she insisted to herself that she understood it was over between the two of them, Peggy ached
for a final glimpse of the handsome doctor, as she didn't want
the memory of that furious grimace he had shot her to be the
last one she had of him.

'Go on wi' yer!' Mabel laughed. 'Take advantage o' t' sunny
weather, an' that lovely figure o' yours in that nice dress, an'
who knows 'ow it'll turn oot?'

Peggy pushed the perambulator down the road to the hospital,
sharing less and less of Mabel's optimism as they went along.

There didn't seem to be many comings and goings there
from what she could see, and so she wondered whether maybe
the staff rotas had been altered.

There was a bench outside the entrance and Peggy felt she
needed a moment, and so she lifted Holly out and sat them
both down in a patch of sunlight. There was a gentle gust of
wind, and Peggy felt her curls lift in the breeze. Holly insisted
on wriggling her feet towards the ground, where she stood
straight in her knitted bootees as she clutched Peggy's knee
for support while Peggy held her arm.

'Who's a clever girl?' said Peggy, and Holly gurgled happily.
Peggy felt an overwhelming rush of love. Holly certainly looked
very sweet, with two small front teeth now and eminently
kissable apple cheeks.

Lost in the moment, Peggy leaned to her side and put her hand
out to encourage Holly to move towards it, and Holly tottered
several tiny steps on her own before she clasped her mother's
hand, and mother and daughter smiled at this achievement.

A shadow fell, and Holly beamed gummily at something over her mother's shoulder. Peggy looked up.

Her heart gave an uncomfortable pitch upwards as she realised James had come out of the hospital's entrance and was now nearby, staring awkwardly at Peggy with a scowl on his face, as if the unwelcome sight of her had completely halted him in his tracks. For a moment she remembered what his face was like when it was close up and laughing, but then this was pushed out of her mind by the memory of James's eyes turning to anger as Bill swung him around by the shoulder and tried to land a punch on the doctor.

James looked to Peggy as if the sight of herself and Holly had served only to remind him of Bill's fury, and not in the slightest of the romantic moment they had shared.

Holly kept on grinning because she really liked James, but for the very first time he didn't reward her with any acknowledgement, although Peggy didn't notice Holly's happy expression becoming more puzzled, so intent on James was she.

Peggy's mouth became dry, and she felt a rush of heat throughout her body while her heart beat furiously.

Now she was actually faced with James it wasn't nearly as pleasant as she had imagined it might be.

And then Peggy noticed with an almost overwhelming crush of her spirits that hovering immediately at his shoulder was an extremely attractive nurse.

A nurse whom nobody would deny was younger and trimmer and more beautiful than Peggy. A nurse who looked as if she had washed her hair in actual shampoo, and had bathed using much more than a sliver of soap.

A nurse who was regarding James in a manner that

suggested to Peggy open admiration of the manly physician merely inches in front her.

Then the nurse turned her gaze to follow James's stony expression and it fell on the inelegantly seated Peggy, frozen in mid-twist and still leaning skew-whiff to one side with a hand awkwardly extended and Holly holding it with both of hers while, comically, the small girl stood on the toes of one foot as she lifted her other leg in the air looking for all the world as if she were a ballerina doing her exercises at the barre.

The nurse's expression tightened for a moment around her mouth, Peggy fancied, before her whole visage relaxed into something that looked something more than a little like triumph, although others might have seen a smile.

Damn and blast!

Broodily, James ignored the nurse, but he continued to frown at Peggy and Holly through uncharacteristically narrowed eyes.

The sun dappled his hair, and made the irises of his eyes very vivid. James was more heart-stoppingly handsome than Peggy remembered, even though it was only a few days since she had seen him last. She tried not to look at his lips. She didn't want to be reminded of how she had thrilled to his kiss.

Red-hot with embarrassment, Peggy couldn't think of a single thing to say to him, and most certainly not in front of the pretty nurse who – irritatingly – clearly had decided she wasn't going anywhere soon.

Of course this was how it was going to be, Peggy immediately understood, and as her heart plummeted even further, she knew she'd been kidding herself if she'd hoped for even an instant that it might be any other way.

What was unfurling before her eyes between the doctor and the nurse was always going to be the case, as any doctor would be spoiled for choice these days given the high number of women now working in hospitals. For James to find a new and very attractive companion would be akin to shooting fish in a barrel.

To Peggy's disappointment, there wasn't a single spark of attraction ricocheting backwards and forwards between herself and him, nor the faintest glimmer of what they had almost shared.

Peggy sighed as quietly as she could, although the flicker of the nurse's victorious eyelashes told Peggy she'd failed to hide it.

'I'm such a stupid, stupid chump,' Peggy berated herself, 'what a mug I am for having put on my best summer dress and having taken trouble with my hair.' She tried not to focus on James's strong hands and handsome face.

A moment passed where Peggy felt a sob uncontrollably gathering and rising in her throat, and although she didn't really believe in God, she silently blurted a quick private prayer to herself of 'Please, God, don't let me cry in front of them and make this worse than it already is'.

God didn't seem to be listening though, as Peggy felt the sure-fire prickle of tears.

Looking down, Peggy blinked furiously as she groped under the pram's blanket with trembling hands to find her handbag, from which she hastily snatched the envelope for James.

She waved it in his direction, taking care not to look at his face again.

James snatched it from her and stuffed it into his pocket without so much as a glance at it, although he managed a grunt of what Peggy hoped was thanks rather than irritation, and then he turned his back on Peggy and began saying something about bandages in an unnecessarily loud voice to the nurse.

Peggy stood up abruptly at the same time as she made to swing Holly up and into the perambulator in a single movement. Holly felt heavier than Peggy remembered, and before she knew it she had dashed her daughter's legs on the pram's rim in a way that caused the springs supporting the cradle to squeak and wheeze in a parody of a merry tune.

Ignoring Holly's cry of indignation at being manhandled so curtly by her normally very gentle mother, Peggy marched away after a brief struggle with a foot brake that suddenly didn't seem to want to release, although not before she risked a last peek towards James and the nurse.

Pointedly, James still had his back to her, but the nurse was playing provocatively with her uniform's nurse's cap and smiling triumphantly over his shoulder with a slight curl of her lip in Peggy's direction, she thought.

Peggy assumed the nurse was touching her hat simply to draw James's attention to the proximity of it to the perfect Cupid's bow of her lips; Peggy told herself the young nurse was probably no better than she should be. She risked a second glance at the hand again and was pleased that the nurse looked to have short and quite thick fingers.

Peggy shook her head in what she hoped looked like a devil-may-care gesture of defiance, but she could feel an unbecoming slash of crimson pulsing across each cheek that rather spoilt the effect.

She marched away as quickly as she could, her back ramrod stiff with tension and the loss of dignity, knowing that if James did turn round to watch her retreat, her gait would look awkward and rigid as she stalked along, very much at odds with the gaiety of the summer dress.

Peggy risked a sideways look under the guise of pushing Holly across the road to the shady side.

James wasn't looking in her direction at all. Instead he had his head inclined towards the nurse, very much as if she were saying something to him that he was *extremely* interested in, and especially so now that she had his full attention.

Peggy's chest stabbed with pain, as this felt almost worse than if they had been staring at her with amusement.

Peggy could have crept under a stone, and hidden from the world for ever. And, for the merest second, she hoped with all her heart that she and James would never set eyes on each other again.

Chapter Seven

'Ah!' said June twenty minutes later, once Peggy had finished describing her and Holly's visit to the hospital. 'So, dropping off your letter not an unbridled success then?'

'On a scale of one to ten, with ten the best I could hope for, I'd say it was a big fat nothing,' replied a morose Peggy.

'Okay, exactly *how* lovely was she?'

Peggy knew June well enough to know she meant the young nurse alongside James. 'Extremely,' said Peggy, and then she added a jokey snarly face to bring a little comic drama to the moment.

'Oh dear. Pert, and shapely too, I bet?'

'Very.'

But Peggy's eyes twinkled naughtily when she couldn't resist adding then, 'Stubby fingers though, if my eyes weren't deceiving me.'

'That's a relief.'

'Isn't it?'

They laughed, and Peggy thought that this was what friends were for: to pull you up when you were down in the dumps and feeling sorry for yourself.

'Anyway, I'm not going to think about James anymore,'

Peggy declared. 'I need to conserve my energies for other things. And I'm definitely not wasting any more time on that nurse.'

'That's the ticket. You just keep on telling yourself that,' June said, raising an ironic eyebrow, an eyebrow Peggy chose to ignore.

It wasn't long before they fell to talking about the horrifying BBC news reports on the weekend's air raids that some had dubbed as Black Saturday, as more and more information had come to light on Jerry's aerial offensive.

The bombers that Peggy had seen once the back yard had fallen quiet following Bill and James's fisticuffs had been merely the prelude to a much stronger aerial offensive. It was the first cohesive home attack deemed to be major by the press and the BBC, and each evening at Tall Trees, everybody knew they'd be gathering around to listen to the nightly news broadcast from Roger's ancient wireless that would crackle out a string of woes.

Across the country so far as many as 430 people looked to have been killed in that single night, with London coming in for a real drubbing, exactly as Ted predicted would happen. And if the papers were to be believed, the skies over strategic targets had continued to be lit up over the land each night since with tracer fire, spotlights arcing into the sky and flashes when bombs exploded.

Gloomy depictions of the attacks when the aftermath of the raids could be properly assessed were already in the broadsheets, along with the occasional image of the damage wreaked revealed huge craters and spaces where buildings should be, sometimes with members of the public pictured as they stared downwards or upwards at the damage with bewildered and shaken expressions. London was taking a pasting, but it seemed that just about anywhere in the country was vulnerable.

It felt like dark times indeed, and although it was disturbing, it could well be that they were likely to get darker, Peggy and June agreed, as they wondered if the Government was perhaps keeping back from the general public the very worst of what was going on, and they looked around the café to gauge if any of their regular customers were unexpectedly absent. It was a relief to see everyone sitting pretty much where they ordinarily did.

And then these good friends nodded at each other as if in agreement.

As one, they stood up and returned to their work with resolute and surprisingly calm expressions on their faces, each reflecting that this was what other people would be doing right at that very moment the length and the breadth of the land: everyone trying to keep working hard, exactly as usual, without any unnecessary fuss or palaver.

Whether they be man, woman or child, all would be determined to show Jerry that those left at home in Blighty could, and would, pull together to keep life going on each and every day in as productive and as normal a way as possible, no matter how great the blows of catastrophe the country was suffering.

Later in the morning, June put a piggy bank near the till so that any spare pennies given in change could be donated to the war effort.

It was a small gesture of defiance, but it felt empowering to both Peggy and June.

*

All the same, it was a thoughtful day for a whole variety of reasons for Peggy, as she described later that night when she wrote to her sister.

Dear Barbara,

I hope that you and Ted got back to Jubilee Street from Harrogate without problem, and there weren't any delays (or not for too long) on your train, nor disrupting bomb damage to the roads on the bus down from the station, and that if there has been destruction that you've seen, it's not been too horrid in dear old Bermondsey.

What blighters flying those aeroplanes that night, and since!

There have been some simply terrible pictures printed of the carnage wreaked, and I confess the sight of it makes my blood run cold, and customers at June's café haven't been able to talk about much else.

Bad as this is for us though, I'm sure too that those responsible are just acting on command and they probably don't harbour a personal animosity towards us as such.

That's what I'd like to think anyway, as anything else seems intolerable. If this is indeed true, I hope it's the same for our boys over on manoeuvres across the Channel or up in the skies on the continent or on our ships at sea, as I just can't bring myself to believe that it is ever good for our spirits deep inside that we start to think of anyone in the world, German or no, with pure hatred. It seems so against logic and honest human decency, although I suppose that for those who have lost their homes in the bombings, or loved ones, it might feel in the heat of anger and sadness a very different state of affairs.

I'm hoping too that the fact that you haven't telephoned to say you are back safely in Jubilee Street is because you both are well and there hasn't been a disaster, and that Fishy is safe and happy too, keeping up with catching lots of mice and doing all the things that a good puss should do.

It was lovely having you here in Yorkshire, simply <u>lovely</u>!

I can't tell you how much we all enjoyed spending time with you and Ted, even if the visit didn't end quite as planned. I am supposing that you both hadn't expected ringside seats for a brawl between two grown men, or that you'd spend ages sitting with me waiting for the vet (pony doing well, by the by). Still, the less said about all of that, the better, I daresay!

Connie and Jessie are well and the new school begun at last, but Connie is most vexed by the teachers not putting her in any of the same classes as the other children from the rectory, although she did say she quite liked the look of the school itself as it felt more grown-up than their last school and she could see it might offer 'opportunities'. But she is definitely down in the mouth about not being with her chums, and I had to remind her at teatime today that she's only just started there, and if she applies herself and works hard, then it might not be too long before she is back up with Tommy and Angela at least, as they are in the form that is immediately above hers; and even Larry, who nobody (not even he!) would claim to be the brightest spark in a box of matches, is in 1D too.

To spare Connie's feelings, Jessie is trying not to look too pleased that he and Aiden are in the top form, but I think he must be proud of himself. I do hope so anyway, as Jessie is a bright lad who works hard, and as he is by nature very unassuming and always happy to take a back seat in a crowd,

I'm sure it's good for him to see recognised what a clever boy he is, as it might help bolster his confidence. He looks a bit tired tonight though, but it's not long since he was in hospital after his run-in with those nasty lads, and so I've made sure he's had an early night.

More generally, I think Hull might have taken a bit of a drubbing from Jerry since you left if the Yorkshire Post *is to be believed, but so far it's continued to be quiet here at Tall Trees even though Harrogate is probably only sixty miles or so from the coast, and so please don't worry about any of us as everything and everyone is bearing an equal strain.*

Naturally I've found myself dwelling on what happened between Bill and James, and it still feels awful. In fact it's almost as if I have a newsreel of the fight playing in my head again and again, never coming up with the result I'd like to have happened, which is that Bill had just <u>stayed put</u> in East Anglia.

To which end, I took the bull by the horns and wrote a note of apology to James, and went by the hospital on the way to June's teashop with Holly this morning. I bumped into James in the road outside as it turns out, but it was incredibly awkward, and I wished very quickly that I hadn't gone as I saw him and a pretty nurse hanging on every word the other was saying. I could have howled in pique and envy.

Goodness, what a mess it all is.

So, Barbara, I think I need the advice of a London solicitor, wouldn't you agree? I'm sure the ones up here are very good and all that, but the longer I think about it, the more I can see that any divorce proceedings might drag on and on if Bill decides to be obstreperous, which I have no reason to believe he won't be. They are still saying the war might be over in a few months, and so it seems sensible for me to take legal advice from someone close to Bermondsey. We may all be home in London before too long, and once Holly is toddling properly there may be a time when I'd be grateful for a solicitor nearby. Do you think you might ask around for me? I daresay one of the regulars at the Jolly might be able to recommend someone, although come to think of it, perhaps I am risking trouble by asking for legal recommendations from patrons of a Bermondsey public house!

If I can get Mabel to look after Holly, I may come down early next week, provided I can stay with you and Ted. It will be a year since I was last in London, and so I am sure that I will notice a lot of changes. I do feel like escaping Harrogate for a few days; suddenly it seems very oppressive in a way I've not found it before.

I'm tired now, and so I'm off to bed. You and Ted are very much in my thoughts now Jerry is on the warpath, so please write soon.

Your loving sister, as ever,
Peggy

As Peggy licked the sticky flap of the envelope to seal it, she thought she would instantly fall asleep once she lay down as she ached with exhaustion from her head to the tip of her toes. But when she climbed into bed Peggy found her eyes wouldn't shut nor her body relax, and so she spent a long while staring at the ceiling as the shadows from the trees outside slowly shifted under the changing position of the moon, reliving James's kiss again and again, and then berating herself for doing so.

Her eyes were only just starting to feel heavy at close to eleven o'clock when her roommate Gracie crept past the door, cradling a slumbering Jack.

Peggy watched across the corridor from her bed as Gracie laid Jack in his cot, and when Gracie noticed that she was still awake, she came into Peggy's room and leaned down and whispered in Peggy's ear, 'You're never going t' guess, but I'm going to be married *tomorrow*, an' Jack and I will be moving out *first thing*!'

Any vestiges of Peggy's weariness bolted instantly, as she heaved herself upright in bed instantly.

Kelvin, Gracie's sweetheart, was Aiden's older brother and the father of little Jack. Gracie had been thrown out by her parents when she was fifteen and pregnant, and Peggy shuddered to think what might have become of mother and baby should Mabel and Roger not have taken Gracie in and later, when Jack was born, acted as if Gracie had nothing to feel ashamed about.

If the death toll of the war was anywhere near as high as some pundits claimed, then Britain was going to need every new birth, no matter how these babies arrived.

Peggy had always assumed that if Kelvin and Gracie and Jack all survived the war that there would be a marriage to welcome peacetime. But clearly, Kelvin and Gracie had thought they'd jump the gun, and do things their way.

Peggy smiled and lifted the covers on the side nearest to her friend so that Gracie, still dressed, could kick off her shoes and slip beneath them out of the chill of the early autumn air and keep warm as she told Peggy all about it.

Chapter Eight

The next morning it wasn't long before the whole of Tall Trees was agog with Gracie's surprise news.

As the children gathered around the kitchen table for breakfast, Gracie announced that Kelvin had come home on a short period of leave before being posted abroad, and unexpectedly he'd popped the question to Gracie at lunchtime the day before and she'd been thrilled to say yes.

The excited couple had then spoken to Kelvin's parents, and Gracie's too, because at just eighteen and sixteen they were too young to marry without permission, even though little Jack was already getting on for nine months old.

In haste the families had rallied around, Gracie's parents delighted their shamefully unwed daughter was finally going to have a ring on her finger, even though Kelvin hadn't followed protocol by asking Gracie's father for her hand in marriage.

Time was of the essence, and so a special licence had been procured just before the civic offices closed for the day, Gracie explained, and the town hall marriage ceremony was going to take place at eleven that very morning.

Rather than spending money on wedding presents, the happy couple hoped that everyone would be able to chip in to help them have a brief honeymoon. Gracie and Kelvin wanted two nights on their own in a bed and breakfast before Kelvin had to return to his barracks.

Peggy had already broken the news of Gracie's forthcoming nuptials to Roger and Mabel first thing, and they had said they would be pleased to add to the bed and breakfast fund.

She gave Gracie six shillings as the B & B contribution from her and Holly. What with this outlay, and Milburn's veterinary bill, Peggy's purse strings felt very stretched, but she couldn't begrudge Gracie and Jack – of whom she was very fond – the chance of their happy-ever-after.

'We know everyone is busy, what wi' school an' t' like,' Gracie went on, too excited to eat, 'an' so it'll just be me an' Kelvin at t' ceremony, an' we're going to ask two people from t' street t' be our witnesses, which'll be *so* romantic!'

Mabel looked as if she was going to chip in to say something, Peggy thought, but before she could, Gracie continued, scarcely seeming to draw breath, 'My parents can't come as they're workin', an' Kelvin said it'd be unfair if 'is were there in that case. So we want it just t' two of us, as time is so limited an' we want every second there is to count an' fer us t' make some special memories o' our own. I'm goin' t' leave living 'ere today, kiddies, an' take Jack an' move in wi' yer granny, Aiden, yer Granny Nora! You an' I will be proper family by t' end o' today, Aiden – just think on that. Yer Granny Nora is lookin' forward to 'avin' us, so I 'ear.'

Aiden was left, quite literally, open-mouthed at Gracie's words. Once baby Jack had arrived, like Peggy, Aiden had expected that Kelvin would get hitched to Gracie at some point, but he hadn't thought it would be so out of the blue. And he would never have thought that Granny Nora, who could be something of a harridan, would be persuaded to take in Gracie and Jack. What a turn-up for the books.

Roger and Mabel seemed shell-shocked by the news too, although they'd rallied enough by then to be able to say that while they would, of course, very much miss having Gracie and Jack living at Tall Trees, they quite understood Gracie's desire to get married and move both herself and Jack to live with her husband's family. War meant that everything was different to how it had been pre-hostilities, but it did take a bit of getting used to, wasn't that a fact.

Peggy nodded enthusiastically as if to reinforce the unvoiced notion that this indeed was a wonderful thing for Gracie and Kelvin to do, even though Gracie was only sixteen. To aid a positive atmosphere, she raised her cup of tea towards Gracie with a 'Congratulations, to Gracie and Kelvin!', which made the children do likewise with their morning glasses of milk.

Nobody mentioned how young Gracie was, or that living with Kelvin's Granny Nora with Jack might not be as much of a bed of roses as Gracie seemed to think it was going to be. Aiden had used the word 'battleaxe' to describe his granny more than once, Peggy remembered. And to judge by the way that Jessie glanced across at her, she thought that he recalled the comment too.

Still, Gracie was clearly so ecstatic at what was about to happen to her and Jack that nobody wanted to spoil the mood, although Peggy couldn't help but wonder for an instant if Roger's feelings were just a tiny bit hurt that he hadn't been asked to officiate at a church marriage. Of course, Peggy told herself then, with Kelvin having to return to barracks so soon, there almost definitely wouldn't have been time for a church

73

service as didn't that need a timetable for banns having to be read? Peggy wasn't sure. Anyhow, because it was spur of the moment, it meant that if the happy couple were determined to wed, then a simple civil ceremony was the only way it could be, and as far as Peggy could tell, if Roger's nose was out of joint, then he was making an excellent job of hiding it.

There were many youngsters across the land doing likewise to Gracie and Kelvin, Peggy suspected, and superstitiously she crossed her fingers as she silently wished all these impulsive lovers health and happiness, and hoped that they would manage to come through the war unscathed in order that they could pick up their proper married lives once peacetime resumed, and then make a better fist of marriage than she and Bill had managed.

'Gracie, I have a length of blue silk ribbon in my hankie case – please let me lend it to you, and then you can wear it as a garter. It will kill two birds with one stone, being something borrowed and something blue,' said Peggy, trying her best to get into the wedding spirit.

Mabel got the point and said, 'You have that lovely cameo brooch that was your great aunt's, Gracie, and so that could be your something old.'

'And I've been saving an unopened pair of stockings,' said Gracie, 'and so that can be my something new. That was easy. Why on earth do people make such a fuss about weddings and marriages?'

Peggy and Mabel exchanged a significant look, but neither commented further. Gracie would learn all about marriage very quickly, Peggy knew, and it wouldn't all be beer and skittles.

*

Although Gracie's news was full of hope, it was a strange start to the day all the same, as at this point everybody realised that they needed to make haste in order to get to school or work on time.

At once there was a cacophony of chairs scraping on the stone flags of the kitchen floor as they were abruptly pushed back, quickly followed by the sound of running feet, and in a trice it was almost as if Gracie hadn't only moments before been sharing her big news.

And by the time Peggy had given Holly her breakfast and then returned to the bedroom, already Gracie and Jack were nowhere to be seen.

Their room felt abandoned and distinctly empty, almost as if the young mother and her baby had never been there at all, Peggy thought, as she searched for her own coat and hat.

For while Holly had been eating, Gracie had found time to strip both her bed and Jack's cot; and all of her possessions that would be going to Granny Nora's were now crammed into a bulging suitcase even more battered than Peggy's that was now placed by the door, waiting to be picked up later.

Gracie had scribbled a note she had left on Peggy's pillow:

You have been a brick, Peggy – I cannot think of any other word for you, and we will never forget how kind you have been to us, or what wonderful chums you and Holly have been. I am going to miss you both. Wish me luck, and here's to YOU finding a new daddy for Holly. Gracie x

Holding the note, Peggy took a minute to sit on her own bed and gather her thoughts. It wasn't every day she was compared to a brick, and although she knew that Gracie meant it as a compliment, it wasn't quite the image Peggy hoped she presented to the world.

More importantly, Peggy couldn't decide whether she felt genuinely pleased for Gracie, or whether she was more worried that such a rushed proposal and resolution might end up as a bad idea. She didn't feel envious, that much was certain, Peggy told herself, quickly quelling an unbidden thought of James's smiling face. She knew all too well from her own bitter experience how painful it was when a marriage fell apart, especially if there were children involved. But perhaps Gracie's young age would make her resilient and strong. Or would it make her more vulnerable? Peggy couldn't make up her mind.

If Kelvin survived the war, he and Gracie might in time feel they had rushed things unnecessarily, she supposed.

But if Kelvin didn't make it through the hostilities, or perhaps either Gracie or Jack became casualties too, then Peggy found she couldn't begrudge the young couple the chance to have two nights sleeping wrapped in one another's arms. It really didn't seem too much for them to ask, and of course if the worst were to happen to Kelvin, that certificate of marriage meant that Gracie would be eligible for some government funds for losing her husband that she could use to help raise Jack.

Peggy gazed around the bedroom, feeling slightly at sea at the way Gracie's presence seem to have been erased so quickly. Was this symptomatic of the fleeting nature of life? And could it be a clarion call for Peggy to seize the day as soon as possible, and do what she could to build a better future for herself and Holly?

Peggy thought hard for a few minutes, and then she decided that if June could manage without her, and Roger and Mabel were willing to step in to take care of Holly as she didn't want to risk having the little girl accompany her on the jaunt because there was no sign of Jerry lessening the aerial offensive, then Peggy would head to London the first thing the next morning with the express purpose of seeing a solicitor.

In fact Peggy thought that she might even arrive in Bermondsey before the letter that she'd written to Barbara, which she had already bribed Jessie to pop in the postbox at the end of the road on his way to school as he would be passing just in time for its first collection of letters.

Gracie's unexpected marriage was perhaps an abrupt but judicious reminder to Peggy that life never stands still, and that all it offers should be embraced with both hands, both the good and the not so good.

She remembered the saying 'it's always later than you think'; it seemed more poignant now, and to have a deep resonance. It was time for Peggy to set things in motion.

And then she smiled to herself in the realisation that it felt satisfying to think this way, almost as if she might be in charge of her own destiny. Well, as much as she could be during these uncertain days of war, but it was a feeling that she was in charge of *something*, nonetheless.

Chapter Nine

'You're going to have Gracie as your aunty by the time we are walking back the other way, Aiden! Just think, she'll be your proper Aunty Gracie. And this will mean that you're going to be a real Uncle Aiden for little Jack yourself, have you thought about that? What a turn-up for the books, isn't it!?' joshed Connie as she pushed Aiden quite roughly on his shoulder.

This was after the children had posted Peggy's letter to Barbara and were then well on their way to school, a walk which still felt too new an experience to be properly part of their daily routine, and it was exactly the same moment that Peggy was staring at Gracie's suitcase.

Aiden nodded, but he didn't seem to want to be drawn further on the subject and, most unlike him, he didn't say anything else all the way to school, although he softly touched Connie on the arm as she peeled away from the others to go to her classroom. It wasn't nerves that prevented him from speaking, as he and Jessie were pretty confident they'd be top of their class as they had both done so well at primary school, and their new form master Mr Graves, while old (he'd been pulled out of retirement for the duration, according to Roger), seemed a decent enough chap who knew his stuff, but the shock of his brother and Gracie's surprise decision that had made him so quiet, even though he was very fond of both Gracie and Jack.

Even so, Aiden had tried to buoy Connie up about 1E without drawing obvious attention to the gesture, but he was obviously distracted.

Unused to not having Aiden's full attention, Connie was left puzzling whether Aiden's silent but gentle touch had been to bolster her confidence, or more as a sad reprimand to Connie for teasing him, or had it been to cheer himself up? Then Connie wondered if even Aiden had known himself quite what he had meant.

Either way, she could sense without looking around that Aiden and Jessie had halted and were now watching her pause for a moment outside the open door to her classroom.

She took a fortifying deep breath to steady herself – her heart was really thumping in an insistent reminder of how loathsome school really was – and then Connie paused to take in the depressing sight of the seen-better-days wooden desks and chairs, and the inkwells with the black stains around them, and the canvas atlas half rolled above the blackboard showing Australia and the South Pole, and a pile of new jotters on the teacher's desk at the front of the room. There were a few pupils scattered about the classroom, no one daring to be the first to sit down, and everyone turned to look towards her.

Connie could see that a pecking order was being established and so she deliberately ignored them all. But as she speculated as to whether everyone else from Tall Trees' classrooms looked as unremarkable at this one, she squared her shoulders before marching inside with a rebellious toss of her head, trying for all the world to appear as if she owned the place and wasn't as rattled as she felt deep down inside. And as if she was expecting everyone else to treat her as if she really was their leader, much more so than any teacher might be.

Outside Jessie muttered to his pal, 'Typical Connie, queening it over everyone! Come on, we'd better get a shufti on, Aiden, else we'll be in detention. And at breaktime—' it still felt odd for Jessie to be thinking of it as breaktime after their first two periods of the day, rather than the mid-morning 'playtime' of his still-recent-feeling primary school days '—let's see if you and I can come up with a plan of action to get Connie back to where she belongs, away from those tykes in 1E.'

'Roll on break,' said Aiden, and although he sounded still a little down in the mouth, this didn't prevent the boys sharing a conspiratorial look.

And then, once they were certain there were no teachers behind them to tell them off for running in the corridors, they bolted up the stairs to their form room on the first floor, Aiden taking care to let Jessie win their race but not by so very much that Jessie could ever be suspicious of Aiden not putting up the prerequisite fight.

Chapter Ten

E vents didn't quite go to plan however.

The telephone trilled at Tall Trees after everyone had gone to bed that evening.

Late-night telephone calls rarely brought good news, and it was only by chance that Peggy was nearby as she'd realised that she hadn't wrung out her stockings that were soaking in the scullery.

And so it proved; this was most certainly not good news.

It was a distraught Barbara telephoning from the Jolly public house, only a street away from number five Jubilee Street, with desperate news – Ted was missing.

What her sister was saying was such a shock that Peggy struggled at first to take in the meaning of Barbara's words, and for a second she felt wobbly and had to grab the back of Roger's chair in his study for support.

Barbara – her voice full of panic and fear – gasped out that a bomb had fallen in the early hours of the morning on a ramshackle warehouse at the docks, and by chance Ted had been nearby, on his way home from his nightly stint on the river ambulance. He'd charged into the building to check for people inside, whereupon the warehouse had collapsed without warning. And poor Ted hadn't been seen since.

Peggy could only gulp with horror at her sister's words. This was terrible news to hear, and she wished she was in Bermondsey as she felt too far away to be much help or able to give Barbara the support and comfort that she needed.

Barbara sobbed as she went on, 'It's been chaos and I've not been to bed for thirty-six hours as I'd spent the night after a full day's work helping in a mobile canteen for bomb teams up near the Elephant. There's been so much damage everywhere, and so it hasn't just been that building on the docks. But we've searched everywhere – all the regulars at the Jolly have joined in – but we can't find Ted anywhere. I held back from calling you all earlier as I thought we just *had* to find him, for better or for worse, but it's getting on for nearly twenty-four hours now, and so I think you're going to have to tell the children what's happened. I fear we must all prepare ourselves for the worst outcome.'

'Oh Barbara, what a calamity,' cried Peggy. 'I'm *so* sorry.'

Peggy heard a noise behind her as Barbara let out a pent-up breath of tension, and she turned to see Connie and Jessie standing side by side, drawn to Roger's study as if by black magic, their eyes dark with trepidation and their arms around each other.

'Barbara, hold on, the children are here already,' Peggy said.

Peggy put the telephone receiver down on the desk and turned to face the twins, a hand on each of their shoulders.

'I've bad news, and you're both going to need to be very strong and grown-up. There's no easy way to say this, but poor Daddy is missing,' Peggy told them quickly. 'But the fact they've not been able to find him yet could be a good thing, rather than not, please do remember that. You need to talk to

Mummy, but don't be scared if the call is short – she's having to borrow the telephone at the Jolly and I expect other people need to use it too.'

Peggy stepped back to stand in the study doorway to give the children a little privacy. She knew her sister would have heard what she said to her niece and nephew.

The twins held the phone between their ears so that they could both listen at the same time to what their mother was telling them, the crowns of their heads touching as they made sure to catch every word.

Then Peggy flew up the stairs to break the news to Roger and Mabel. She knew they'd be very cross if Peggy didn't alert them to the unfolding crisis. Aside from it meaning the twins would need extra care, both Roger and Mabel had become very fond of Barbara and Ted, and Peggy was certain they would be distressed at the thought of him being missing.

Used to dealing with all manner of crises, because as a rector Roger could get called upon at any hour of the day or night when awful things occurred, he and Mabel rose magnificently to the occasion, haring downstairs in their dressing gowns and slippers.

Mabel went to make hot drinks for the twins that she told Peggy she would lace with a spoonful of precious sugar for the shock, while Roger and Peggy both hovered in the doorway to Roger's study to wait for the twins to finish talking to their mother.

The twins were still listening in horrified silence, too shocked just then even to cry, and then Roger shepherded them into the kitchen, leaving Peggy to pick up the telephone receiver once more to say to Barbara, 'I'll be with you as soon as I can. You try and get some rest now as you must badly need it, and you won't be helping anyone if you make yourself ill with exhaustion.'

It was advice that Peggy found impossible to follow herself, and she lay in bed tossing and turning for hours after the call. The thought of Ted possibly dead was sickening.

Worse was to come though, as the next morning the twins' beds were empty and they were missing, Peggy discovered at six o'clock when she went to whisper to them that she was going to London and she would give their love to Barbara.

A hastily written note had been left on the kitchen table.

'*We have gone to look for Daddy,*' it said. The twins hadn't needed to add anything further.

Chapter Eleven

Although ordinarily it was Connie who came up with a plan, and Jessie who dutifully followed in her wake, this time the plan was Jessie's.

After they had finished their cocoa, the twins had gone back to bed but neither had been able to sleep, even though Jessie had left the boys' dorm and had snuck into Connie's bed, the twins taking tremendous comfort in being with each other at this traumatic time.

After a long while, when dawn wasn't too far away and he thought Connie might have dozed off, Jessie got up as quietly as he could.

'What are you doing?' muttered a sleepy-sounding Connie. 'It's still dark.'

'Connie?' he whispered. 'Go back to sleep. I'm going to go back to Bermondsey. I know I can find Daddy.'

'You're not going!' hissed Connie, instantly alert. 'Mummy and Daddy would be furious if they thought you were even thinking of it. And Peggy too.'

'Want to bet that I'm not going?' said Jessie, cross now that he'd let his sister know what he was about to do – he should just have said he was going to the lavvy. 'I don't care what the grown-ups think.'

'In that case, you're not going on your own,' Connie said, already fumbling for her own clothes. 'I'm coming too.'

'No.'

'Yes.'

'No! Connie, no. It's too dangerous.'

'YES.'

Connie was clearly not going to let him slip off easily without her, Jessie could tell.

He realised he was going to have to give in and so to save face, he muttered grudgingly, 'Oh all right. I suppose two heads are better than one. We'll have a lot of things to work out.'

'You'll be glad I'm there, you'll see,' said Connie with a confidence her brother didn't share.

'Shake a leg then. We'd better get a move on, before Peggy is about, as with our luck Holly will have her up early,' said Jessie, and even in the dark he thought he could detect his sister nodding.

They knew they were about to have an adventure of the sort their aunt wouldn't countenance for a minute, and she would definitely put the kibosh on their plans.

'Let me write a note,' Jessie added, after they'd carefully crept down the stairs, paying great attention to avoiding all the creaky floorboards, 'we don't want anyone to worry.'

'Good idea,' Connie said in as convincing a way as she could muster. 'They won't mind *too* much, as long as we leave a note.'

Neither twin believed that for a second.

And as the first hint of the coming dawn lightened the sky to the east, the twins snuck out of the back door – each with a slice of bread and dripping, and their rain macs' pockets bulging with things they thought might be useful – almost tripping over a snoozing Porky who was lying on the other side of it. Luckily the piglet didn't wake, although Milburn watched them go, his head over the stable door on the other side of the yard and his ears pricked with interest at the unusual activity.

The pony let out a soft breathy sound.

'He's wishing us luck,' said Connie.

'Let's hope we don't need it,' Jessie answered. 'And fingers crossed he doesn't call to us.'

The twins glanced at the window overlooking Milburn's stable door, which was where Peggy slept. Milburn had a very piercing neigh when he wanted, and if he really let rip, Peggy would definitely be woken.

'Shhhhhh,' Connie whispered to the pony, and quietly Milburn watched them jog around the house, the soft soles of their summer sandals making barely a sound on the stone flags of the back yard.

Once outside the garden gate, the twins ran at full speed down the road away from Tall Trees, their faces determined. As far as they were concerned, it was unthinkable that they wouldn't return to London when their father needed them.

They reached for each other's hand and then they ran all the faster.

It was a long way to go, even though they weren't totally sure of the way, and they wanted to be there as soon as they could.

Chapter Twelve

'We have gone to find Daddy.'

No matter how Peggy stared at the piece of paper weighted down under the salt cellar on the kitchen table, she couldn't make the words mean anything else, other than the twins had done a bunk and now were, well, who knew where?

'This is terrible,' said Peggy to Roger a few minutes later, after she had charged noisily up to his and Mabel's room clutching the note, 'Barbara's never going to forgive herself, or any of us, should they come to harm. How on earth do Connie and Jessie think they are going to get to London? They've no money, no maps and very likely no idea of how trains or buses work, or the main roads heading there, and they're completely unused to embarking on long journeys all by themselves. And they won't know the telephone numbers of the Jolly or Tall Trees either if they run into trouble, I'll be bound. And I bet they've not thought of food or drink. They'll be cold and tired, and this will make them easy prey for anybody with malicious thoughts …'

'Peggy, calm down, dear. Do try not to catastrophise,' said Roger sensibly as he interrupted her panicky train of thought, reaching a little wearily for his dressing gown and slippers; still heavy-headed with sleep, it didn't feel very long since he had taken them off. 'Both of them are resourceful children, remember, and we must take heart from the fact that Jessie and Connie are together – that will make them much less vulnerable, as I'm sure they won't let themselves be separated from one another. Still, I think you must catch the next train to London. I'll drive you over to Leeds to speed up your journey a little as it will save you changing trains. You go and get ready, and I will telephone the police to report Connie and Jessie's absence from their billet.'

Mabel told Peggy that she would be happy to look after Holly for the next few days, adding Holly could 'help' her with the parish accounts.

Peggy thanked Mabel profusely as having someone else care for her lively daughter would give her one less thing to worry about during a long train journey and, following that, what was likely to be a very stressful and difficult time.

She was almost certain that Mabel's jokey comment about Holly 'helping' might be something Mabel would regret uttering, as looking after Holly was a lively business and it was difficult to do much of anything when she was in full flow, and so Peggy very much appreciated the always busy Mabel's selflessness.

Peggy knew too that Holly would find it less disruptive to stay put in Harrogate, although the mere thought of them being separated for a few days gave her a real pang. It was the first time they had ever been parted, and Peggy hoped she wouldn't miss Holly too much, and vice versa.

It wasn't long before she was packed and ready to go, and

was ruffling her daughter's hair as she told Holly that she must be a good girl for Mabel.

Holly took no notice whatsoever of her mother's words; she was already much too intent on what Mabel might be about to give her to play with before she went to wake the rest of their children for their breakfast before school.

Mabel had also promised that she would telephone June when it was a bit later to explain the situation, and tell the school about the twins' absence. Peggy realised that she had felt so anxious about Ted and Barbara, that she hadn't even thought about letting both June know she wasn't going to be at work for a while, or informing the school. She sighed that she wasn't better at coping in a crisis.

Still, Peggy was standing ready by the car clutching a basket containing a change of clothes for herself as well as for each of the twins by the time Roger came outside as he tried to remember which of his pockets held the keys to the car. If the worst came to the worst and there had to be a funeral, Peggy had made sure that these outfits would do, but she had felt too at sea to sort through other clothes to take, telling herself that what they stood up in would have to be rinsed out overnight should they get grubby.

They drove to Harrogate station, but there was neither hide nor hair of the twins, and they then drove along various bus stops, and then the main road out of the town, but however much Peggy peered around, it remained resolutely twinless.

'Let's head for Leeds,' said Roger, and Peggy nodded in agreement.

Once the suburbs of Harrogate dropped away, Peggy realised it felt unusual to be going anywhere by motor, as Roger rarely drove anywhere these days. Petrol was firmly rationed, and in order to save the car for emergencies he ordinarily drove a well-behaved Milburn in the trap for his run-of-the-mill parish visits, or else he walked or cycled. And when he was required to go to Leeds, he nearly always went by train. The fact that he was driving Peggy to get the direct train showed that he thought Jessie and Connie missing was a circumstance that mustn't be ignored.

'I'm so thankful to you for taking me to Leeds, Roger,' said Peggy after Roger told her the police had promised that they would keep an eye out for the twins. 'We must all be a nightmare for you and Mabel, I do know that, especially when you have both been so terribly kind to all of us evacuees. I don't know what we'd have done without you. And we've repaid you by bringing the police to Tall Trees on more than one occasion, and the less said about the set-to between James and Bill the better, and now there's this.' She sounded at the end of her tether, Peggy knew, and as her bottom lip began to wobble, it was a struggle to hold it all in.

'There, there, Peggy, please don't take on so. It's my pleasure to be able to help,' Roger replied. 'You just concentrate on the best way of finding Connie and Jessie.' There was a pause, and then Roger added, 'I have to say though that life is never dull when your family is about!'

Peggy gave a tiny smile. She did feel bad for the disruption that she and her loved ones had brought with them to Tall Trees, and she felt very, very worried, both about the twins' whereabouts and regarding what might have happened to Ted. None of it was nice to feel, and Peggy was full of an extra twist of dread as to what the next few days might bring.

But to distract her from these maudlin thoughts, Roger began to speak about Gracie and Kelvin's marriage, proving to be remarkably sanguine about the whole matter.

'Um,' said Peggy after a while, finding it very difficult to follow the conversation, her nerves feeling so shredded.

But she didn't want to appear rude when Roger was being so nice, and so she rallied to say, 'Gracie wrote me *such* a sweet note. And I thought as I read it that she's braver than me, and perhaps I should take a leaf out of her book, and so this is why I'd already planned to go to London, although leaving at this godawful time is a bit earlier than I'd expected. Gracie made me feel that I need to move things forward in my own life myself. I hadn't planned on having to give chase to Jessie and Connie though, or feeling so concerned about Ted.'

'This will all work out, Peggy, you'll see.' Roger had such a compassionate tone in his voice that it quite undid Peggy, especially when he added, 'And the fact there wasn't another telephone call from Barbara during the night might well be a positive sign.'

Peggy blinked quickly a couple of times as she pretended she needed to poke about in her possessions in the basket on her knee, after which she had to clear her throat.

Then, to her relief, Roger lightened the mood a little by adding, 'I'm not sure how easy Gracie will find it once she has got her knees under the table alongside the fearsome Granny Nora though.'

'Agreed,' said Peggy, and she and Roger shared a smile, a smile that was distinctly feeble in Peggy's case.

There was no sign of the twins at Leeds station, and Peggy felt flat with disappointment.

She hadn't realised she had been hoping against hope that they would be there, but in the sense of crushing defeat caused by their absence Peggy saw that indeed this must have been the case.

'I wonder if Jessie and Connie have tried to cadge a ride with somebody by sticking their thumbs out, and are trying to get to London by road instead, in which case their trail will be hard to follow. But to do that would be quite an undertaking for them, especially with all the road signs taken down and me having locked away all our maps, and so I think you should take the train anyway to London, as it could be you'll be more help to everyone if you are there,' said Roger.

Roger bought Peggy a train ticket, and then he began to escort her to the platform the London-bound train would be leaving from in just a couple of minutes.

'I don't know what to do for the best, Roger,' cried Peggy as they crossed the station concourse, her voice tight with disappointment that the twins were nowhere around. 'And I don't know what Barbara would want me to do. Should I stay in Harrogate, or get to London? I really hope—'

And then she let out a cry that made Roger visibly jump, followed by screams of '*Jessie! Connie!*' at the top of her voice.

'*Peggy!*' came an answering screech.

Roger turned to the direction Peggy was staring, to see the rather comical sight of a guard heading their way, firmly holding onto the twins as he strutted along between them, their nearest ear in each of his hands.

The guard looked cross and as if he was holding on to the children very firmly, and although presumably this was quite an uncomfortable way of being led along, the twins were, for a moment, clearly delighted at the sight of familiar faces, although this quickly gave way to trepidation at what Peggy and Roger would do now that they had been caught out.

'Do you know these children?' the guard said testily to Roger and Peggy, who had both run forward. 'I caught them hiding away in the guard's van. These reprobates seem to think they could travel *without paying*, and so we are off to see the station master.'

Peggy thought that Jessie and Connie appeared more regretful that they had been caught in their attempt of stowing away on the train, than in any way contrite about their actions.

They looked like what they were – children who had had precious little sleep – but their expressions remained incredibly determined that they were going to London to try and find their missing father.

Then Peggy noticed something she found almost unbearably touching. They were each clutching tightly to their chests the knitted toy bears that had accompanied them up to Harrogate over a year earlier.

Jessie and Connie, although in many ways quite grown-up now, had clearly thought that they might be in need of the sort of childish comfort that only holding a treasured toy could provide.

Bless them, she thought, and then Peggy had to fight manfully yet again with another lump of emotion that had come unbidden to her throat.

'These are my niece and nephew,' Peggy hastily admitted to the guard, as relief flooded through her that the twins hadn't come to any obvious harm, despite the rashness of their impulsive and potentially dangerous actions. 'I'm sure they didn't mean to cause you trouble.'

With a sniff of what seemed like disbelief, the guard continued to look very affronted, and he kept tight hold of the children's ears although Peggy noticed the two of them relax when they realised she sounded more cajoling rather than cross as she spoke to the guard.

'They learned very late last night that their father is missing in London, and so they wanted very much to get home to Bermondsey, come what may. I'm sure you can understand what a very big shock to them that news was,' Peggy added in as persuasive a voice that she could muster as she appealed to the guard's better nature. 'I don't think they set out to commit an offence on the railway.'

'Ah,' replied the guard, the wind taken out of his sails at Peggy's words, although he then added, 'Well, that's as maybe. But we can't have all and sundry riding on the railways for free, can we? No matter what the reasons are.'

The guard was a jobsworth, Peggy decided, and she felt too weary and fraught to be polite any longer.

But as she opened her mouth to give him a piece of her mind, Roger nudged her arm in a way that warned Peggy that she was in danger of making things worse, and quickly he stepped in to smooth things over, saying that of course he'd pay for the children's fares from Harrogate to Leeds, and after that he would take them home with him in the car, while Peggy went on to London.

'No!' shouted Connie and Jessie as one. 'We're going to London to find Daddy! We're *not* going back to Harrogate.'

'That's not possible, I'm afraid. You must both go back to Tall Trees,' Peggy told them very firmly. 'Now the bombing has started, it's too dangerous for you in London, and you know that. Mummy will let you know the very moment there's news, whatever it is. I promise.'

'NO!' Both twins were adamant. 'We're going to London. With you, Peggy.'

The whistle was blown by an exasperated-looking guard for the final stragglers to get on to the London train. The Tall Trees contingent looked at him, and he stared pointedly back at them. A decision had to be made right away.

Roger and Peggy stared at each other helplessly as the sound of closing doors clanged up and down the train platform.

Peggy didn't want to miss the train as she'd have to wait an age for another, but she didn't want the twins to risk hurting themselves if she got on alone, should they give chase as the locomotive pulled out of the station and attempt to jump into a moving carriage.

'Would I be able to buy them tickets from here to London on the train?' said Peggy, and the guard nodded.

Roger pressed some money into Peggy's hands just in case she didn't have enough, and then he said, 'I'll sort those other fares. Off you go.'

And with a whoop of triumph from the twins and Peggy saying, 'Don't either of you make me regret this', the three of them climbed onto the train in the nick of time, and the moment the guard banged the door to, off the train chugged.

Five minutes out of Leeds, Connie said, 'We're starving. I don't suppose ...'

'You suppose right,' said Peggy a trifle snappily. Well, a bit more than a trifle snappily, truth be told.

She'd had a rotten night's sleep and had had an early start marred by a cartload of worry. And now she felt very put out at being ambushed by the twins into having them accompany her.

For a few seconds it all seemed a bit much, and she fiddled with her gloves in a thoroughly disgruntled way.

But then she calmed down when she saw Jessie catch his sister's eye and then from their seats opposite her, both twins looked at her with downcast expressions.

It didn't take Peggy long to feel overcome by guilt; the poor things were only eleven after all, and they would be tired and hungry, as well as beside themselves with worry over what might have happened to their father.

Peggy smiled to let them know they were forgiven properly now, and putting her basket on the floor she opened her arms and they both came forward for a hug, a hug that Peggy found she valued every bit as much as both of them.

Once the twins had been persuaded to sit down, gently Peggy tried to prepare them for every eventuality that they might find when it came to Ted, but their serious expressions and glistening eyes told her they were fully aware of what they might have to face.

They needed distracting, Peggy decided.

And so at the next sizeable station, Peggy had a word with the guard waiting on the platform, explaining the situation, and he directed her to a stand selling sandwiches, indicating that it was all right for her to jump the queue. Peggy apologised to those she was pushing in front of, and then she bought food and drink, running victoriously back to the carriage with her arms full.

After they had eaten, the clackety-clack of the train's wheels on the metal tracks as it rattled along quickly lulled the children to sleep.

Although Peggy felt weary, she didn't feel sleepy as such. But while restless at first with her worries over Ted refusing to lessen, nonetheless she found the gentle rocking of the train's carriage to be soothing, and as the miles passed she started to feel stronger and a little recovered.

As the fields rolled by, punctuated by the train stopping at various stations, stations often overshadowed by depressed-looking red-brick factories and other industrial buildings, most of which seemed to be belching out thick clouds of smoke, Peggy stared out of the window and wondered if those inside – who'd be nearly all women, these days, often even right up into the ranks of management – were making armaments. She fancied that in many ways in these dank buildings the war was being won by an army of selfless workers.

And slowly, although the view was sometimes dour and her thoughts downbeat, Peggy felt her spirits settle, just a tiny bit.

As the train paused for a minute or two at yet another station – Peggy wasn't quite sure where they were as all the stations had had their name plaques removed to confuse Jerry should there be an invasion, and of course that this meant that ticket collectors or guards no longer shouted out the stops – she noted that somebody was still taking the trouble to make sure the wooden planters along the platform had abundant foliage and cheery flowers spilling over the sides.

The sight of this riot of colour and verdancy suddenly made Peggy infused with optimism about Ted's fate. It was impossible not to be uplifted by such a joyful sight, and she couldn't believe the flowers would be so colourful if Ted were no longer in the world.

Chapter Thirteen

An hour or so later, the twins were awake and the train gave a very loud yet comically wheezy toot to its whistle to signal their arrival at Kings Cross in London.

The mere thought of the station's name brought its usual flush of warmth to Peggy, as whenever any member of the family could be persuaded to say Kings Cross, Jessie and Connie had nearly always immediately responded with 'And the Queen's not too happy either', and so this had become something of a running gag at Jubilee Street. It was a small joke, but a sweet one, Peggy felt, and she rather hoped the children wouldn't grow out of saying it too quickly, although she knew that day would come at some point.

The twins' faces remained stony though, and Peggy knew that today wasn't the day to remind the understandably trepidatious Jessie and Connie of such jokey things. They had serious matters in hand they needed to save their energy for.

As she stepped a trifle stiffly down from the carriage onto the platform, the more positive mood of earlier threatened to evaporate as Peggy felt just to be in London was unaccountably odd, and for her to be there without Holly even more so.

It didn't help that she couldn't help comparing the sight

before her now with how it had been when the three of them had been at Kings Cross last, on their way up to Yorkshire the previous September for the duration as evacuees.

Two more contrasting views would be hard to come up with, Peggy thought.

Back then, just over a year earlier, the whole station had been crammed to the gills, simply awash with excited evacuees jostling against one another.

A million and a half people had been in the first wave of the Government's evacuation, and a large proportion of those evacuees had left from Kings Cross in just a matter of days. The evacuees gathered in the station back then were a raucously noisy mix of children who were often accompanied by their school teachers, or pregnant women – Peggy had been both – or mothers with toddlers or those who were blind or otherwise disabled.

Some of the poorer children had absolutely nothing with them other than the filthy summer clothes they stood up in and holey plimsolls or badly scuffed sandals on their feet, many without even a cardie or a pullover, even though autumn was just around the corner, and Peggy had been left horrified that some dear children came from poverty-stricken families that had so little.

She'd been touched, too, by the luggage labels many parents had pinned to their children's clothing, with the kiddie's name and address scrawled, and sometimes their age, and their likes and dislikes. Peggy had found the sight of this both optimistic yet almost unbearably poignant.

Peggy remembered that there had been long queues for the station's lavatories and refreshments, but people waited patiently in line as others were herded past them on the way to their trains, although nearly everyone shared the same pensive look on their face as they wondered quite what it was they were heading towards.

The hullabaloo in the station had been chaotic, with people milling antlike everywhere, and an almost deafening din of excited chatter rebounding from the high rafters in the station's roof as everyone tried to find where they needed to be. Those keeping the melee under control had glared down at their clipboards of lists of passengers, and shouted crossly into megaphones or blown whistles to try and get the right evacuees' attention; some even waved flags in the air to marshal together the group of evacuees they would then escort to the correct platform where they could find their trains.

Peggy had found it very disorientating and she had been understandably scared that such an upset might be harmful for the baby she was carrying. Jessie and Connie had shrunk very close to her side as they pushed their way through the station, determined to stick to her like glue.

Certainly, many of those evacuated alongside Peggy and the twins had gone on to hate where they had ended up, and Peggy knew that a sizeable tranche of evacuated children had soon returned to London when their parents couldn't bear their families being split up. Some evacuees had been woefully treated as little more than slave labour by the households that took them in, and so who could blame them for wanting to go home?

Peggy and the twins had understood immediately that their billet at Tall Trees was one of the really good ones, and that they had well and truly fallen on their feet when Roger and Mabel had picked them as their evacuees. Tall Trees was comfortable and spacious, with inside plumbing and the luxuries of a telephone and even a refrigerator, plus it had the added bonuses of a large garden for children to play in and lots of books and musical instruments for the evenings. And even a pony and a piglet who were very much part of the new family they all now belonged to.

Over the last year Ted remained insistent that they were all staying in the right place. Harrogate was much safer than Bermondsey, he swore, adding, 'It's nought but a matter of time before these docks 'ere are bombed. You all need to be out of it, you mark my words.'

Peggy started when she realised that almost everyone from the train down from Leeds had now departed, leaving the twins staring up at her questioningly as she stood frozen in thought.

She said, 'Right, you two, let's find the bus stop,' and Jessie and Connie looked relieved.

As they made their way through the station, everywhere was dusty and grubby, and smoke from the dense number of hearths nearby caught in their throats and prickled their eyes. The station looked much more depressed and shabby than Peggy remembered it being when they had been there last time, and the glimpses of London streets as they had chugged into the city suggested this was the same outside of the station as well as in it.

Peggy couldn't recall London being like this before, but then she thought that maybe she was just more used to the griminess when she had lived in the city.

Large propaganda posters had been pasted up on every conceivable space, reminding people to Open Their Door to strangers should there be a raid, that they all should Grow Their Own veg, Wear Something White in the blackout, and – most pertinent to Peggy and the twins, being evacuees – Leave The Children Where They Are.

Harrogate had the same posters but there in the sharp Yorkshire air they seemed fresher and brighter-hued some-how, offering a more uplifting sense of Britain's bulldog spirit. Here the posters seemed faded and worn and verging on the mournful.

Perhaps most noticeable to Peggy of all though was that the excited high-pitched clamour of the evacuee children of a year ago had given away to the deeper, huskier hum of what sounded to be almost totally men's voices, emanating from a mass of soldiers in army uniform standing around gossiping as they waited for, Peggy assumed, their trains up to various camps and airfields.

Peggy could see virtually no women in the station and she was struck by the sight of each Tommy having a huge sausage of a canvas bag containing his kit upended on the ground beside him, big enough in which to hide almost anything. To a man, these chaps smoked cigarettes as they chatted, many casting an appraising eye over Peggy's figure as she made her way past.

There was a lewd catcall made in Peggy's direction despite the presence of Jessie and Connie, followed by a bawdy shout of 'Oi, I'm over here and ready for you, lady', followed by somebody else saying 'Hello beautiful' and another calling 'Smile, it might never happen'.

With a chippy toss of her head, Peggy tried to ignore these comments and bawdy whistles. But it was difficult as many of these men refused to look elsewhere if she caught the glint in their eye, and she could feel herself growing flustered.

The twins were unhappily silent and seemed to share their aunt's discomfort, and Peggy's cheeks began to colour although she tried very hard not to let them, quickly darkening from her customary pale shade to a flush of becoming rose and on to an uncomfortable fuchsia.

Luckily the promenade past the soldiers didn't last for too long, and once Peggy and the twins were safely upstairs on the bus that would take them through Blackfriars, across the River Thames and down to the Old Kent Road – they would walk to Bermondsey from there – she began to feel a bit less hot under the collar.

Then, as the bus made its way slowly around the next corner, suddenly her and the twins' attention was transfixed by the sight before them.

The sheer extent of damage the slew of night-time bombing raids had already inflicted on London was plain to see.

Peggy was shocked and her mouth fell open. The London in which she had grown up, and which she loved, was clearly badly wounded and bleeding.

After a while Jessie summed it up, saying, 'It doesn't look like London,' and Peggy had to agree.

Although it had only been a few days since Jerry's aerial offensive had begun, collapsed buildings were numerous, sometimes with depressed-looking people standing around as they surveyed the damage. There were wisps of smoke curling upwards still from some of the heaped masonry on the pavements and shattered glass everywhere. Just as shocking were the large craters left by the blasts here and there in the road, sometimes meaning the bus had to divert from its normal route into side streets, once almost getting stuck trying to navigate a particularly sharp corner to a very dingy back road.

At one point Peggy looked down at a pavement, and saw an abandoned, soggy-looking dolly lying there blackened with soot and with an arm missing, the other arm waving at her as if the dolly were drowning. It was only a little thing that Peggy spied for a second or two, but even so she found her eyes filling with tears at the distressing sight. She hoped neither of the twins had noticed the filthy toy that had probably once been very loved by a little girl. And she hoped that by having the twins with her, she wasn't leading them into physical danger or a horrible situation to do with what might have happened to Ted.

With a final glance at the grubby doll and then across at the contrast of the twins' knitted toys, more robust and much cleaner, Peggy felt washed with shame that she had just been wrapped up in herself, lost in the trivial embarrassment of the few minutes earlier that her left her feeling upset and affronted by being given the once-over by a few men in uniform. Ordinary people had had their homes disappear into nothing; this is what she should find upsetting, and certainly not an unwelcome leer or two from some men on their way to war.

It was a salutary lesson that she'd do well not to forget, Peggy told herself, and then, as she and the twins sat in total quiet, too stunned to speak, she spent a mile or two of the bus journey reminding herself very firmly of the myriad things and people in her life she should be grateful for.

*

'Peggy! And my darlings!' squealed Barbara when they tapped on the front door in Jubilee Street.

Barbara's broad smile was heartening to see, and immediately Peggy felt as if the weight of the world had been swept away in an instant from her shoulders.

She knew Barbara wouldn't be smiling as she was if Ted had been badly hurt or worse. And the fact her sister wasn't surprised to see the twins told Peggy that either Roger or Mabel had telephoned the Jolly, to beg someone to pass on the message to Barbara that the three of them were on their way to Bermondsey.

'Ted's all right,' Barbara cried, her eyes shining with happiness.

Jessie and Connie both yelped with pleasure and threw themselves against their mother who hugged them back as tightly as she could.

Peggy smiled at her sister, as she mouthed, 'How is he really?'

Barbara pulled the children close once more for a final hug, and then she said to all of them, 'Ted had a concussion that temporarily affected his memory, and he doesn't seem to have suffered any other obvious injuries other than some cuts and grazes to his hands.

'He went missing as after he'd had his head bumped, he was helped out of a hole made in the rear of the building by an ambulance crew who didn't pass the information on to the relevant authorities, or to those working at the front of the building where most of the damage was. And so we found him this morning in a shelter all the way up in Camden – no, don't ask me why he was there as I have no idea, but I suppose all the ones around here must have been full – when somebody thought to check all the shelters outside the immediate area. He'd lost his memory, but although he was groggy this morning, I hear that now he seems to be getting it back quickly. He's being brought down from Camden in an ambulance and I'm just about to meet him at the doctor's. Shall we all walk there together to give him a lovely surprise?'

Peggy suddenly felt overwhelmed with fatigue, and she knew that she'd rather have a moment to herself than to go with the others to collect Ted. 'You three go to meet him – it will be good for you to have a special family moment. I'll have a sit-down and wait for you to come back.' Peggy grinned at Jessie and Connie. 'And then you two rascals can tell me all about it.'

'Thanks, Peggy, and I'm delighted you're here,' said Barbara, 'I've got warden training tonight, even though I feel a bit that I'm running on empty, and so it's good that you'll be able to keep an eye on Ted later. I think I told you I'm being moved from helping with the mobile canteens to assisting the Chief Warden as he deals with bombed-out people and moving those affected to safety, but you and I should have time for a catch-up before I have to go out again.'

As she put the kettle on to heat once they'd gone, Peggy wished she was able to buy some food to chip in with Barbara and Ted's provisions, but unfortunately her and the twins' ration books were for use in designated local shops in Harrogate only.

Peggy told herself that she should make the most of whatever Barbara had in the house already and see if she could surprise them with a ready-prepared supper. After a little sit-down, that was.

She looked around her as she slumped in a chair.

It was undeniable that number five Jubilee Street seemed much tinier, and tattier, and colder inside, than Peggy remembered. How odd.

It was verging on the dingy in fact, which she had never previously thought, with its familiar metal bathtub hung on a strong peg from the scullery wall ready to be lifted down and filled with kettles of hot water for the whole family to take turns in on bath night in front of the range in the kitchen, with no indoor plumbing, or Hoover Model 150 vacuum cleaner or electric iron, all of which Mabel owned.

With a little jolt Peggy understood that without realising it had been happening, she had got used to the generous proportions of the large rooms at Tall Trees, and the pleasures having central heating and devices to help with the housework, as well as a proper bathroom and not one but two inside lavatories.

But there was something here that Tall Trees didn't have, Peggy realised, as then a warm welcome bounded into the kitchen, purring a happy welcome that instantly made Peggy grin.

Fishy, Peggy's beloved puss when she and Bill had lived a couple of streets away, was clearly pleased to see her.

And as Peggy sat with the little tabby on her lap, the cat's rhythmic purrs and her paws paddy-padding soon lulled Peggy into a doze from which she started awake only once the twins and Barbara and a tired-looking and slightly woozy Ted arrived back home.

Seeing Ted with an arm around each twin and Barbara and him smiling at each other was a very sweet sight, Peggy thought, as her mood lifted and she thought how nice it was to be back somewhere so familiar, feeling almost as if she had just slipped her feet into some warm and comfy slippers. She really liked Harrogate, but there was something very comforting nonetheless to be found in the wonderfully familiar tiny kitchen in Jubilee Street.

Barbara was bearing a large newspaper-wrapped package as well as some bottles of Mackeson stout and some lemonade to celebrate having everyone back together again.

It was going to be fish and chips for tea, Barbara announced, as she placed the parcel of food on the kitchen table, and told Connie to look lively with the cutlery then reminded Jessie that he was going to need to let go of his father so Ted could sit down. Oh, and they'd popped into the Jolly on the way back to Jubilee street to ring Tall Trees to let everyone know the good news.

They decided to eat their food directly from the newspaper – as who didn't know that that was the *very* best way to eat fish and chips? – and there was a separate, much smaller package that Jessie pushed Peggy's way. Peggy smiled as she knew just what this contained, and how thrilled Fishy would be.

Peggy's belly rumbled at the smell of the fish and chips. With so many to feed at Tall Trees, a treat of somebody else cooking their supper beside her or Mabel was practically non-existent, and she felt very spoilt as she folded back the newspaper to douse her food in salt and malt vinegar, and then spoon herself out a couple of pickled onions from the jar that Barbara had made with produce from her and Ted's allotment.

The twins' happy faces broadcast loudly that they were really pleased about the fish and chips too, but not nearly as pleased as they were about Ted being safely home with a child sitting as close as possible on either side of him.

Fishy was, however, the most thrilled of all about the food as she had a particular fondness for scraps, which was what the local chippy called the bits of batter that had dropped off in the fryer, especially if there was a tiny morsel of fish tucked away now and again inside. Peggy laughed at the way the treat made Fishy purr squeakily and lash her tail with pleasure. It was how she had got her name, and it was the heart-warming sight of the tabby cat and everyone's contented munching that made Peggy's heart feel full to bursting.

'A toast,' she said, raising her glass of stout. 'To our dear Ted, and to all of us. And a big phooey to Jerry!'

'Hear, hear!' the others said as glasses of stout or lemonade were clinked together. 'Phooey to Jerry.'

Chapter Fourteen

After Fishy scoffed a second helping of scraps with such speed that Peggy told her she was a greedy trencher-woman and she'd be sick if she didn't slow down – not that Fishy listened – Peggy deftly cleared away, insisting that Barbara and Ted remained seated at the kitchen table while she made them all a pot of tea.

As it was still light, the twins were allowed outside for half an hour so that they could visit some of their old haunts, provided they didn't go anywhere near the docks, or as far as their old school, and that if the siren sounded they ran home as fast as they could.

'What on earth happened, Ted?' said Peggy in her most serious voice, once the twins had gone off to explore.

'I don't rightly know, to be honest. I remember kissing Barbara before I left for work, an' then nothing until this morning when it was more than thirty hours later an' I was in a strange place with no idea of my name or where I lived,' said Ted. 'Then somebody asked me if I might be called Ted, and did I live in Jubilee Street? An' I thought, I like the sound of "Ted" an' that street, an' so I said I might be. Barbara arrived then, an' I remembered who she was. And since then people 'ave told me about the warehouse, an' it coming down while I was inside – I was in a doorway in the back I'm told, an' this was why I wasn't badly hurt as the lintel took the strain when the wall collapsed. And then I was taken out the other way an' whisked up to north of the river before anyone knew.'

'I should jolly well think you would remember who Barbara was! Thank goodness, Ted, it wasn't worse,' said Peggy. 'You gave us all a huge scare, you know.'

'It'll be nothing to the scare I'll give him if he does it again,' said Barbara grimly. Peggy didn't think her sister was joking.

Barbara sounded quite indignant as she added, 'Do you know, when Ted noticed me picking my way between the beds, he told a man sitting nearby that he'd never seen me before in his life, and I *heard him!* I knew he was joshing, but all the same … I told him to give over, or else I'd leave him there.'

'Risky, Ted. A very risky strategy. Barbara might then have said to them you were suffering from delusions, once you claimed afterwards that you did know her,' admonished Peggy. How naughty of Ted to lark around at that point as he must have known that Barbara would have been beside herself with worry, Peggy thought, but then he'd always enjoyed a prank and it must have seemed a perfect moment to have a moment's fun after the fright of what had happened.

Ted was very pale still, and he admitted to having a headache, so Barbara insisted that he have a couple of aspirins and go to bed for an hour, while she and Peggy caught up.

After he'd disappeared upstairs, Barbara poured Peggy and herself another cup of tea, and said, 'He'll be out for the count now. Tell me once again about going to the police station to see Bill as I only had the time to hear the bare bones when I was up in Harrogate. And I want to hear about how you found the twins had done a flit.'

It was quite some time before Peggy paused for breath.

Once she and Barbara had mulled over every nuance of the distress at finding the twins gone, and she'd reminded Barbara what had been said between her and Bill, Barbara told Peggy that she had already put out feelers locally to see if anyone knew of a good solicitor who might be able to offer advice at short notice. Barbara didn't for a second urge Peggy to think long-term and hope her marriage could survive, and for this Peggy was grateful.

Peggy took special care not to paint Bill to be blacker than he was, even to Barbara, as of course Bill and Ted's friendship went back a long way as they had known each other since they were three or four years old, and so Peggy reiterated that she didn't want Ted to ever feel that he was in the awkward position of appearing as if he had to choose between Bill or her, which could conceivably also put Barbara in a difficult position. Peggy hadn't asked Ted recently what he thought of it all, and Barbara hadn't commented either about what her husband might be thinking. But Peggy knew he had taken a dim view of Bill getting Maureen pregnant, and he hadn't enjoyed seeing Bill fight with James. But good friends were good friends, Peggy knew, and so she assumed that Ted would probably keep these feelings to himself when he was with Bill, and that their friendship would go on much as before, as long as Barbara and Peggy weren't around.

As the twins arrived back and Barbara stood up to put her coat on to go to her training session, Peggy told her, 'I do hope Ted understands that I don't want this to come between him and Bill. I think Bill may be in need of a good friend come the war's end, and so it would be awful if the pair of them were estranged.'

Barbara listened with a sympathetic expression. 'I'm certain Ted knows that. Meanwhile, Peggy, you are stronger than you think, you know. In fact I think all of us women are, and once it's peacetime again it's going to be very possible that we're not going to love returning to how it was, standing endlessly in front of the kitchen sink. I was terrified for Ted last night, but now he's safe, I can see that I dug into reserves I didn't know I had, and I am sure that the same is true of you too.'

Peggy knew exactly what Barbara meant. The sisters looked seriously at each other in agreement, and then as one they leaned across the table to grasp their hands together. It felt good, and for a minute or two as if there was nothing they couldn't conquer.

Barbara broke the moment. 'Well, this isn't going to get the old woman her ninepence. I must get off to ARP training. Peggy, you understand that you're going to have to nip into the Anderson shelter tonight if the air-raid alarm sounds, don't you?' Peggy nodded, and then Barbara said, 'You'll be in charge of making sure the twins and Ted get there, if I'm not back by then.' Jessie and Connie looked quite excited at the prospect. 'That shelter will be an experience for all of you,' Barbara added with a grim look that made Peggy feel apprehensive.

Before hostilities broke out, the Government had supplied those who had their own gardens with all the parts of an Anderson shelter that were needed, with instructions of how to construct it from sheets of galvanised corrugated steel. It was, apparently, a design excellent at withstanding blast and shock, but it was quite a Herculean task to get one ready. Homeowners had to bolt the sheets together, making sure the arch for the roof of the shelter felt strong and sturdy. The sides of the shelter were straight, as were the front and back, with the front having a narrow door in its middle.

Ted had constructed the shelter and then grumbled mightily when he'd had to dig a pit four feet deep to wedge it into. It had been back-breaking work, and Barbara had had to help, but at last the shelter was in place. Ted had then banked up the displaced earth around the dome of the corrugated steel, bolstered by rather a lot of sandbags to bring the protection on top of the curved roof up to the fifteen inches of cover the Government specified.

Peggy knew that once they had finished in their own garden, Barbara and Ted had then helped the elderly residents of Jubilee Street with their shelters, as well as a couple of young mothers whose husbands had already been conscripted. Jubilee Street had always had enjoyed a tremendous feeling of community spirit, and everyone liked to muck in together, both in good and bad times. Still, it had been fortunate for a huge number of people that Jerry kept the Phoney War going for as long as it lasted, as it had taken quite a few months to get everybody's shelters up and functional.

Peggy had noticed earlier that the sandbags and the heaped earth over the shelter in Barbara and Ted's back garden had been there long enough to have sprouted some tufts of grass.

As Barbara went out of the door, she said, 'You'll have to wrap up warmly if you need to go in the shelter, do you hear me, Jessie and Connie? Take a Thermos in with you – maybe Peggy can make it beforehand – and eiderdowns and cushions, and I've a spare torch you can use. The shelter isn't exactly roomy, but it's what we have. Try to take Fishy in with you too.'

The evacuees hadn't had personal experience of an air raid yet in Harrogate, and the plan back at Tall Trees was that if the siren went, then everyone would charge like the clappers the length of the garden path in order to take refuge in an old mossy icehouse down at the bottom end of the garden, in a dark and shaded area under the fir trees that gave the rectory its name. Roger had made them all practise this several times, and Porky was yet not to be the first into the icehouse; he clearly wasn't going to risk being a piglet left to fend for himself when everyone else was taking refuge.

The icehouse had been there for donkey's years and was made of a double layer of large stone blocks, strengthened when Roger had put in struts for extra support as it was very spacious inside. Luckily, it had been built largely underground in order to keep a constant low temperature to prevent the large blocks of ice it would once have contained from melting. A motley collection of camp beds and ancient garden seating had been put inside. For now, its big colony of spiders remained in charge, as the siren in Harrogate was yet to sound.

'We'd best give it a once-over,' said Connie, sounding very practical and grown-up, and Jessie, Peggy and Fishy followed her outside to see what was what as regards the Anderson shelter.

The entrance was only feet away from the outside WC, the only 'facilities' the Jubilee street house possessed. In fact the wooden door to the lean-to toilet was so close to the entrance down to the shelter that Peggy's elbow touched the latch as she passed.

Once down a couple of steps and inside, it was immediately obvious that it wasn't roomy.

Peggy had of course seen Anderson shelters from the outside, but she had never ventured into one before. It was 'compact', to say the least. She estimated it couldn't be even five feet wide nor much longer than six feet. Ted had laid some boards down on the earth to give it what passed for a floor, and there was a small drainage sump and so Peggy assumed that this must mean that either it leaked from the rain or that if people were inside, then perhaps the warmth of their breath would cause condensation to gather on the inside walls of the shelter and then pool on the floor, neither of which were appealing thoughts.

Ted had decorated the shelter's internal walls with some yellow paint, and there were two Tilley storm lanterns hanging from hooks in the roof that Peggy could light (there was a box of matches on a small shelf at the far end, placed beside a metal box with 'First Aid' scrawled on its lid). There was plank trestle seating about eighteen inches off the ground the whole length of each side so there was seating, or even a bed if one didn't mind it being very narrow and not having a mattress to lie upon.

It all felt very cramped to Peggy, and the shelter certainly wasn't tall enough for her to stand upright in. Even the twins were hardly able to do this.

Peggy couldn't prevent an involuntary shudder when she turned on her torch and then pulled the wooden door shut for a minute to see what it would be like if they all had to use the shelter later, and she felt a bubble of claustrophobia course through her.

But if it were a choice between protection inside the shelter and possible death or maiming outside of it, then Peggy knew what she would choose; she owed it to Holly to look after herself as best she could.

While it would be a tight fit for herself and the twins, and Barbara and Ted to huddle up together inside the shelter, they could manage, Peggy knew, and she suspected she would feel most comfortable having other people sharing the space with her, even if was a bit of a squeeze.

Goodness knows though how some large families were faring if this was all they had to protect them; Peggy knew the shelters had been designed to take six adults – six! – but that simply didn't seem possible to her.

She knew tube stations were providing shelter for some once the last trains had run, with the underground platforms then being turned over to become makeshift sleeping areas. But Peggy didn't like the idea of nestling down to sleep with a load of strangers around her, as who knew how well behaved or how honourable these strangers would be, and she doubted the sanitary arrangements would be anything other than the most basic kind, probably just a bucket with a blanket slung up in front to give a semblance of decency. Perhaps it was just as well that in this part of London tube stations were non-existent.

Dusting her hands off, Peggy headed back inside Barbara and Ted's house, and switched on the wireless to listen to the news, leaving the twins in the shelter as they wanted to stay there for a bit.

She realised that this was the first time since the onset of war that she had heard the daily evening broadcast from the

BBC on her own. It felt quite strange, she decided, and she was grateful when Fishy jumped onto her lap for a stroke.

A pensive Barbara returned home a while later, and she told Peggy that from the following week, she would be out on her volunteer stints three nights a week, and possibly more often if Jerry's bombardments remained heavy.

Ironically, in the light of the system not having worked when it came to Ted, Barbara's nightly duties would include maintaining a record of the various hospitals the injured had been sent to (or, although this hardly bore thinking about, the temporary morgues), while she also would also have to establish exactly who it was that might have been injured if any private homes were hit and whether anyone might still be missing, as they could possibly be lying gravely injured somewhere buried in the rubble. Barbara would then attempt to make sure relatives were matched up with where their loved ones had been taken. She would also make a note of which emergency centres bombed-out families would be offered temporary beds in.

'You're going to be brilliant, Barbara,' said Peggy as reassuringly as she could as she didn't like to see Barbara looking so nervous at the thought of such responsibility. 'You're so organised and you know this area like the back of your hand, plus you know who all of your neighbours are. And your experience with having Ted mislaid this week has shown you how traumatic it is when good records aren't kept and somebody can't be accounted for. I know that if I were in trouble then I would really want someone like *you* looking after things, and keeping records, and telling me what had happened.'

'I'm not so sure, Peg. We were reminded tonight that we might be first on the scene and this means we could well see some mortal injuries, and that we should prepare ourselves for such an eventuality. I'm not good with blood and gore at the best of times, and I can't bear the thought of somebody dying. What if it were a little baby that I found ...?' Barbara's voice had become quiet, and then quivery with pent-up fear.

'Barbara dear,' Peggy began, deliberately sounding quite firm as she wanted to buck up her sister's spirits, 'you are simply wonderful in a crisis, I promise you, and the fact you are thinking about this as you are, is precisely *why* you are going to be such a boon to Bermondsey's war effort. I know you may well see some frightful things and it's possible you won't be able to save or even help everybody you have to deal with, and I'm not in any way trying to make less of you being worried about this. But you will make a tremendous difference to many other people, an absolutely *tremendous* difference, do you hear me, and at one of the most difficult times of their lives, for which they will be eternally grateful. That is a privilege, you know, and something for you to embrace, safe in the knowledge that without you these affected folks would be having a much worse time. And it's something you should feel very proud that you can do. I am in awe of you, Barbara – in *awe*, do you hear me? – and whatever life throws at you in the next months, I want you to know that I love you and *nobody* could have a better sister than you are, or be more perfect for this new volunteering role than you. And I know Connie and Jessie, and Ted too, feel just as strongly as I do about how wonderful you are.'

Peggy leaned over, even though Fishy wasn't happy about

being a bit squished on her soft lap as she did so, and the two sisters spent quite some time with their arms wrapped around each other in a heartfelt hug as they each felt that tears were hovering very near.

And then Jessie came in and said as if it was just an ordinary day like any other, 'Is there anything to eat? We're starving,' and the sisters pulled apart.

Sure enough, within an hour the air-raid siren droned out its message that Jerry was coming and everyone should race for shelter, and Peggy thought there was no sound quite like it.

The hairs on her neck quite literally stood to attention; the sensation made her shiver with another rush of adrenaline and she was surprised to discover her tightened nipples pushing against the cotton of her underwear.

She ran up the stairs to find Ted on the landing about to come down, and then grabbed first her coat and hat, followed by cushions and eiderdowns that she thrust at Ted, and finally a discombobulated Fishy, before she followed the others out to the shelter.

It took a while for everyone to get inside, and so Peggy had time to pause and look upwards at the dramatic sight of the enormous tethered barrage balloons floating high above in the night sky as searchlights sent beams upwards around them to deter the bombers, accompanied by the alien sound of muffled retorts from what Peggy took to be British anti-aircraft weapons.

'Oh ...' escaped her mouth as she stood mesmerised, and she shivered as Fishy tried to burrow deep inside her open coat in fear.

'Peggy, do come *on*, else you'll be the death of us!'

Barbara's anguished entreaty interrupted Peggy's reverie, and with an effort she tore herself away and hurried down into the Anderson shelter, feeling very small and insignificant after seeing such a huge and panoramic sight stretching right across the heavens above the cityscape as far as her eyes had been able to see.

The light from the one Tilley lamp they lit – Barbara saying they should save paraffin by just using the one – threw sinister shadows that turned them into a parody of dancing figures who shimmied up and down the walls as they settled themselves as comfortably as they could. Ted had the end space, and closed his eyes and seemed to fall instantly asleep while Fishy mewled to go out, but Peggy told her no.

Peggy didn't know what she should do once she had fussed about and had finally become still. It felt very strange, and she realised that what she hadn't expected was quite how noisy the bombardment would sound from down in the shelter, even when the dropping bombs going off felt quite a way away.

There were terrifying crashes and thumps, and Peggy experienced wave after wave of fear and excitement pulsing through her, and she got used to the way the blood rushing through constricted veins seemed to pound deep within her ears.

Peggy could hear Barbara breathing quite heavily and so presumably her sister was experiencing many of the same physical sensations as she was. She looked at Jessie and Connie who, a bit to her surprise, looked exhilarated rather than afraid of all the commotion, and Peggy rather envied them. She realised that what was as bad as the noise of the destruction being caused by the falling bombs were the brief moments of respite, punctuated by shouts and awful cries made by people nearby, which gave free rein to the worst that her imagination could conjure up.

The shelter became warm very quickly, and then oppressively hot, with not quite enough air, but Barbara wouldn't let Peggy crank the door open even an inch.

As Fishy's cries faded to a whimper and then nothing, and the cat slithered under a bench to hide behind Ted's legs where she crouched in fear with eyes so terrified they'd become opaque and opal-like, Peggy and Barbara agreed that the pungent and earthy smell of being inside the shelter would be remembered by them both long after the war's end.

'It pongs,' said Connie, and Peggy thought that was exactly the right word.

There was one very loud blast that seemed to vibrate through and then upwards within the shelter, and Peggy fancied she could clearly hear the corresponding crack of shattering glass, and then some horrifying smashes as if nearby roof trusses and brick chimneys were cascading to the ground, followed by the deafening snaps of what might be roof tiles smashing to the earth in smithereens.

Whatever had been hit seemed terrifyingly close. Peggy was sure that Barbara's saucer-like eyes, looking blacker than Peggy had ever seen, such were the size of her sister's panicked dilated pupils, would be matched by her own reflecting equal horror at what was occurring outside.

'I've made a will, Peggy,' cried Barbara.

'So have I,' Peggy answered. She looked at the ground,

and then she added in a wavery whisper, 'I hope we don't die tonight, Barbara.'

And that second comment immediately felt such a daft thing for her to say – as of course nobody wanted to die that night, or the next, or the night after that either – that in desperation the sisters caught each other's eye, and the madness with which they looked at each other ignited their tickle bones and then they began to, quite literally, howl with uncontrollable laughter.

The twins stared on with wrinkled brows as if they were rather embarrassed by the behaviour of the older generation, and Ted let out a loud snore.

'Stop it, Peggy, else I'll be needing the lavvy,' gasped Barbara.

'Well, at least it's nearby,' said Peggy. 'In fact, any closer and we'd be sitting on it.'

At this the sisters rocked their bodies and screamed with such hysteria bordering between the happy and the panicked that their bellies began to hurt. The humour was contagious, and although quite sleepy now despite all the noise, it wasn't long before the twins joined in the laughter too, even if they didn't quite understand what all the merriment was about. Peggy thought she should probably say that she and Barbara didn't know what was making them laugh either, but immediately there was another deafening bang that made the shelter feel as if it were shuddering with aftershocks of a bomb exploding for quite some time, and it killed stone dead the sounds of laughter of just a second earlier.

And as the judder didn't seem to abate, in abject terror the sisters then threw their arms around each other and the children, with Barbara having linked her arm through Ted's, as they all buried their faces in each other's trembling shoulders, fully expecting these to be their last moments on earth as Ted slept on.

'I think I'd rather be at Tall Trees,' said a muffled Jessie, and Connie nodded that she felt the same.

Peggy knew what they meant; the only good thing she could think of was at least she wasn't exposing Holly to this terrible danger.

'I know,' said Barbara. 'This is horrible, and very frightening for all of us.'

'Even Daddy?' said Connie.

Everyone looked at Ted, whose mouth was now slack as he slumbered.

'Yes, Daddy too,' Barbara insisted, 'even while he is asleep. Being scared is nothing to be ashamed of, Jessie and Connie. You both, and Peggy too, will be back at Tall Trees soon, I promise.'

'Really?' Jessie sounded as if he wanted very much to believe his mother.

'Yes, really,' said Barbara in the sort of voice that allowed no argument.

The bombardment seemed to go on for ever, but when the all-clear sounded they hadn't been in the shelter even an hour, Barbara said, although Peggy felt it had lasted for what could well have been the whole night.

Barbara tapped her wristwatch and nodded as she listened to her timepiece continue faithfully to mark time passing with its ticking, and said in that particular older-sister-being-smug manner that had always irritated Peggy, 'No, not even an hour, Peggy. You are very wrong about that.'

Peggy didn't say anything back although that was more because she felt used up and weary now and not quite up to thinking of a smart retort, than because she agreed with her sister.

As the sound of the all-clear faded, cautiously the twins opened the door to the shelter and peered outside as Peggy and Barbara began to fold up the bedding tidily, and then Barbara shook Ted awake.

Once outside, it was a bit of a surprise for a stiff-legged Peggy to see that everything looked exactly as if it had done when they had gone down into the shelter, with no obvious damage that she could see. While they had definitely heard bombs striking homes, it seemed as if Jubilee Street had managed to come through the bombardment unscathed.

Peggy squinted as she peered about to see if she had missed anything, and then she noticed various neighbours also hesitantly venturing from their shelters at the same time, staring around themselves with equally confused looks on their faces – exactly as Peggy suspected she was too.

She chirruped for Fishy to come to her, but the cat stared accusingly back at her and flatly refused to move from beneath the bench.

Finally Ted woke up, and said, 'Is it all over? That was quick.'

As people nearby called to each other to see if everyone was all right – and it seemed as if everyone in Jubilee Street was – a huge wave of exultation suddenly exploded right through Peggy's body.

They were alive! The mere fact of that felt wonderful – absolutely wonderful – to Peggy, and immensely precious in a way that quickly manifested itself into a powerful physical sensation the likes of which she had never experienced before.

In fact Peggy almost wished she had a man at her side who she could passionately kiss at that very moment, so overwhelming was her desire to reinforce her sense of survival and just being *there*. In fact she couldn't recall ever having felt so vital as right at this moment.

The memory of James kissing her outside Milburn's stable flashed into her mind, as that moment had aroused sensations slightly akin to what she was feeling now, and immediately Peggy experienced an answering wriggle of pleasure from a secret place somewhere deep within her.

Peggy looked at Barbara, and Barbara glanced back at her with what seemed to be a similarly exultant look. Presumably others were likewise feeling a joy in simply being alive, as spontaneously several people had started to clap.

'It wouldn't surprise me if there's not a surge in the birth rate round here nine months on from tonight,' Peggy commented dryly. 'Ted had better watch it.'

'Peggy!' cried Barbara, acting as if she were more than a little shocked.

But Barbara couldn't help then laughing once more, as what Peggy had said was so obviously true.

At breakfast the next morning, Ted had shaken off his headache of the night before and was much less dozy and more like his usual self, and he had been out early to see what the damage was locally. Doctor's orders were that he wasn't to return to working on the river ambulance until the following week, and although normally Ted hated sitting around, Barbara and Peggy had agreed it was good that he could spend a little time with the twins.

Barbara had already left for her daytime job at the haberdashery, and the twins had just got up and were sitting blearily at the kitchen table with sleep-tousled hair, when Ted came back to announce that the Jolly had taken a hit, but in spite of that the landlord was still managing to provide pints of ale to thirsty rescue workers in the wee small hours.

'I told 'im 'e were taking the "'ole in the wall" for serving drinks to those outside a bit too literal,' said Ted, 'for the 'ole of the pub's porch 'ad been knocked off an' most of the outside wall to the ladies bar 'as gone too. Oh, we did roar!'

Peggy smiled, although it was only a little one as she hadn't been able to get to sleep for ages once she had got into bed and she felt quite drunk with exhaustion. Her excitement of the previous evening was quickly fading to a dull-feeling memory.

'Oh Peg, I almost forgot to say but you 'ave an appointment with Mr Ainsworth, a solicitor, at eleven o'clock this morning,' said Ted. ''E's also on the river ambulance team, an' I saw 'im this morning on 'is way 'ome, an' so I asked about solicitors, an' 'e turned out to be one an', best of all, one with experience in divorce law. 'E said you'd be best advised not to get your 'opes up as it's still a man's world endin' a marriage. 'Is office is in Borough. Me and the twins'll attend to the allotment while you 'ead over there.'

Ah, yes, the solicitor. The other reason she had come to London. It was the last thing she felt like doing that morning as she was quite done in, but Peggy knew that she would be furious with herself if she didn't go. She poured herself a second cup of tea from the pot and tried not to feel nervous at the prospect.

Chapter Fifteen

Mr Ainsworth seemed exhausted, with charcoal shadows that looked like bruises under his eyes.

Peggy thought this wasn't at all surprising as he had probably worked most of the night on the river, with time only to snatch a couple of hours sleep before he needed to go to his office for his paid employment.

She knew she wasn't at her best either. The resulting comedown from the excitement of the hour that Jerry's bombers attacked had left her feeling groggy still, and unable to focus easily.

And this was infuriating when she very much wanted to be at the top of her game for the solicitor's visit, she thought as she gave a small sigh of frustration.

Peggy wriggled about in her chair as tried she to get more comfortable, and then she realised that actually she felt a little queasy too and this was probably caused by nervous anticipation over what she hoped would be a clarification of her position.

She hadn't been able to face any breakfast other than the tea, and now she thought not eating anything hadn't been a good idea as she felt peculiarly light-headed. Damn and blast!

Peggy wasn't sure what she should think about the advice Mr Ainsworth had given Ted about not her getting her hopes up, although now that she was finally here she wanted to find out the truth of the matter as quickly as she could, for good or ill.

She had been asked by Mr Ainsworth to take a seat on the other side of the desk to him, with her back towards his office door as he faced it with the window behind him. His hair looked fluffy in the backlight of the window, and his ears bright pink from where she was sitting as the sun hit the back of his head. Peggy knew this meant her face would be illuminated by the window, and that presumably this helped Mr Ainsworth read his clients' expressions so that he could better understand what they were trying to tell him.

She could hear the quick rat-a-tat of a secretary's sit-up-and-beg typewriter in another room, and the faint ding of the bell when the end of each typed line was reached.

Mr Ainsworth's desk was dusty and untidy, and Peggy noticed motes swirling in a shaft of weak sunlight coming in through the window, which badly needed a clean. The solicitor seemed quite a kindly man though, and as Peggy scrutinised the face that was regarding her very seriously, she decided that she could trust him.

They exchanged a pleasantry or two about Ted and how worried they'd been at his disappearance, and what good news it was that he wasn't badly hurt. And then they agreed that Peggy would pay a non-returnable sum and for this she would have thirty minutes to set out her position and for Mr Ainsworth to offer his advice.

Once Peggy had given Mr Ainsworth the fee and he'd put it

in his petty cash box, slipping the key back into his waistcoat pocket, she set out the situation between her and Bill as quickly and as clearly – and with as much essential detail – as she could, as she felt the clock was running. She had practised in her mind what she would say on the walk over to Mr Ainsworth's offices, and now she was pleased she had done this as it definitely saved a lot of time.

The solicitor listened carefully to Peggy as she spoke, occasionally scribbling a few notes onto a legal pad.

He waited for Peggy to finish, and then he cleared his throat. But when his advice came, it was blunt.

'Mrs Delbert, you are likely not to enjoy what I am about to say. I'm sorry to tell you that you are almost definitely going to be at a disadvantage should you take this to the divorce courts, and the situation is likely to remain that way no matter what you do. It seems as if you have grounds for a divorce, as least in the technical sense, under the Matrimonial Clauses Acts of 1923 and of 1937. But the technical tenets of the legalities do not always carry through to the perception of the court, nor their consequent decisions, and I cannot stress that strongly enough to you. This means that, while you might have a case in law, in the actual court you might appear before a judge who personally believes a wife should stick by her husband at all costs, and there will be an innate disadvantage to you in this.

'In your case, should you choose to go further, then the courts are likely to demand further proof of Mr Delbert's infidelity – the existence of the child alleged to be his but born to another woman will not necessarily be enough on its own if he doesn't formally acknowledge the paternity, and your case is very much weakened if he is not named on the child's birth certificate – which you say you don't know – and thus you will need sworn testimony of at least one witness who has seen and is prepared to swear in court as to his adultery, and ideally more than one witness. This is why, in terms of a legal requirement, it will usually mean adultery going forward, rather than adultery that has already occurred, if you take my meaning,' explained Mr Ainsworth.

Peggy frowned. He was quite long-winded but so far she understood what he was telling her. He was right: his assessment of her case wasn't what she wanted to hear.

The solicitor continued, 'Even if you could persuade Mr Delbert that he allow himself to be caught in a compromising position with a woman who is not you – most people arrange for a chambermaid to disturb them in a hotel room – the fact that you have been spending time with Dr Legard is likely to also be taken into account by the court, and very probably it will be extremely difficult for you to prove that you have *not* been a guilty party as well, no matter even if this is a completely innocent relationship, and so this might reduce your husband's culpability to even-stevens. And if you set yourself up to be proved the guilty party – the adulteress as it were – it would, almost certainly, very much damage your own position in terms of the custody of your daughter.

'Before you make your decision, you should bear in mind that in spite of there having been a fracas between Mr Delbert and Dr Legard, the courts are likely to pay more heed to the fact your husband is working, and is not and has never been either demonstrably cruel to you and/or your daughter – according to how the courts might define cruelty – nor has he been violent to you and/or your daughter, nor is he a habitual drinker or work-shy husband, and nor is he insane.

'The court will almost definitely assume that the length of your marriage in excess of ten years suggests that it has generally been a happy one, as signified by your daughter of that union not yet being a year old.

'It is inescapable too, in terms of the opinion of the courts, that Mr Delbert has never wavered from telling you that he wants still a relationship with you and that he is against the ending of your marriage. The courts would take note of all these factors, and I remind you once again that in addition, you would do well to pay great heed to the fact that some judges are very biased against women speaking out against their husbands, and that many judges view it as their duty to make divorce as difficult as possible.'

Peggy's teeth were uncomfortably clenched, she realised, and then she felt an icy bead of sweat inch down her backbone.

But Mr Ainsworth was not finished yet, for he added, 'And even *if* you are granted a divorce, it is no means certain that the courts would necessarily award you custody of your own child, especially should your husband contest the divorce petition; or, if the court so did do this, that your husband would subsequently be ordered to pay adequate support for your daughter. While in theory all of those events could be decided by the courts to be in your favour, in actual practice they might very well fall in favour of Mr Delbert's position. You must remember that the courts are of the opinion that divorce should only ever viewed as a final option, and the system tends still to be skewed in favour of the husband's interests, and in keeping marriages together. Furthermore, if Mr Delbert refused to hand over any upkeep, there's maybe no recourse for you to make him, at least in practical terms. If you divorced and ended up with shared custody of your daughter you would be expected to discuss every situation to do with her with Mr Delbert, and in my experience that is rarely a happy outcome for any of the parties, including the child.

'My advice to you, Mrs Delbert, would be very strongly that you should try to mend your marriage, otherwise you are in for what can only be a time-consuming, painful and financially exacting experience, in which there is also very likely to be a scandal and resulting personal loss of reputation that you might very well find immensely hard to weather, and with no guarantee that you would get what you want, as your divorce might not be granted. And even if it is, there is a risk that you could still lose custody of your daughter if Mr Delbert were deemed the more reliable parent. And of course if Mr Delbert, as a serviceman, were to die during the war while you are married to him, then that makes it simple over you receiving his widow's pension, even though that would be taken as taxable income.'

The tick of the grandfather clock at one side of the office seemed very loud as Peggy tried to absorb what she had just heard. Her position was worse than she had imagined.

Mr Ainsworth said, quite kindly, 'Have I made the position clear to you, Mrs Delbert?'

Peggy felt numbed to her very core by the solicitor's words, and she nodded blindly as if she were a puppet on a string as she managed to croak out, 'Quite clear, thank you.'

Mr Ainsworth obviously had expected this reaction, presumably from having prior experience with similar cases, because he added in a more sympathetic way, 'You can go to one hundred solicitors about this, I promise you Mrs Delbert, and ninety-nine will say exactly what I have. The one that doesn't is not to be trusted, I fear.'

'I see,' said Peggy, standing up abruptly. 'I won't take up any more of your time then. But it sticks in my craw that a man faces little censure for not putting emotional investment into his marriage to anywhere near the same extent that his wife is expected to commit to the relationship, if I understand you correctly as to how the courts would be very likely to interpret my situation. Is this the case if Bill is named on the other baby's birth certificate?'

'Even in that eventuality, I would still remind you that the courts would not necessarily rule in your favour.'

Peggy had to fight herself not to stamp on the floor in temper at the solicitor's reply. It was all so unfair!

'It is not a perfect scenario, I agree,' said Mr Ainsworth, his voice mild. Peggy thought this was because at this point of similar meetings, it was probably where some wronged wives would become furious and raise their voices.

'Good day,' was all that Peggy could manage at that point as she stood up abruptly; she tried to keep her voice reasonable, as it wasn't the solicitor's fault that it was a man's world.

She felt impolite for not thanking the solicitor properly, and in her being what could only be described as curt with him with these final words. But she didn't trust herself not to break down if she tried to say more.

Gathering her possessions with hands made shaky by the tide of emotion sweeping through her, Peggy left the office as quickly as she could, determined not to cry, and a last glimpse of Mr Ainsworth through the bannisters as she went down the stairs showed him looking concerned and sad.

Peggy stomped back to Jubilee Street as quickly as possible, and it was only once she was inside that she allowed herself to give in to a violent volley of sobs, an outburst that alternated with her punching the pillow on Connie's bed as hard as she could, and that was how Barbara found her when she came home to tell Peggy she'd decided she was going to join Ted and the twins for the rest of the day, and they were going to have an afternoon out together, if Peggy didn't mind.

Chapter Sixteen

While going with their father to his allotment sounded okay in theory, in practice it wasn't a lot of fun, the twins agreed.

Ted realised quite early on that the difference between two types of onions that he was growing, or how he'd made the frames for the runner beans from odds and ends, wasn't going to be enough to distract his two eleven-year-olds for long.

'Can we go to the warehouse that fell down with you inside it?' asked Connie.

'I don't think yer ma would approve,' answered Ted. 'I'd be for the 'igh jump if I took you there as she would think it would make you miserable.'

The twins thought about it, and then they nodded in agreement, albeit reluctantly. Their father was right; Barbara absolutely wouldn't want them to see where Ted could so easily have lost his life.

They decided to head to Greenwich Park and climb up to the Royal Observatory, and so they jumped on a red double-decker bus going that way.

The park wasn't as either of the twins remembered it, as the bits of it on the flat had been given over to Grow Their

Own cabbages and other root vegetables, but the hill to the Observatory was still grassy.

'What a view,' said a rather puffed Ted a while later as they stood right in front of the Observatory, looking across the River Thames and the dome of St Paul's Cathedral, and on towards the northern part of London.

They sat down on the grass in order to take in the view better. It was spectacular and they could see for miles.

'If you look at London quickly,' said Jessie, 'it looks normal. But if you really stare you can see where some of the bombs have dropped.'

Connie was silent for a moment. And then she said softly, 'I wonder how many people died in all those buildings we can see when Jerry dropped those bombs? Are their families sorry we are fighting, do you think, Daddy?'

Ted's first impulse was to encourage his daughter to think of happier things, but then he thought that perhaps he shouldn't be too quick to do this. Sometimes not talking about things didn't help, and the twins must feel strange and frightened by the harsh times they were all living through. The actions and decisions of the politicians and the grown-ups around them would help forge the world that Connie and Jessie would be living in and bringing up their own families in once they were grown-up, and perhaps, therefore, it was time for the current grown-ups to start listening to the younger generation and taking their thoughts and fears seriously.

Resolving to make sure that he and Barbara took the children for a proper treat later in the day so that they would go back to Harrogate with some nice memories of their surprise trip to London, Ted said, 'That's a thought, Connie. I'm sure there are lots of folks un'appy down there. Do *you* think we are right to be at war?'

'Hitler seems a bully,' Connie answered. 'And in the playground if somebody stands up to a bully, often the bully is shown to be a coward. I think we are standing up to a bully.'

Ted felt proud of his daughter. 'I couldn't 'ave put it better meself,' he told her, and Jessie's nod told Connie he thought too that she'd been very clever.

Privately, Jessie didn't wholeheartedly agree with Connie's assessment, as the situation seemed more complicated. But Connie had a point, most definitely, he was happy to concede.

Ted put an arm around the shoulders of each twin, and looking very serious, he said, 'What I do know is yer ma an' me are right lucky to 'ave such good 'uns as you two. I'm right touched you tried to come an' find me – I'll never forget that. But it was a lucky day that none o' it were worse. An' you must both promise me an' yer ma that you'll never do this again. Jubilee Street ain't safe for you, an' we don't want to worry about you. Do you hear me? An' you both promise me yer won't be getting' up ter this malarkey again? You're the most precious things in our lives an' we couldn't bear it if anything bad were to happen to you.'

The twins nodded they had heard, and they each promised their father very soberly not to run away from Harrogate again to come back to London.

Then, to lighten the mood, Ted said, 'Now, who wants a florin?'

And, no surprises, naturally both Connie and Jessie wanted a florin, and by the time Ted had placed the silver coins in their hands, all three of them were smiling at each other, even though the twins' grins were slightly tempered by them realising that they had just made a vow to their father that at some point in the future might be difficult for them to keep.

But then Jessie noticed that Connie's fingers were crossed, and he knew his had been too. And wasn't it the rules of vows that if one's fingers were crossed when making them, it wasn't totally binding as a promise?

Jessie and Connie shared a look. It said that they would do as their father asked, and certainly would while the bombing held. But in the coming years, it might be that they wouldn't be prepared to honour his wish for all time.

They helped a stiff-jointed Ted stand up, and as they walked down the hill, they smiled at each other, their eyes shining at the thought of having two bob of pocket money all of their own to spend exactly as they pleased. It was a rare, rare luxury.

Chapter Seventeen

All while the twins were out with Ted and Barbara, Peggy devoted herself to getting quite – well, extremely, truth to tell – tipsy back in Jubilee Street.

Before they had left, Barbara had done her best to jolly a teary Peggy out of the fug she'd fallen into after seeing Mr Ainsworth, mainly by repeating again and again that it must be all very irritating for Peggy, but at least she knew the divorce position for certain at last, and this meant that now she could make her plans accordingly; and *of course* she and Holly never had to live with Bill again; and anyone with an ounce of intelligence could see that Bill was a total fool, that much was obvious; and Peggy should never forget that all the family and everyone at Tall Trees loved – no, simply *adored* – Peggy and Holly; don't you *dare* let the thought of Bill get you down … And so on.

Barbara felt quite weary after not too much of this, and her cheeks ached with her putting on a smiley, brave face for Peggy's benefit. But irritating as it all was, Barbara kept going, as she knew that Peggy would have done exactly the same for her, should their positions have been reversed.

Peggy was a pragmatist by nature, and once she was feeling a bit less angry (no one could have kept up that level of fury for too long!), she wiped the last vestiges of moisture away from beneath her eyes and smoothed Connie's pillow from the angry thumps she had given it.

Then Peggy looked at her sister with a wicked cast to her eye as she announced, 'Well, maybe I'll be able to rely on Maureen putting pressure on Bill to do the right thing by her and the baby, and eventually he'll want to divorce *me* in order to keep the peace in Norfolk, and Maureen will make sure that he does the right thing by me in order to give her and her own baby a clean slate.'

'Hold that thought, Peggy!' said Barbara, clearly relieved that her sister's spirits were starting to perk up, and she quickly stood up as if to go downstairs just in case Peggy would take on again should she hang around, although she did pause in the bedroom doorway to add, 'You give yourself a wash and spruce-up, missus, and I'll nip and get ready for our outing.'

Peggy decided that even though an easy divorce might be a pipe dream, at least the knowledge of her position made her feel a little bit more in charge of her own life.

She might not be able to alter some things, but she could alter how she *felt* about them.

And so Peggy thought of Holly, and how lucky she was to have given birth to such a wonderful and perfect little girl. It might be a mess between herself and Bill, she thought, but Holly was certainly something they had managed to get right between them, very right indeed, and for that Peggy felt blessed across every cell in her body.

Once the others had left on their outing, Peggy poked around in the small, rarely used parlour until she discovered the bottle of port that had been lurking in the sideboard for years.

Peggy enjoyed her first glass so much that she ignored the Spam sandwich that Barbara had made her, instead pouring a second glass that she sipped as she looked at the newspaper. It was full of how the Royal Chapel in the South Wing at Buckingham Palace had taken a right battering from at least one bomb, and with King George VI and Queen Elizabeth being resident in the palace at the time. This upset and devastation at their home hadn't stopped them being photographed later in the day visiting the East End to keep morale up of other people who had suffered through being bombed out.

Peggy thought the reporting of this would be sure to bring those on home shores closer together, the precise opposite to what Jerry intended. If the King and Queen, and the princesses, could soldier on regardless as a wonderful example, then so everyone else would as well. And the stoicism of the royal family could be echoed by Peggy herself, now she knew how difficult it would be to get a divorce.

By the fourth glass of port, Peggy's mood had slipped to the maudlin as she declared to Fishy, 'Those *dear* little princesses Elizabeth and Margaret – fancy them giving up their toy saucepans for the war effort to be melted down. They'll have a fancy little kitchen somewhere with no pans to play with.'

Fishy's eyes seemed to reply crisply that really the princesses would have lots of other toys to play with, and the story was more about how the Palace wanted the general public to feel that the Royal family was just like the rest of the nation in having to make sacrifices, but to Peggy at that moment it seemed easier just to pour another glass of port than to grapple much more deeply with this thought.

Peggy was hit by a wave of hiccups as she pulled the Spam

from her uneaten sandwich to little pieces, which she threw to Fishy one by one. She felt bad for not eating it, as she knew Barbara would be offended – there were hungry children in Africa after all, and many others too who were starving probably much closer to home – but she really didn't like tinned luncheon meat, although fortunately it was another one of Fishy's favourites, not that she was allowed it these days.

Peggy reached for the bottle of port again, and topped up her glass, before turning up some dance hall music on the wireless.

She lifted Fishy up, and as the puss licked her whiskers after her unexpected treat, Peggy buried her face in Fishy's soft fur and danced slowly around the room with her eyes shut.

By the time the siren sounded that evening, Barbara and Ted and the twins had just come in from a lovely double bill at the pictures and were standing in the kitchen, staring at the slouched and sleeping form of Peggy slumped over the kitchen table with her head on folded arms, the now empty bottle of port at her elbow, clearly oblivious to the siren's call.

'Can you carry her into the shelter?' Barbara said to Ted above the drone of the siren, 'I'll collect everything else.'

'She's only a little thing, but she's 'eavier than she looks,' said a red-faced Ted a minute later, once he'd lugged the comatose Peggy down into the Anderson and heaved her onto a bench, '*A lot* 'eavier, it 'as to be said.'

'Sssh, Ted, don't you dare let Peggy hear you say that, for goodness' sake, else we'll never hear the end of it,' said Barbara, although she couldn't stop a twinkle of merriment seeping into her expression. 'And I'll be betting that tomorrow, Peggy will be saying she must have picked up a bug as she feels so queer, conveniently ignoring the fact that she single-handedly drank almost a whole bottle of port. I don't know whether to be impressed with her or cross! I know I couldn't drink that much, no matter what the provocation.'

Fortunately there was much less aerial activity this second night, and it wasn't long before Ted, with a fair amount of huffing and puffing and 'who needs this late at night?', carted a still lifeless Peggy up the stairs to Connie and Jessie's bedroom and deposited her ungracefully onto Connie's bed, whereupon Barbara slipped off her shoes and then pulled an eiderdown over her.

The twins thought Peggy's obliviousness to be one of the funniest things they had ever seen, although Barbara made them solemnly swear that they must *never* let on to anyone how Peggy had behaved once they were back at Tall Trees.

And as sure as eggs were eggs, the next morning Peggy was convinced she was coming down with something as she felt riven with aches and a bad head, and she must have picked up a bug when she was over in Borough seeing Mr Ainsworth.

Ted and Barbara and the twins had to stare at their breakfast plates for quite a while not to laugh out loud as they exchanged amused raised eyebrows over their morning toast.

Peggy perked up enough a while later to go with Barbara to the East Street outdoor market off the Walworth Road, while Ted walked with the twins over to their old primary school, to see if it had sustained any obvious bomb damage.

At the market Peggy was able to buy a bundle of second-hand comics for the children, a small wooden jigsaw for Holly, and some home-made marrow and blackberry jam for Roger and Mabel, and a second pot for Barbara and Ted.

On the way back to Jubilee Street, a spiv came up to Barbara and Peggy, and hissed 'Lipstick?' out of the corner of his mouth as he stood near to them while he pretended he had stopped in order to light a cigarette.

Barbara looked very disapproving, but Peggy inched closer to him, and said quietly, aping the way he was speaking out of the corner of her mouth, 'Are they new?'

The spiv nodded.

'How much?'

'Five bob.'

'Daylight robbery,' Peggy answered. 'Four bob.'

'Four and ninepence. I've got five kiddies to feed.'

'Rubbish. Don't listen to him, Peggy, he's just trying to fob you off,' hissed Barbara disapprovingly.

Peggy ignored her sister, who was now glancing anxiously up and down the street in case there was a policeman nearby, as black market trading was illegal.

But as far as Peggy was concerned she had already bought the two pots of jam illegally, and now felt she might as well be hung for a sheep as a lamb, and she didn't care a jot if a bobby came upon her mid-transaction.

'Five children is excessive. Four and three,' countered a prim Peggy, although her eyes twinkled in merriment.

'You'd take the clothes from my back, missus. Four and six?'

'Done.'

And with that the spiv held open one side of his moth-eaten jacket, and Peggy laughed to see inside, each in a tiny fold of fabric looped in a line from one side to the other, a long row of brand-new lipsticks, all Auxiliary Red from Cyclax. Goodness knows how the spiv had come by them but, my, they did look tempting!

Quickly Peggy chose two lipsticks, and handed over a ten-shilling note. But she shook her head when the spiv said 'Powder?' and quickly flourished the other side of his jacket open to display a selection of white cardboard circular boxes of face powder ready to be decanted into the metal powder compacts that most women owned, as if this would change her mind.

Peggy shook her head again. Reluctantly he dug about in his trouser pocket for a while and then dolefully he handed her back a shilling, before he and Peggy parted with a 'Nice doing business with you' and an answering 'And you'.

'You idiot,' said Barbara a hundred or so yards down the road. 'He saw you coming, you ninny.'

'You'll be laughing out of the other side of your face! One of those lipsticks is for you, as a thank you,' said Peggy.

'In that case, what a bargain you struck.'

Three hours later Peggy and the twins were on the train heading back to Leeds. They hadn't been going fifteen minutes when all three were firmly asleep following an inconclusive discussion on what more they could do to help the war effort as they were all a little shaken by the obvious signs of bombing they had seen, Jessie and Connie each resting their head on one of Peggy's shoulders.

As the train rattled along on its way northwards, it felt to all of them as if it were taking them home.

Chapter Eighteen

'How was it this morning, Connie?' said Aiden at breaktime a few days later as they huddled outside the main building of the school trying to get into the lee of an unpleasantly nippy wind.

Jessie and Connie's trip to London was already old news at Tall Trees, although all the children were still enjoying reading the comics that Peggy had bought them at the market there.

'All right, I suppose,' said Connie, 'although the teacher had problems making everyone be quiet in the second period. It turns out though that three of those Hull lads have just been moved back to the same class as me – I think they've been held back a year, or it might even be two, as they're having problems with reading. One of them tried to trip me up when I went up to help the teacher make the blackboard higher—'

'No!' cried Jessie, the crack in his voice more a sign that he was imagining the humiliation of one the Hull lot trying to trip him up than indicating concern for his sister.

'He did!' said Connie, not noticing that Jessie might not have been wholly thinking of her. 'And right under the teacher's nose too. But I don't think Sir's eyesight is too good, or otherwise he'd have seen the way that Hull lad looked at me and drew a finger across his throat to mime cutting mine with a knife.'

Jessie felt quite faint for a second, and as if his knees were knocking together in fear. This sounded exactly like the gesture he'd seen one of the Hull boys make the day after Milburn had been hurt in the road accident.

Connie was undaunted. 'Well, that lad's got me very wrong if he thinks I give two hoots for such a babyish threat.'

It hadn't looked a babyish threat to Jessie when he had seen it, but he didn't say anything. Connie went on, 'And so a little while later I put my hand up to be excused so that I could go and spend a penny, which Sir allowed although he said it would only be this once. And on the way back I jabbed the Hull twerp really hard in the ribs with my thumb as I went by as Sir was writing something on the blackboard and had his back to the class. The one who tripped me is called David, and the other two are Hugh and Stuart, by the way.'

Jessie and Aiden looked at each other as if to say that they didn't give two hoots what the Hull boys' names were.

Connie took no notice as she added, 'And what's really bad is that right before break the four of us were then told that we had to sit for all of our lessons *in a line together*, as apparently our reading is the worst in the whole school – and I'm not even allowed to be at the end of the four of us in the row! Then, when those boys tried to rile me, I pointed out they are getting on for two years older than me, and are now having to sit with a *girl*, which means the joke's on them and not me. But at this, David said to me that I'd missed out a word, which was "stupid" before girl, which was a nerve, the damn cheek of it, don't you think?'

Jessie thought David was taking a big chance by calling Connie stupid.

'And the other two are Jared and Sam, I think it is, and they are already in 3E,' Connie finished.

'You should be a spy, Connie,' said Aiden, as if he were trying to lift her spirits, although to judge by the quite jolly expression on her face, he wasn't too sure that her spirits had been dented in the slightest. 'You're very good at getting information, you know,' he added, and Connie nodded her agreement in a way that showed it was obvious that everyone should naturally accept she would make a brilliant spy and be a wonderful interrogator.

'It's not difficult when they're so stupid, and—' But whatever Connie had been going to say was drowned out by the bell ringing to announce the end of breaktime.

Ninety minutes later, after lessons had broken for lunchtime, it looked to be a slightly different story unfolding as for the very first time Connie didn't seek out her brother or Aiden.

Instead, she spent a long while talking outside with the three Hull lads in her class, even laughing with them at one point, almost as if she was having a good time.

Worse was the fact that all three boys then guffawed back at whatever it was that Connie had just said, Jessie and Aiden agreed as they watched from the other side of the playground.

Jessie wasn't sure what he thought about his sister's brazen behaviour. It seemed strange. He did know that he wasn't happy about it, but he knew already he probably would wait for her to tell him what she was up to rather than asking her outright what she was about.

Aiden stared at Connie in silence, and Jessie thought that,

to judge by his grim expression, he wasn't taken by this turn of events either.

'Let's make sure we get Connie away from them as soon as we can, I mean generally, and not just today,' said Jessie, wanting to give Aiden something else to think about other than whether Connie might be flirting outrageously with the enemy.

Jessie didn't think Connie seemed as if she was giving the Hull lads the glad eye as such, but he knew he was very inexperienced in these things which meant he couldn't be sure, and so he added, 'Why is it that she is in the lowest class, do you think?'

With narrowed eyes, a stern-looking Aiden ignored Jessie's question, saying instead, 'Jessie, I don't want to talk about Connie.'

Jessie tried again with, 'Well, what shall we do about marking Gracie and Kelvin's wedding then?'

'Ugh, I can't be bothered to think about that either,' said Aiden in a more grumpy way than was usual for him, as normally he was a boy who seemed always cheerful. Then Aiden added in the sort of voice that suggested he was making a huge effort, 'Look, shall we see if we can join in that game of football over there?'

If there was one thing that Jessie disliked more than the Hull lads, it was football.

But although Jessie cast an eye around for his other Tall Trees pals so that he would have a good reason not to play, unfortunately Larry, Tommy and Angela were nowhere to be seen, and this meant to Jessie that the fear of being stuck on his own, which might make him an easy target in the eyes of Jared and Sam and the others, became stronger than his aversion to football.

'Good plan, Aiden. Let's,' Jessie heard himself say. He didn't know if he or Aiden was the more shocked at his apparent desire to play football.

Aiden gave Jessie a sideways look at these words, as to show even the slightest enthusiasm for something sporty wasn't like Jessie at all.

Then Aiden shrugged, and called 'Over here!' to the footballers as he ran towards them.

And with nothing more than that, the two boys from Tall Trees were quickly swallowed up in the kickabout, Jessie (to his huge surprise) even scoring a screamer of a goal when Aiden flipped the ball his way.

It was his very first goal ever, but although Jessie felt inordinately proud of himself for a moment or two, he realised immediately after that his foot was stinging uncomfortably from hoofing the ball too hard between the two woollies that had been bunched on the ground to signify the goalposts, and he hoped that football wasn't going to be a regular occurrence every lunchtime at this new school as he didn't think he could stand the pain.

Gallingly, Connie meanwhile didn't even seem to notice that Jessie and Aiden were playing football, or that Jessie had scored a goal.

But both Jessie and Aiden heard her tinkling laughter ring out and David's deeper answering guffaw just as the bell rang for them all to head back to their classrooms.

They looked at each other, but didn't say anything. They had never thought they would have to listen to Connie fraternising with the enemy.

There didn't seem to be the words to describe what they felt.

Chapter Nineteen

That same afternoon, after leaving June's at the end of her stint, an incredibly unsettled and restless Peggy had to push Holly's perambulator smartly up and down the steep hills of Harrogate in an attempt to wear herself out.

She'd felt flustered ever since returning from London, but she found this physical exertion did little to alleviate matters.

A surprised and uncertain Holly stared seriously at Peggy as she was bounced about, as if this were very strange behaviour indeed on her mother's part, after which Peggy slowed down a little as it did feel a little demeaning to be so openly judged by her daughter who wasn't yet a year old.

At last, finding herself near the train station, Peggy stopped at a café for a cup of tea while Holly napped in the pram.

There were some khaki-clad soldiers standing around the station, and a few men in Royal Air Force or Navy uniforms, but Peggy didn't find them to be anything like as threatening as she had the groups of servicemen just a couple of days earlier when she had been stalking through Kings Cross station on her way to Bermondsey with Connie and Jessie at her side.

Peggy looked at Holly with her eyelashes now adorably touching her cheeks, and then realised that although she was still a little restless in the physical sense, in her mind she felt calmer than she had in a long while.

She wondered if the intense rollercoaster of emotions that had coursed through her over the past week had proved to be cathartic on some levels, or was she instead just emotionally and physically drained and she was mistaking exhaustion for feeling psychologically calm?

It was worth thinking about some more.

There had been, of course, the horror of the escalating set-to between Bill and James, the realisation that she and James were not to be, then finding Bill so pathetic over at the police station, before feeling unexpectedly embarrassed under the scrutiny of the leering soldiers when she'd first arrived in London, and there'd been the terrifying and relentless waves of adrenaline during the bomb raid, the disappointing visit to the solicitor, and the normally forbidden naughtiness of drinking the port and larking about with the spiv.

All the feelings generated by these experiences had melded at last into something that felt a lot like resilience. A resilience that had something fortifying about it too, Peggy hoped.

It was as if she had experienced almost the whole gamut of emotions a person could feel over only a very short time, and the upshot was, Peggy decided slowly, that although blasted by life she was also ready to turn a fresh cheek to the world. It was liberating.

To celebrate her new-found resolution, she treated herself to a toasted teacake.

Peggy sat in the window of the tea shop contentedly watching people scurry by until it was time head back to Tall Trees and get Holly's tea on, ideally before Holly woke up.

But before she stood up to leave, Peggy fished around in her basket and pulled out her old compact. Bill had given it to her as an engagement present and it had put in sterling work over the years. Although it was now tarnished and dented, Peggy loved it still, and felt it was good for a few years yet, even though at that precise moment the compact was bereft of face power (she probably should have taken the spiv up on his offer of buying some, Peggy thought now).

Then, while thinking that she, exactly like the compact, was tarnished and dented but was hopefully good for a few years yet, Peggy flipped it open and angled the mirror so that she could apply the Auxiliary Red lipstick she had bought from the spiv.

It looked very striking, if perhaps a little too bold for ordinary daytime wear.

But the lipstick's waxy texture felt luxurious on her lips, and Peggy couldn't help turning her head this way and that as she pushed her lips into a come-hither pout and admired her handiwork in the mirror's reflection, then patted her hair into shape.

It seemed as if a brand-new Peggy was staring back at her. It was also the first time since Holly had been born that she had had any lipstick to wear, and that added a sense of optimism and positivity to Peggy's mood.

As Holly sat up and gazed in fascination at her mother's lips, Peggy began to make her way back to Tall Trees.

There was an appreciative wolf whistle attesting, Peggy thought, to the glamorous impression the lipstick bestowed.

This time Peggy smiled and gave a nod of acknowledgement to the soldier who'd whistled, and politely he raised a finger to his forelock in reply.

This time Peggy enjoyed it because she knew she had discovered a new confidence in herself. She had to admit that just at that moment, the man's whistle made her feel good, and appreciated.

The insecure and rather prickly Peggy of just a few days earlier, who would have hated such attention, seemed but a faded, jittery memory, almost a different person in fact.

While naturally Peggy wanted to be thought of as more than a pretty face – she'd always been very firm in this opinion – there was something nice about, just now and again, having a stranger notice she was attractive.

Peggy smiled again as she pushed the perambulator along, although this time it was a more complicated smile, being one directed at herself and in large part a private acknowledgment of how complicated life could be, and how one's attitude could alter in just a day or two, with neither the earlier or the later attitude being wrong in themselves, but just different.

Certainly, Peggy didn't consider herself now as just a sex siren, any more than she would have considered herself earlier in the week as nothing more than a dowdy woman who eschewed something as frivolous as make-up.

The truth, Peggy knew, was that she was neither of those two interpretations, and yet there were aspects of both of them inside her, alongside a lot of other versions of Peggy too.

She looked forward to meeting them all.

After Holly had been put down for the night, Peggy reached into her basket for her pen and a notebook and envelope from the new writing set that Barbara had pressed on her as a goodbye present before she left London.

Dear Maureen, wrote Peggy,

I hope you are well. I am not sure if you have had the baby yet, but if you have, then I trust that all is as it should be and mother and baby are doing well.

It may be too soon after the birth for you to think about what I am going to write – I was very all over the place right after Holly was born and so I will understand perfectly if that is the case, but that phase does pass, I promise.

The reason for this letter is that I want you to know that at some time I think you and I should have a telephone conversation as it strikes me that we could be of useful support to one another.

I must reiterate that as far as I am concerned my marriage to Bill is over, and although legally there are problems in us separating formally, I do think Bill must do his best to look after both of his children, mine and yours.

I absolutely do not want to argue with you, Maureen, please do be assured of that, and while I think you and I should be in touch, even if only for the sake of the children, who after all are (or will be) half-siblings to each other and may well want to know each other in time, do please also understand also that I won't pester you if right now the thought of speaking to me feels too much.

You have my details so that you can get in touch, should you want to do so. For myself, I would welcome it.

Yours faithfully,
Peggy

Ordinarily Peggy would have signed a missive like this as 'Peggy Delbert (Mrs)' but it seemed that if she were to do so now it would be too harsh, and would risk unhelpfully rubbing Maureen's face in the reality of Peggy's legal connection to Bill, when really – although Peggy didn't like the woman or, more precisely, she hadn't liked a heavily pregnant and distinctly testy Maureen the one time they had met – that was the last thing she felt like doing.

It was more that Peggy could see that divided, she and Maureen were weaker than if they banded together to share some common aims to look after their children.

Bill wouldn't like it if they did unite, but that was his problem to deal with in whatever manner he deemed fit.

So, for now it seemed a simple 'Peggy' at the end would have to be enough to close the note, even if not strictly correct in terms of etiquette.

Peggy made sure the Tall Trees telephone number and address were without mistakes, and with no further ado she folded what she'd written, and slid it into an envelope she'd addressed from memory.

Before she retired for the night, Peggy nipped out and trotted down the road as quickly as she could as there was an autumn chill in the air and she'd dashed out without a coat so that she could drop the envelope in the nearest post box to the rectory.

She thought she had better do this immediately, in case she got cold feet overnight about doing so.

All in all, Peggy thought as she made her way back to Holly, it had been an interesting few days that meant she had returned to Harrogate in a much more positive frame of mind than she might have expected at the time she was leaving Mr Ainsworth's solicitor's office.

Or when she had been watching James and that attractive nurse together, for that matter.

Peggy decided that although it had been a long way to go to see a solicitor, it had done her good to leave Harrogate for a few days, as without her knowing it, the experience of the visit and the appointment with Mr Ainsworth had definitely lessened her feelings of ire towards Bill. Things were stacked in his favour, but she couldn't really blame him for that; it was just how things were, and understanding this had definitely helped her feel a little calmer.

She was fairly certain, too, that she had done the right thing by extending an olive branch of friendship towards Maureen.

Peggy suspected that the other woman might need all the help she could get; and in spite of her and Maureen's shouting match in the street outside Tall Trees in the height of summer, following her own run-in with Bill the other night Peggy discovered that she had a lot more sympathy for Maureen than previously.

Chapter Twenty

After school several days later, Connie told Jessie she was going to walk home with Tommy and Angela, while Larry and Aiden headed over to June's café to do some washing up for her.

When they had still been at primary school the two boys had given June a hand clearing up in the café most afternoons after they had finished their lessons, but now that they moved up to senior school and there was a greater emphasis on academic achievement, Roger had limited this work, for which June paid them each sixpence a shift, to an afternoon a week, and this was only provided their grades didn't slip. If their marks went down, then all pocket money earning in the café would have to cease immediately. Aiden and Larry, and June, understood they must keep up with their lessons if they were to go on with their stints at the café.

Aiden had been to see his parents the evening before, and he'd reported back that they had told him that Kelvin and Grace had enjoyed their honeymoon, and now Kelvin was back at barracks, and Grace and Jack were settling in at Granny Nora's

Aiden had promised the other children that he and Larry

would bring all the previous week's old newspapers home with them that evening from June's café.

This was because the children had decided that morning at breakfast that their wedding gift to Kelvin and Gracie was going to be a scrapbook of what was going on around the world in the week they got married.

'In the years to come, they'll love knowing exactly what was happening at the time of their marriage,' Connie had said, after she'd come up with the idea. And once she had, then everyone agreed it was a very good plan indeed as it would be a nice keepsake to help the young couple remember their happy occasion and, best of all, would cost the children virtually nothing to make.

Roger overheard the conversation, and he offered to provide the scrapbook as he had a spare one he'd never used, while Mabel said there was some Gloy left over from making the Mothers' Union jumble sale posters that they could use for the sticking down part. The children were delighted as it meant they could do all of this without having to dip into their pocket money.

'It might be nice if at the back of the book you each write a goodwill message to the happy couple,' Mabel added.

Connie piped up, 'In that case I'm going to say to Gracie she needs to watch out for Granny Nora!' and then she begged Mabel to donate her weekly copy of *Woman's Own* too so that the final selection of clippings wouldn't be too gloomy or news-heavy. Although they would choose a selection of news and photographs, they'd hopefully be able to find some funny stories too, and they could add smaller snippets such wireless schedules, recipes, and hair and beauty tips, as it would probably be Gracie who spent more time reading the scrapbook than Kelvin.

'And we can include the women's problem page from that week's *Woman's Own* as Gracie loves to read this section first when the mag is doing the rounds here, and it always makes Peggy laugh,' added Connie.

But Jessie knew that all the scrapbook stuff was going to be for later that evening, after they'd had their tea and everyone's homework had been done.

And before that he had something more important that he wanted to do while everyone else was otherwise engaged, and so he slipped out when nobody was paying him any attention.

'Hello, Doctor Legard. Might it be all right if I came in?' Jessie said tentatively after school, as he tapped on the open door to James's office over at the hospital.

Jessie knew his way around the hospital quite well as he had been treated there after being knocked unconscious, and now he had found his way easily to the correct office. Or should it be examination room? Jessie wasn't sure, but he didn't allow it further thought, even though usually he was quite pedantic about giving things their correct description, as the important thing was that he had tracked down the very person he was searching for.

James had been writing something on a thick pad, and he looked up quickly in surprise when Jessie spoke.

He stood up and hurried over to the boy, asking in a worried way as he led him to a chair beside his desk, 'Is everything all right, Jessie? Is there anything wrong? Nobody has been hurt at Tall Trees, have they?'

Jessie wondered if, in a roundabout way, James was quizzing him about Peggy, and so he replied, 'I need some advice and I am hoping you can help me with this, but everyone is well, I think. Peggy and me and Connie have been in London, but Holly didn't seem to be missing her mother as Roger says Mabel allowed Holly to get away with murder while Peggy was away. And Gracie has got married and moved out. And we've all started our new school.'

'Goodness, you've all been busy,' said James a trifle thoughtfully, as he reached deep into a pocket of his starched white doctor's coat to touch Peggy's letter as if it was a talisman.

He had read the letter again and again, and the envelope was now looking quite crumpled from where he had been taking it out of his pocket and then putting it back again.

James felt ashamed he hadn't replied, especially as he had no excuse for this other than he had been putting it off, in part because one moment he missed Peggy intensely, but the next he was furious with her for putting him in such an awful situation of making him care about her when she wasn't really available.

Pushing thoughts of Peggy aside, James asked, 'How is the new school going, Jessie? It sounds as if you have all been very busy. That's a turn-up for the books, with Gracie leaving so quickly and getting married to boot. How quickly life moves on, doesn't it?'

Even to James's ears, his chatter was inane, and the look on Jessie's face suggested the boy thought likewise. But Jessie's surprise arrival had thrown James rather, there was no denying.

Then James, to his relief, had an idea, and so he said, 'Why don't you come with me to the canteen, Jessie, and you can tell me all about it?'

Meekly Jessie walked beside James and then sat at a table while the doctor went and fetched them each a cup of weak tea, before he encouraged Jessie to confide in him with a raise of his eyebrows.

'It's Connie I'm worried about,' Jessie began. 'I think she's very clever, and Aiden does too, I know.' James nodded encouragingly at this, and Jessie went on, 'But me and Aiden have been put in the top stream at school, and she's been put right down at the bottom of the lowest stream because of her reading, and it doesn't seem fair, particularly as there are three of those awful Hull boys she's been made to sit with, and none of them can read properly either. Connie can read but she does it in a funny way, and Aiden and I tried to help her over the summer. But we couldn't make her take it seriously, and now she's larking about with those *other* daft lads and it's going to cause trouble, I just know it. Aiden looks very bad about it all, but he won't say much or do anything about it, and I don't know what to say to make it stop without really annoying Connie. But I think Connie must be ill or something, as I can't see why she's like she is, if she isn't poorly.'

'I see,' said James. 'Message received and understood. Let me have a day or two to think about this. I can see it is quite a tricky problem though.'

James knew how viciously Jessie had been beaten up by the Hull evacuees and so he quite understood why he wouldn't want Connie to become friendly with them.

But he knew too that someone a lively as Connie was likely to become a ringleader wherever she was, and if that meant bringing some of the Hull contingent under her sway, then James doubted she would see a particular problem in that. Obviously, the others at Tall Trees wouldn't interpret it in quite those terms, James suspected. All in all, Connie's attitude could indeed bode looming trouble.

Jessie was an observant lad, James knew, and the fact he had gone out of his way to appeal for help from the doctor, said a lot. The more he thought about it, the more James was convinced that Jessie's instincts would be proved correct.

Jessie seemed reassured by James's placating words though, and he gave such a smile of gratitude that the young doctor's heart quite went out to the boy.

In his experience of the lad, Jessie being concerned about a problem somebody else was having was very typical, even though he was only eleven and of an age where he should be getting into his own scrapes and naughtiness, and not always being worried about what others were up to.

And James thought as well that Jessie might actually have a point regarding Connie and her lessons. It did indeed seem very peculiar that Jessie found his schoolwork came so readily, yet his twin sister, who always seemed so whip-smart when anyone spoke to her, had clearly struggled tremendously from the start of her education. Peggy had talked about this more than once.

Whatever the reason behind this was, James agreed with Jessie that nothing was going to help Connie much if she had now been lumped with others who were toiling equally ineffectively.

James wasn't sure whether he could be of any practical use in the situation, but he thought he would see what he could do.

A fleeting impression of a warm smile that Peggy might bestow on him if he managed to get Connie to read with confidence and ease sprang into his mind, but James managed to damp that down without Jessie noticing the doctor's distraction.

'Now Jessie, tell me all about your first few days at the new school. I remember feeling very strange when I moved up from my first school,' James said to encourage Jessie further, and Jessie was happy to chatter for quite some time.

A little while later James popped back to the counter and was able to beg a rock cake for Jessie to enjoy on the way home.

He waved Jessie on his way, and then James gave himself a metaphorical pat on the back for not openly questioning the youngster as to what Peggy had gone to London for, much as he had been itching to nudge the conversation in that direction.

What had been brought home to James by seeing Jessie was that at some point he was going to have to speak to or write to Peggy. He wasn't sure whether he was excited or perturbed by the thought.

Jessie felt much more cheerful as he made his way back to Tall Trees. He might not be able to help Connie ultimately, but the fact that he had tried to do *something* – and the manner in which James had treated him as if he was in no way a silly nitwit for being concerned about his sister – filled him with a sense of achievement all the same.

Once he was back at the rectory, as it wasn't yet teatime because both Mabel and Roger were involved in something over at the church hall that meant everyone's supper was pushed back an hour, Jessie popped a peckish-looking Milburn (if the whinny in Jessie's direction and the pony's velvet nose poking insistently over the top of the stable half-door were anything to go by) into his rope halter.

Then Jessie slowly led him up the road to where the grass verges were particularly lush following some rain the previous week.

Now that the pony had had his metal horseshoes removed, his hooves were almost silent on the road as he walked, and Jessie was delighted to see that Milburn was moving as if his various cuts and bruises weren't badly paining him any longer. He certainly had lost the noticeable hobble he'd had following his brush with the police car.

As the road became more of a country lane and the verge widened, Jessie stopped and allowed Milburn to graze. The pony kept his nose close to the sod as he tugged at mouthful after mouthful of the bright green grass and hedgerow herbs that he pulled with his yellow teeth in what looked like a continuous motion that didn't allow time for chomping or swallowing, while he stood in the lee of a drystone wall that was taller than his withers and rump.

The weather was warm that afternoon, and it wasn't long before Jessie slumped down, sitting on a large stone as he toyed with Milburn's loosely-held lead rope. For a while it was all very relaxing and Jessie even closed his eyes in contentment.

He listened to birds singing their getting-close-to-bedtime songs, which were accompanied by the hypnotic sound of Milburn grazing, and all felt well with the world.

Until, that was, the unmistakable ring of Connie's

commanding voice rang out from somewhere that sounded like it was only just over the other side of the wall to where Jessie was sitting.

Presumably she was messing about in the field that the wall separated from the lane and the green verges, but that didn't mean it was anything other than a disturbing discovery for Jessie, as his eyes sprang open and he slipped off the stone to crouch in as small a way as he could down in the ditch beside the wall.

Milburn flicked a toffee-coloured ear in Jessie's direction although the rhythm of his chewing never altered.

It was Connie's utterance that had so shocked Jessie.

'Dave,' Connie had giggled, and then she laughed in a sing-song, almost saucy way. Her voice had a coquettish timbre her twin had never heard come from her mouth before, and it was as if she and whoever she was addressing were quite alone.

Where were Tommy and Angela? There was certainly no sound of them there, and in any case Angela's wheelchair would have made it difficult for her to be in a field in the middle of nowhere. Jessie knew that Connie had been going to go home with them – she had definitely told him that – and he didn't think Mabel or Peggy would then have allowed Connie to go out again on her own, being a girl. And so this must mean that Connie had never walked home from school with Tommy and Angela in the first place.

And 'Dave' had to be that Hull lad, Jessie realised, as they didn't know any other Davids or Daves. And if *Dave* were there with Connie, then it was most unlikely that Tommy and Angela would be there too, at least so silently.

What an awful and unexpected to-do!

Jessie's face was a caution as quickly he ran through the ramifications of what might be occurring nearby, although he didn't dare stand up to take a peep over the wall to see if he was correct in any of his assumptions.

Connie gave another uncharacteristically girlish tinkle of laughter, one that was answered by a boyish chuckle, but a boy with a deeper, more on-the-way-to-being-a-man laugh than anything Jessie and his friends could manage.

Jessie recognised the laugh, definitely. He didn't think he'd ever forget the sounds of the bullies laughing as they had viciously kicked him as he lay on the floor to the alley and they rained blows on to his small huddled frame. They had thought that giving Jessie such a pasting was hilarious.

Jessie didn't approve in the slightest that Connie's tone now verged on the downright flirty.

How could his twin sister be a girl aged only eleven in the morning, and by the very same afternoon, while not yet a woman, have grown into someone who was definitely no longer just a girl? Jessie didn't understand it.

Worse was to come, as then Connie said quite distinctly, sounding much closer to the wall, 'I don't want anyone to know, remember. It can be our secret.'

'You're a one, Con,' said Dave. He chuckled back at her in a way that Jessie suspected very probably could be described as lustily.

Con! Jessie felt quite sick. Now Dave was daring to take liberties even with Connie's name.

And then Connie laughed back at her companion again.

Worse! Connie *liked* being called Con, Jessie knew what this must mean.

Jessie wasn't totally sure why, but he felt at that moment almost as if he could die with shame.

He didn't have any idea exactly what was going on all too close to him, but it sounded far too much like one of those things that a brother should *never* see or hear a sister doing.

And the fact that Connie was choosing to do whatever it was that she was doing with a Hull lad – and not even Aiden on whom Jessie believed she'd had a pash for months – was deeply shocking. Not that Jessie would have approved of Connie messing about with Aiden either, of course, although this would definitely be the better option than her experimenting with one of the yobs who had scared him so just a few short weeks ago in the summer holidays.

And almost as bad was that Jessie felt well and truly trapped.

He didn't dare move now in case Connie looked over the wall and saw him.

He hadn't meant to spy on her, but now he had, in effect, been doing just this, and Jessie knew that Connie would certainly describe whatever it was that he was doing as spying.

And this meant that if he were discovered after he had been listening to her and Dave for a while, then she would never believe that it had all been a huge accident as far as Jessie was concerned.

This would make Jessie a 'dead man walking' as far as the gang from Hull were concerned, Jessie was sure.

Jessie wished with all his heart that he had moved away instantly the second he had first heard Connie, before he had had any thought – or heard even a smidgen of evidence that could suggest her possibly canoodling with Dave.

But he hadn't, and this poor choice had now put him

in a real bind, with the terrible fear of being discovered growing in seriousness the more the situation went on and the longer he crouched down beside the wall.

As Jessie's legs started to ache and then grow numb from his low crouch, there was a lot of whispering that he couldn't quite make out, followed by far too much giggling from both Connie and Dave. Whatever they were up to was being enjoyed overmuch in Jessie's opinion, and – worse – weren't they taking an age about it.

At one point Milburn seemed to realise it was Connie who was nearby, and he swung up his head so that his nose was pointing in the direction from which Connie seemed to be speaking. For a heart-stopping moment it looked as if the pony were going to give Connie a nicker of recognition or, worse, stick his nose over the wall.

Jessie had to poke Milburn in the shoulder in order to disrupt his concentration, and then hiss an anguished 'oi' at him, with a tug on the halter's rope.

Milburn turned his face to look at Jessie, his liquid brown eyes indignant and accusing.

To add insult to injury, once Connie and Dave had finally left, Connie rubbed salt into Jessie's wounds with a final 'I'd better hurry, Dave, else I'll be late for tea and Mabel will flay me alive', which she said in such a jolly way that nobody could have taken her words of being flayed alive seriously.

There was a boyish giggle in response, definitely as if flirting, and although Jessie suspected that Dave would probably laugh right now at anything Connie said, nevertheless he felt quite queasy again.

Connie leaving the scene of her crime wasn't to mean,

however that poor Jessie didn't have to lurk around on the verge for a fair while after she had long gone.

He felt quite paranoid, and that he should make doubly sure that there was no danger of his sister seeing him and Milburn coming down the road back to Tall Trees in Connie's footsteps. Or of *Dave* seeing him either; that would spell d.i.s.a.s.t.e.r.

Of course, by the time boy and pony were home, and Milburn ensconced safely back in his stable, it meant that Jessie was very late for tea, and consequently Mabel was quite short with him as it had been hard for her to ring-fence Jessie's share of the Woolton Pie as Connie had turned out to be extremely peckish.

Playfully, Connie wagged a finger at her brother as if it were him who had been the naughty one, and Aiden stared back at him with a curious expression when Jessie found it hard to look him in the eye.

And then Jessie had to go through all sorts of shenanigans to stop himself and Aiden being alone together afterwards as they cut out news stories from the newspapers, just in case Aiden asked him what the matter was.

It all felt very unfair, and Jessie was relieved once the damn scrapbook had been finished, the good luck messages written inside it to Gracie, Jack and Kelvin by all the children, and they had finally been sent to bed.

After what seemed like hours, eventually Jessie heard the sound of Aiden's faint snores drifting across the dorm where the four boys slept.

But although the imminent danger of discovery had now passed, Jessie lay awake for ages, feeling much too tense and crabby to nod off.

He wasn't sure what to make of what he had heard,

although it seemed for the best if he didn't say anything about it to anyone, and most particularly his twin as Connie would be very quick to throw it all back in his face and make him out to be the bad guy.

What Jessie found most infuriating of all was that he had only been up the lane when he had because he'd had a little time to kill after he'd been trying to help Connie by going to see James on his way back from school.

Connie, meanwhile, had been the picture of innocence the whole evening, apparently quite happy to spend ages rather sloppily pasting the various cuttings into Gracie and Kelvin's scrapbook that Angela had just cut out with her own customary carefulness.

In fact, Connie looked for all the world as if butter wouldn't melt in her mouth, and as if she would never share a secret with a maggot called Dave, and as if she were able to wilfully ignore the fact that Dave had been one of the lads that had kicked him so hard in the head that he had ended up in hospital.

Jessie felt very hard done by, and he had no idea what was going on with his sister. What he did know for certain was that his own feelings were badly hurt as he couldn't believe Connie was being so disloyal to him, although he was sure it would be sensible if he tried very hard never to let Connie realise how easily she had cut him to the quick. A large part of this was because he was no longer sure – in the way he always had been – that, come what may, his twin sister was always in his corner as his biggest ally.

And the more he thought about it the harder he had to fight not to gnash his teeth together in frustration, just as happened in the comic strips he had been reading.

Chapter Twenty-one

The next month or so passed in a bit of a blur for most of those at Tall Trees.

Peggy had a couple of letters from Bill, neither of which she opened, instead putting a line through the address of Tall Trees and then boldly scrawling 'RETURN TO SENDER' on the envelope's front before crossly shoving them back into the postbox.

At least Bill wasn't making the plaintive telephone calls that he had earlier in the year, and she didn't for a moment think he'd be writing to say he was sorry for all that had happened and that he was happy if they divorce, so she thought she was doing the right thing reminding her husband she wasn't, and nor was she going to be, a pushover.

To take her mind off Bill and how annoying she found him – and the way she would almost always immediately contrast this with the memory of the innocent freshness and her hopeful excitement that still surged through her body when she thought of James, even though inevitably this was followed by the crushing disappointment that they were no longer speaking – Peggy did some long shifts at June's café. She felt she needed to make up to her friend for her four days' absence, but meanwhile Holly's walking improved with every day, and it was clear to anybody who cared to look that she was growing into a very independently minded toddler. This meant that Holly made it increasingly clear that she was b-o-r-e-d with the playpen at June's.

Peggy knew she had to do something about this, but she wasn't sure what, a state of affairs she found disheartening.

It proved hard to hold on to the optimistic mood with which she had returned to Tall Trees when she'd enjoyed wearing her 'special occasion only' bright red lipstick, and over the next few weeks Peggy realised what a lot of time she had been devoting previously to thinking about James (and wondering if he would think her crimson lips alluring or too much, not that she'd ever find out, of course), and what a void in her life his absence was now making. She was missing James very much, but she felt too proud to attempt to see him again, her last try having been so bruising to her ego.

One afternoon, as she was buttoning Holly's coat, a hand-me-down a customer had given Peggy, to get them ready to walk back to Tall Trees from the café, Peggy glanced up and, to her surprise, there was James walking along on the opposite pavement.

Peggy stopped what she was doing and stood up straight to look at him better, as her heart flip-flopped around and her mouth felt suddenly dry.

James was every bit as enticing, and handsome, and strong-looking as she remembered, and it made Peggy feel quite undone as the hairs on her arms rose and she thrilled in every part of her body.

It seemed that while her mind knew that what they had

shared was over, her body certainly didn't. It was a delicious sensation, but Peggy didn't know whether that was a good thing or not.

James stopped and turned towards her, their eyes meeting through the window as several cars drove down the street that divided them. Peggy couldn't read James's face, and then she thought that she might have been staring at him open-mouthed, which wasn't at all the impression that she wanted to give. It was an awkward moment, but despite this it felt significant and important, at least as far as Peggy was concerned.

But before either could nod hello or raise a hand or do more than blink, there was a resounding crash and thunder of broken crockery, and an ear-piercing scream from Holly, and an aghast Peggy looked down to see that Holly had toddled at the speed of light to an empty table, where a pile of clean saucers had been left waiting to be stacked tidily away.

Unfortunately the part-time waitress had just left the saucers there rather than putting them away on their shelf, with a tantalising corner of a tea towel flopped over the side of the table, and the saucers balanced on the towel. Holly had grabbed the tea towel and upended the crockery on to the floor.

The toddler's howls of fright were out of all proportion to the mishap. And she was difficult to quieten, much to Peggy's discomfort, as well as that of a proportion of the customers; Peggy couldn't help but notice several clench their shoulders at the sound. It couldn't be denied that Holly's bellows were very grating on the ears.

As Peggy brushed away her daughter's tears, she saw the incident for what it was: a warning about the dangers lurking in that café and an insistent wake-up call that Peggy needed to get her skates on and make sure that Holly had proper, safe daytime care.

No one had been injured this time, but it might have been a very different story if a hot cup of tea or a sharp knife had been involved. Peggy shuddered at the very thought.

And then, as she picked up a panting and wailing Holly to give her a final comforting cuddle, Peggy remembered James, and she looked out of the window.

He was nowhere to be seen.

Naturally he wasn't, Peggy told herself dejectedly as all the excitement of seeing him so unexpectedly left her body in a fizzle of disappointment.

As she and Holly trudged homewards, there was a squally shower and Peggy felt it aptly summed up her downbeat mood, while a still gulping Holly began to grizzle in earnest in protest at how badly her own afternoon was going.

Peggy's suddenly sombre mood seemed reflected at the rectory by the children being very affected by the news of a torpedo scuttling the SS *City of Benares*, which had been sailing with ninety evacuee children from Liverpool to Canada. Seventy-seven of the evacuees died in the attack, and people across the nation felt devastated to see so many young lives being cut down too soon. Prime Minister Winston Churchill immediately cancelled the Children Overseas Reception Board government-funded plan that had been to send 24,000 evacuated children abroad for the duration. Peggy wondered how many of these 24,000 children would now die or be badly hurt at Jerry's hands on home soil.

Roger, Mabel and Peggy were deeply saddened by the news of these poor evacuees, of course, although not so shaken as the children obviously were. They talked endlessly about it in awed voices, and these sessions usually made Angela sob uncontrollably, which made Peggy wonder if this was a result of the head injury she had sustained in a silly road accident when larking about in the blackout with the other children the previous Guy Fawkes night that had left the little girl in a wheelchair and made her very sensitive to any sort of bad news.

The Tall Trees adults had to navigate several difficult conversations about death and dying that always seemed to take place when everyone was seated at mealtimes, and as this seemed to kill their appetites, soon Mabel had to ban any talk of the *Benares* when everyone sat down to eat. This helped, but the children remained quite subdued for days after they had heard the news report on the wireless.

The adults wondered if the story had hit home with the youngsters especially because this was the first time the Tall Trees children had understood properly that others the same age as they might actually die or be horrifically maimed during the hostilities, while the fact the casualties were all evacuees had added an extra poignancy.

Obviously the children had seen several very distressed parishioners arrive at Tall Trees at all hours needing to talk or to have Roger comfort them when a son had been lost or maimed when fighting abroad, but what those adults had experienced hadn't really made much sense to the younger members of the household and so they hadn't been anything other than mildly curious.

And as Peggy knew from her own experience, it was remarkable how quickly she and the children had got used to living with a constant low level of anxiety about what might be going on back in London. It wasn't that one wasn't worried, but more that thoughts of the danger everyone back home was in quickly stopped being all-consuming because – as the Government encouraged – everyone just tried to carry on with 'normal' life as much as was possible as a collective show of defiance to Jerry.

But what had happened with the *Benares* felt different. It was a shocking turn of events, and one immensely hard not to consumed by.

Roger, Mabel and Peggy had agreed from the outset of the evacuees arriving that any bad news coming through in the BBC's news broadcasts wouldn't be sugar-coated for the children, as they were convinced that if they attempted this it would only make it harder in the long run for them to accept that unpleasant things could happen. They'd also agreed that they would always answer any of the kiddies' questions honestly. But so preoccupied with the *Benares* story were the children, that Peggy began to wonder if, after all, they had taken the right decision as far as that was concerned, and it seemed Roger might be having similar thoughts.

'I'm going to say special prayers on Sunday for those tragic *Benares* evacuees at the morning service, as I think this particular story will have touched a lot of the congregation deeply,' he said as he sat with Peggy and Mabel as they enjoyed some cocoa at the kitchen table late one night and discussed the situation once the children were all safely in bed. 'And I think I'll write my sermon around the theme of evacuation, and how important it is that we all recognise that sacrifice comes in many shapes and forms, and we must all be very tolerant and understanding of that. And us adults must take care to speak to children in the right way about stories like this, whatever that is.'

'I'm sure Tommy and his friends here will appreciate those words,' said Peggy. 'And Roger, if very casually, while you're about it, you could mention something that could be applied to those evacuees from Hull that could help Jessie especially, I'm sure he'd find comfort in that. Those little thugs are probably missing their families and being at home, and perhaps their parents have lost their homes or maybe worse has happened to those lads, as Jerry is giving Hull a real battering. I'm sure those boys are feeling upset just as much as we all are here, even though it might not seem like it to judge by their brutish behaviour; and Jessie may well never have thought of that, as he probably can't think beyond how big and bullying they can be. I am fairly certain he's worried still about what those lads might do as he's so down in the mouth at the moment, and wondering whether they will attack him again.'

'Poor Jessie – yes, that was atrocious behaviour on their part. I'll see what I can do to mention this in a way that will be helpful but not too obvious,' said Roger.

Mabel nudged a notebook and pencil towards her husband's elbow. Although there was a paper shortage, Roger had bought a whole box of notebooks just before the outbreak of war and so there rather a lot of them dotted around the rectory in strategic positions as Roger never quite knew when the muse for a good topic for a sermon was going to strike, and he lived in fear of forgetting what he had intended to note down if he had to fight too hard to find a piece of paper.

'You scribble that down, Roger, and I'll top up our cocoa,' said Mabel helpfully, and Peggy smiled her thanks at both suggestions Mabel had made, and then at Roger for wanting to help Jessie just as much as he wanted to help the other members of his congregation.

Lying in bed that night, Peggy was struck anew that all this upset might just be a foretaste of what was to come. Should the war stretch on interminably, then it was practically inconceivable that at least one of the inhabitants at Tall Trees wouldn't be hit by some sort of personal tragedy. It hardly bore thinking about.

Meanwhile, although this was out of sight of the adults, tensions escalated amongst all the Tall Trees children at Connie's growing friendship with the boys from Hull.

Now Connie was spending nearly all her breaks and lunchtimes at school with those three lads in her class, and it wasn't long before the two third years from Hull joined those four every day as well.

The Hull lads seemed to have dropped the overt vendetta that they had raged against the TT Muskets over the summer, and there was no repeat of any such gestures of aggressive fingers being run across throats as Jessie had seen on the day his parents went back to London.

It seemed as if those boys had decided that the best way forward was to totally ignore everyone from Tall Trees other than Connie, as if to pretend they didn't exist, or at any rate weren't worth bothering with.

But Aiden and Jessie agreed that this silence was ominous. Such passivity didn't feel natural, and in itself it came to feel almost an act of aggression. It certainly didn't suggest that any of the Tall Trees children were out of the woods yet. The pals dubbed the Hull lads' attitude 'the phoney snubbing' and while normally they would have laughed together about this as both Aiden and Jessie enjoyed a bit of wordplay, to do so didn't feel appropriate in this case.

Tommy and Larry didn't seem particularly bothered either way about Connie sneaking closer to the enemy, while Angela seemed intent only on trying to be alone with Tommy and so, as usual, she never took much notice of what anyone else was up to if it wasn't him.

By the time that Peggy began to twig that all might not be well, noticing that the twins were now sitting at opposite ends of the kitchen table for meals rather than beside each other as normal and Aiden was no longer glued to Connie's side, she chose to probe Jessie, usually the more forthcoming twin, about how it was all going (she didn't need to be specific what 'all' meant as it was obvious Jessie immediately understood what she was driving at).

He shrugged in a despondent way, before he mumbled, 'It's quiet, Aunty Peggy. The Hull lads will talk to Connie, but they don't say anything to the rest of us, and we don't say anything to them. They don't even *look* at us. But it seems as if they are waiting for a chance, or for us to crumble. I think them *not* doing anything is almost as bad as them doing something.'

Peggy couldn't think of anything to say that was particularly encouraging. She thought Jessie may well be right, and the other gang had decided to bide their time and await a good opportunity to strike.

'Well, why don't you concentrate on your schoolwork instead, and so this way you won't have time to worry about other things?' was the best Peggy could come up with. She felt it was something of a feeble response, and she could see Jessie did too.

She tried to pull him close for a hug, but she felt him stiff-backed and tense when her arm was around his shoulders, and so she didn't feel she had managed to soothe his concerns in the slightest.

What Jessie hadn't confided to Peggy was that these days, and apparently with no effort, Connie appeared to all intents and purposes to be pretty much the ringleader of her new group of friends.

Jessie had kept his opinion to himself as far as his aunt was concerned as the mere sight of Connie with her new cronies at school gave him a maelstrom of complex feelings. On the one hand he had to be grateful for not being picked on, but on the other it made him feel peculiar about his sister, to the point that Jessie tried not to think about her at all. This felt very strange, as all his life to this point he felt the fact that he and Connie were twins made them into a team with unbreakable bonds. Connie, it seemed, hadn't felt similarly, and this was a very difficult thought to get used to.

Aiden wasn't happy either, a situation confirmed when one day Jessie heard his disgruntled friend mutter to himself as across the school yard Connie had the five boys standing in a semicircle before her, looking as if they were hanging on her every word. 'Pah! like bees to a honeypot!' he mumbled in a way that Jessie felt he hadn't been supposed to hear;

Jessie was shocked to hear himself respond by suggesting 'goal practice, Aiden?' as a distraction.

Connie had an awful lot to answer for, Jessie thought, as he nursed a headache later that afternoon for having attempted his first header. In fact, more than that, it just wasn't fair.

Fortunately Connie seemed to reserve the Hull boys for a weekday friendship only.

At weekends she appeared happy to spend time with her old buddies, although she didn't seem to notice that arguably Jessie and Aiden weren't quite as keen to spend Saturdays and Sundays with *her* as once they had been.

Connie proved to be remarkably adept at sliding out of any references to the Hull gang, and she had an annoying knack of looking at anyone who dared to raise the subject with an unswerving look of wide-eyed innocence that dared further comments on the matter, and the result was that everyone took to avoiding the subject.

All of this meant though that while Tommy, Angela and Larry looked on in a bemused way as this game of psychological musical chairs played out, Aiden and Jessie became increasingly withdrawn during the weekdays.

The two boys each shied away from saying anything directly to Connie in private, not that she gave many opportunities for either Jessie or Aiden to catch her on their own.

The boys told each other that this was because they weren't sure how to handle it in a way that wouldn't cause an argument that they guessed they were unlikely to win, and they also agreed that to make too much fuss about it would be the best way of making Connie spend even *more* time with Dave and, by association, his Hull cronies.

But although they had declared this in a most emphatic manner, Jessie wasn't really convinced, and he couldn't help but wonder if they were both a little in awe of Connie's boldness, and how much older and more assured than he and Aiden she seemed all of a sudden. Much more the age of the Hull boys, in fact, who were two years older.

Still, whatever the reason for their reticence in tackling the matter, it didn't prevent Aiden and Jessie spending a fair time shooting wounded glances in Connie's direction, and she retaliated by spending a fair time studiously ignoring these looks.

There was an awkward moment one Sunday afternoon when all the Tall Trees children had been grazing Milburn on a patch of scrub ground and, for once, Connie and Aiden were larking around together in the familiar way they once had. Then Aiden had frozen awkwardly when he had noticed Dave and the other four boys standing a distance away, blatantly staring at him and Connie.

Aiden put a proprietorial arm around Connie's shoulder, and while Connie didn't shrug it off as such, neither did she do anything back to Aiden to suggest that she and he were a thoroughly united team, and so, after an awkward minute, Aiden removed his arm rather stiffly.

Dave looked puzzled and, Jessie thought, so did Aiden. Jessie studied the half-smile on his sister's face and found it very hard to read. He couldn't tell who she was taunting and who she was encouraging, and he wondered if Connie knew either.

One breaktime at school Jessie even risked inspecting Dave (from a distance), and he couldn't see anything about the lad that would entice Connie's attention so. He didn't seem particularly funny or smart or strong.

Jessie looked then towards Connie with the same scrutinising gaze. And although he had been meaning to see if she gave Dave the same sort of looks she'd previously reserved for Aiden, instead Jessie was thunderstruck by what he now saw as if for the first time.

Without him noticing, it was undeniable that Connie had started to look quite well-developed in her chest area; and that evening he noticed she was taller than him by at least a couple of inches.

How had that snuck up on her, and him? Jessie wondered. And how had she changed from a sister he felt close to into somebody he hardly recognised?

'Jessie, people grow up, and as they do, they change in lots of ways, and so you mustn't take it personally,' said Peggy in a careful manner, after she had asked Jessie to help her put Porky to bed as she had noticed the way he couldn't stop staring as if he were inspecting his sister.

Peggy had been spurred by a comment made to her by June earlier in the day; she had overheard Larry say something about Connie's antics at school to Aiden while they were clearing tables and washing up one day, which caused Aiden to give only a pained grunt in reply.

'And I doubt that Connie wants to be mean to anyone, although sometimes it might feel as if she does,' Peggy added.

After Peggy had spoken, Jessie thought he'd worked all that out for himself, and that Peggy had let him down rather.

'Hmmm,' was all he could reply, but Peggy failed to see that she had disappointed him.

*

Peggy tried to speak to Connie woman to woman a day or two later.

'Connie, dear, I might be wrong, but you and Aiden don't seem to be quite the buddies you were,' she said casually as she and Connie pegged out damp washing on the line in the garden while Porky rooted around at their feet.

'We are,' said Connie in a firm manner, as if nothing could be further from the truth than Peggy's comment.

Peggy looked at Connie, and similarly to the way that Jessie had been, she was struck by how much Connie had changed in the last year. She appeared by far the oldest of all the children now, quite the young woman in fact. Connie was nearly as tall as Peggy, and had all the makings of a womanly figure starting to fill out her clothes.

Peggy tried again. 'Connie, a little bird tells me that you are becoming pally with David, one of those lads who hurt Jessie. Would Barbara and Ted approve of that if they knew?'

'You can tell your little bird that *Dave*'s not so bad when you get to know him. And Mother and Father aren't here, are they, and so I'm not thinking about them.'

'I don't believe that for a moment, Connie,' said Peggy, who been taken aback by her niece's waspish tone, and Connie had the grace to look sheepish for a second or two.

Peggy didn't want to let Connie off the hook, and so she persisted with her grilling. 'Have you asked Jessie, or the others, what they think about your new friendship?' Peggy tried to keep her voice as non-confrontational as possible.

'I'm sure I don't need to *ask* permission from *anyone* who I'm going to be friends with, Peggy, and that includes you!' Peggy noticed that Connie had dropped the 'aunt' or 'aunty' before her name, which she most definitely would have used during the summer holidays.

Connie's tone now moved from the petulant to the provocative as she added with a distinct note of challenge, 'After all, if I don't make friends with those in my class, school is going to be even more of a pain in the backside for me than it is already. I am in a class on my own, remember.'

'*Connie!*' said Peggy at the vehemence of Connie's response. Peggy knew Barbara most certainly would not approve of Connie using a phrase such as 'pain in the backside'.

They might come from a poor part of London, but Peggy and Barbara had endured hours of elocution lessons when they were teenagers, and Barbara particularly was a stickler for polite and proper speech.

Peggy remembered Connie saying after her first day at this new school that although it wasn't nice being put in the lowest stream, nonetheless she felt the school might offer her some 'opportunities'. At the time Peggy had taken this as a good sign, but now she wasn't so sure.

She wondered if instead Connie had decided to play up to the low expectations the school had placed on her, and that the friendship with Dave had become part of that, designed to show everyone that if they expected Connie to be stupid, then she darn well would behave in such a way to prove them right.

Peggy also thought Connie's bolshie attitude might be something to do with her age and with the shift of leaving childhood and moving into that uncomfortable phase rife with uncertainty of the way adulthood should be embraced.

It had been a tricky time, Peggy remembered, and one that had spanned several long years for herself.

At one point she and Barbara had even had a massive falling-out when she was only about a year older than Connie, over some boy called Desmond Smith, even though – it turned out later – neither girl had actually been that keen on him.

Looking back now at this tiff, Peggy understood that it had been more the intoxicating feeling of taking a stand against anything – and it hadn't much mattered what, or who, the stand was about – that had seemed to have felt so very overwhelming and compulsive at the time. Rather than her and Barbara's behaviour making any proper sense to them then or now, so imperative had this sensation been of doing just *something* that 'sense' hadn't mattered a jot to either of them.

Desmond Smith had grown into a chubby young man with a receding hairline and womanly hips by his mid-twenties, with a penchant for continuously licking his overly pink, too-shiny lips, and Peggy and Barbara had often laughed since that such an unprepossessing physical specimen had led to much door-slamming, shouting and hair-pulling between the sisters when they were twelve and fourteen over who was more taken with him out of the pair of them, and who it was that he liked best.

Neither, it had turned out, when they came across him behind the bike sheds enjoying a quick fumble with a girl from a class a year below Peggy who had been blessed with a very large chest. Years later they had decided they had chosen at the time to carry on their sisterly vendetta despite all evidence that Desmond preferred those of much fuller figures than they.

Peggy decided now that she should talk firmly to her niece. 'Well, speaking woman to woman, Connie, maybe you should bear in mind that we all have to live together here, and I really don't want any more upset if Aiden and Jessie become cross with you, Aiden because he is fond of you although he might not be the type to say that directly to your face, and Jessie because Dave was one of those who attacked him. Connie, please consider that your behaviour could have repercussions, and that you should always remember what Roger and Mabel have had to put up with already over the fracas between Bill and James.'

'Well, that was *your* problem and not mine. And I'm doing Jessie and Aiden a favour, one that they are just too dumb to see. They need to stop thinking about me, and concentrate instead on trying to impress the *clever* girls in their class.' Connie's tone was defiant.

'Connie, I understand why you say that, but I don't think you really mean it …' said Peggy, intending to go on to say that Connie should treat everyone with kindness and in the manner that she would want herself to be treated.

'DO MEAN IT!' interrupted Connie in a shouty manner, and then she hurled the armful of towels she had been holding ready to pass to Peggy for pinning to the washing line back into the laundry basket and clomped furiously away, with Porky happily skittering at her side as if Connie were playing a game.

Grumpily, Peggy watched her go. She tried to tell herself that Connie was still a young girl, and that perhaps she was struggling a bit more than Peggy had realised, what with being at a new school and having been publicly shown up as being less far able academically than the other children at Tall Trees, and with being an evacuee and not having her mother and father around.

190

But all the same it was annoying and rude behaviour that in an ideal world would be nipped in the bud.

Peggy was pretty certain that Connie wasn't really particularly interested in Dave, but was simply keener on making a few ripples around her.

Oh dear, Peggy sighed to herself. Youngsters of Connie's age weren't easy to understand, or to deal with.

Let's hope this damned war is over soon, she thought. The mere idea of all the other children catching up with Connie and then the whole group of them sharing the volatile years together, which would surely happen within a year or two, was a reminder that it would be hard going for Roger, Mabel and herself if everyone was still living together at Tall Trees at that point.

Of course, the war might indeed be over by then, but a year previously the Government had promised everyone it would be over by Christmas, and look how that had turned out; it made it feel hard to be optimistic that they weren't all in it for the long haul.

Peggy tried to console herself that it would be a long time before Holly was at the 'difficult' stage, but that wasn't much solace. She recalled how both she and Barbara had yelled out loud at times, and the way their father, recently returned from WW1, had hated it if either of them ever slammed a door in temper as this made him jump with what their mother called 'his nerves', following his time on the front in France.

Were all generations destined to have their lives tainted by war, or – Peggy was now thinking of the hunger marches in the 1930s – by financial depression and massive social upheaval?

How sobering these thoughts were, but then Peggy reminded

herself that she and Holly were well, the twins were growing up, Ted had been found and had no apparent lasting effects, and life at Tall Trees had opened all their eyes to different things from how it would have been if they had stayed in London. Okay, it wasn't great around the Bill-James fiasco but, generally, things could be much, much worse. Her spirits rallied as the phrase the newspapers loved to bandy about – Bulldog spirit – came to mind.

With a bit of luck, dealing with Connie and the others at this time would be good training for what would be to come with Holly, Peggy hoped.

Meanwhile worrying news came from London, as both Larry and Angela's homes had sustained bomb damage and so the children's families had been placed in temporary accommodation. Peggy had telephone calls with both mothers who were allowed to call from a kindly woman's house, although when she spoke to Larry's mother, it was quite clear that her husband's rowdy behaviour and routine drunkenness was causing her more than a few problems at the temporary housing they had been moved to, which was one room in a shared dilapidated house in Poplar with no inside sanitation nor a proper kitchen, where eight families had been squeezed in, a whole family per room.

Peggy could well imagine how difficult this must be.

She watered down the sorry truth though for Larry by saying to him that his family were all doing as well as could be expected, as this wasn't exactly a fib.

But the look Larry gave her back suggested he could guess all too well exactly what his mother was having to put up with, and it wasn't good.

Chapter Twenty-two

'Peggy. Peggy!' shouted Roger late one afternoon. 'Telephone for you. I'm just going to the garden to check on Porky and the chickens.'

'Damn it,' said an exasperated Peggy, as she got up from the kitchen table where she had been trying to snatch five minutes to herself to peruse a newspaper while keeping an eye on Holly who was overtired and grizzly as she alternated between walking and crawling around the none too clean flagstones of the kitchen floor.

'Will you mind Holly, Tommy?' Peggy said, as he had just meandered into the kitchen in the futile attempt of seeing if there was anything to eat despite Mabel's insistence on the children not snacking between mealtimes. He did this every day, and Peggy always joked it was Tommy's perpetual triumph of hope over experience.

When he nodded that he would, she gave his shoulder a squeeze of thanks as she passed by on her way to Roger's study.

She sat at the desk and lifted the telephone receiver to her ear, saying a cautious (as it was extremely rare for anyone to call her), 'Good afternoon, Peggy Delbert speaking.'

'Good afternoon,' said a woman's voice that Peggy half recognised, but which she couldn't immediately place. Her brow furrowed, and then she realised who it was on the other end of the telephone line.

It was Maureen!

'Peggy, please,' said Peggy, glad to be sitting down already as a wave of anxiety engulfed her.

She knew she had suggested that Maureen ring her, although now that Maureen actually had, Peggy wasn't at all certain what to say.

Eventually Peggy concluded that honesty was the best policy, and so she admitted, 'I'm sorry if I sound a bit surprised, but I wasn't expecting you to telephone just at that moment and so I feel slightly caught on the hop. First things first, have you had the baby, and are you well?'

To Peggy's surprise, Maureen laughed. It sounded quite a cheerful laugh, and Peggy felt herself relax just a tiny bit.

'Maureen please,' she replied. ' I was surprised to get your letter, and I needed to think about it. I had the baby a fortnight ago, and all went as it should and so baby Peter and I are both doing well, although as he was nearly nine pounds it took a while for him to arrive.'

'Goodness,' said Peggy, feeling a bit sorry for Maureen as even though Holly had been quite a lot smaller, Peggy had felt extremely sore for weeks afterwards. 'A big boy then.'

'To anybody else, I'd probably say he takes after his father,' Maureen replied, 'but to you I can say yes, Peter is a big boy with a big heart, while his father remains a toady little weasel of the lowest order throughout his body.'

Peggy had to smile. Indeed, she was rather warming to this different version of Maureen to the one she had dealt with in the summer, who had been very pregnant then and presumably awash with anger-making hormones. And so Peggy said, 'Well, the last time I saw Bill, it was in a police station after he had been arrested for causing a fight here in Harrogate, and he *did* look rather woebegone in a shrunken sense ...'

'Can't say that I'm surprised, although I didn't know he'd been to Harrogate. That's more than I have seen of him, then,' said Maureen. 'He knows Peter is here, but he hasn't been to visit us. To spite Bill, I've put his name on the birth certificate.'

Peggy thought she'd file that away for future reference; it might be useful to her further down the line. To her surprise, the news of Bill being named on another woman's birth certificate didn't give her the slightest pang. The pangs Peggy had once experienced to do with her husband seemed to belong to a Peggy from the past, and not the Peggy she felt she was now.

'Well, maybe he has been very busy at the camp,' said Peggy in a magnanimous tone, rather hoping that this was true, and it wasn't that Bill had spent all his free time in a public house that had prevented him from visiting his newborn son. Or – heaven forbid – he was now gallivanting around with another woman. Or two.

'Possibly,' agreed Maureen.

There was a long silence, and Peggy realised that neither woman believed for a moment that this was why Bill hadn't made any effort to see his son.

'Poor Bill, he's so transparent,' Peggy said at last. 'And I've had my fill. He caused trouble here, and since then I've returned several of his letters unopened. If it were anything serious that I really needed to know, such as him being injured, I'm sure his commander would be in touch with me. But right now I don't need or want any direct contact with him.'

Maureen gave a bark that managed to convey both a mix of hollow irony along with the heavy sense of hopes being dashed to smithereens. 'You've been doing better than me then,' she added after a pause, and Peggy guessed that Maureen had been avoided by Bill altogether.

Peggy thought that now would be a good opportunity to clarify once again her own position.

'Look, Maureen, as far I am concerned my marriage to Bill is well and truly over, all bar the shouting, and actually I think we've done enough of that now, as I find it too upsetting afterwards.' Peggy heard Maureen give something that sounded like a faint groan, maybe a groan of recognition of shared feeling.

Peggy went on, 'I have been to London to see a solicitor who specialises in divorces, and unfortunately it seems not so easy for me to instigate a divorce as I had hoped. At some point I will need to speak to Bill about this, and I can't say how he will react. He does know already, however, that an ending at some point to our union is what I want, as I said this to him at the police station. And so it will be inevitable, in one way or another.

'In the interim, if you still want Bill, and you think there is any chance of you two being able to make a go of things together, then I would not stand in your way if you wanted to cohabit or you wanted to try to get him to start divorce proceedings, although I wouldn't go along with fabricating any evidence of my infidelity as, well, there hasn't been any behaviour of that ilk on my part.

'Bill might say otherwise to you, that of course I would say that seeing as I have a fancy man, but that is not the truth, and Bill has simply got a bee in his bonnet over nothing. There was a time when I had hopes in that direction, I admit, but Bill's visit to Harrogate put the kibosh well and truly on that happening. It's more that I am realistic, and while I don't want Bill for myself, I don't feel there is any reason that anyone else shouldn't have him. If they want him, that is ...' Peggy's words faltered at this point.

'That sounds honest, although I'm not sure what I feel,' said Maureen. 'I am very up and down about it all.'

'Of course you are, Maureen. It's only days since you had little Peter, after all, and so you are going to feel very emotional for a while longer yet. Look, as far as you and Bill are concerned, whatever you decide is *your* decision, and as long as Holly and I are treated fairly, your decision won't be one I'm going to argue with. I think the most important thing for both my Holly and your Peter is that they have a daddy in their lives. A man who remembers Christmases and birthdays, and who pays for their upkeep, even if he isn't romantically tied to either mother. He might not always be much of a daddy, but he is the best those little ones have right now.'

'Well, let's hope Bill takes on board the enormity of what he has done, and that there will no danger of a third mother joining us.' Maureen's tone was incredibly salty, and Peggy rather liked that.

'Maureen, you and I don't have to be friends,' said Peggy, 'but it has to be to the advantage of our children, who are after all brother and sister now, if we both present a united front. I have said to Bill I would expect him to provide for your child, as well as for mine. And I suppose this means that if he chooses to have a child with somebody else, he will have to live with those consequences, or at least he will in my book.'

'Peggy, I think you are a bigger woman than I, as I'm not sure, were I in your position, I could find it in myself to be so big-hearted,' said Maureen.

Peggy laughed. 'Actually, I'm surprised at myself. But every time I look at Holly, I am determined to do the best I can for her, and so to antagonise either Bill or you after all this water has passed under the bridge isn't helpful to either of us up here in Harrogate. And I don't love Bill any longer, and because of this I find it hard to be angry with you. I wonder if you should make a move towards him, as you could be waiting a long time for Bill to get in touch otherwise?'

The sound of Maureen giving a gulping sob came through the telephone receiver, and then Peggy had to move it away from her ear as Maureen gave a loud trumpet as she blew her nose.

To lighten the mood, Peggy added, 'Maybe a bit less of you reminding me of being the "bigger woman" though, perhaps?'

Maureen made a sound that was perfectly balanced between laughing and a strangled sob, and Peggy could remember feeling exactly the same herself quite often in the weeks immediately after Holly was born.

She said they should stop talking now as Tommy had probably been in charge of Holly for long enough, but both she and Maureen could think about what had been said in the conversation and they could pick it up another time.

Peggy sounded quite cheerful as she made her goodbyes to Maureen, and then she sat in Roger's chair in which he always polished up his sermons, thinking about how far she – and Holly – had come in the months since Holly's dramatic and traumatic birth.

For, as she had been ending the call, Peggy had felt the germ of an idea forming.

She smiled, just as Holly toddled through the doorway to Roger's office, beaming a toothily gummy smile at the delight at finding where her mother was,

Peggy nodded to Tommy, who was standing behind Holly to make sure she didn't hurt herself should she take a tumble, that he could go back to whatever it was that he had been doing, and then Peggy put back her head and laughed out loud.

It was a good idea that she had had, a very good idea indeed. And she could hardly wait to put it into action. She felt flooded with a renewed sense of energy, and it felt amazing.

But there was something important that Peggy needed to do first.

She rummaged on Roger's desk until she found one of his notebooks. She tore out the bottom half of a page of precious paper, and began.

Bill,

Maureen and I have just spoken on the telephone. Our conversation was pleasant, and I am sure we will speak again soon. I am pleased that your son Peter has arrived safely. You and I need to have a sensible discussion at some point. However, it may be a bit too soon after you were here in Harrogate for that, and so I think Maureen and Peter would appreciate a visit from you in the meantime.

Peggy

PS Holly is well. She is now walking almost properly, and she has four front teeth, two at the top and two at the bottom. If I can find someone with a camera, I will get a photograph of her to send you.

The note was to the point but Peggy felt it said all it needed to.

She looked at Holly, standing beside her now with a grubby hand on Peggy's knee.

She said to her daughter, 'How about I find a stamp and envelope to send this to your daddy, and then you and I stroll to the postbox to wear you out a little, poppet? And you and I need to go to Granny Nora's.'

Holly clapped her hands as if she were thrilled at the prospect, and gave a burble of baby talk.

'Clearly you've not yet met Granny Nora,' Peggy told her daughter. 'But, to be fair, neither have I, and so I may well be doing the poor woman down.'

Chapter Twenty-three

When Peggy and Holly returned home from the postbox and Granny Nora's, Tall Trees was in uproar and everyone was standing in the back yard.

Milburn's head was alert as it hung over his stable door and he looked on in such interest that his little chestnut ears were so flicked forward as to be almost touching at their tips, and Porky was happily snuffling around everyone's feet. Even Bucky the cat was watching, perched on the stable door close to where Milburn's head was pointing over.

Roger appeared to be almost cranky, Peggy thought, which was extremely unlike him, while Mabel and all the children looked most put out. This was very uncharacteristic of Mabel, especially, as usually she treated everyone and nearly all situations with an enviable equanimity.

'What on earth is the matter with everyone?' cried Peggy, whose heart had given a little flop of panic at the first sight of them all, before she concluded the strange atmosphere of the group looked to be more one of temper and someone having done something wrong, rather than the melancholy feel of there having been a tragedy.

Nobody replied as everyone was staring daggers at Roger,

and so Peggy added encouragingly, 'It was all sweetness and light before I left.'

'Roger says he is going to KILL Porky!' Connie literally squealed then. 'Do something to stop it, Peggy!'

'Yeah, 'e's goin' ter do 'im in!' shouted Larry. He had spoken with more of a gangster swagger than was strictly necessary, and Peggy thought that very possibly Larry had been sneaking into the cinema without paying to watch some Mickey Rooney flicks.

'Well, no, er, it isn't quite true that I am going to "do Porky in",' said Roger, although Peggy thought he looked a trifle shamefaced. 'What I actually said was—'

'It's time t' pig went t' slaughter,' interrupted Tommy.

'Yes, well, er, I did say that,' admitted Roger.

'So 'e *is* goin' ter do in our Porky – I told yer all!' Larry sounded triumphant.

Tommy geed up the excitable mood with, 'Yeah, the knacker man's going to come round an' do fer Porky. 'E'll whack him on t' 'ead, an' 'ang 'im up wi' 'is throat slit to get t' blood!'

''E'll 'ave 'ad 'is chips!' added Larry

'Larry! Tommy!' admonished Peggy.

'But Porky's part of the family!' protested Angela. 'I'm *never* going to eat him.'

'Nor me,' said Jessie, who was looking very upset.

'You'll all eat what you are given, and—' said Roger peevishly, although he was stopped from saying anything further when Mabel gave him a look that would have had a lesser man quaking in his boots.

Porky gave a grunt as if to remind everyone that he *was* there, and listening to what they were saying about him.

The children, and Mabel, all glanced at Porky before they stared accusingly at Roger once more as if he had instigated the most unpleasant thing in the world, which Peggy supposed that, in Tall Trees terms, he rather had.

Roger tried to look authoritative. 'Look, can everyone be sensible, please? And remember that I've always told everyone that the only reason we have even had a piglet here at Tall Trees has been to, er, fatten him up, into a pig. And pigs mean food. So Porky is an animal who is going to feed us, and from which we can have the butcher make us delicious sausages, bacon and all the rest. We can make brawn from his head, and use the trotters as a meal too. And I know that there's not a person here who isn't partial to roast pork and apple sauce, and crispy roast crackling,' Roger said, licking his lips at the very thought. 'There is a war on, after all, and Porky is part of our own private war effort.'

Roger looked down at Porky, who gazed back at him with a trusting look in his eyes. 'In fact, the only bit of a pig that one cannot eat is the oink, so I'm told!' Roger added in an affectionate manner.

Peggy didn't think the rector had noticed that he had been lovingly scratching Porky just where everyone knew the pig liked it, right behind the sprouting of ginger tufts that grew in a little crested patch nestled bang centre between his ears.

Roger was still scratching and so Porky closed his beady eyes in sheer unadorned pleasure, and a hind leg involuntarily lifted and trembled in the air in happy abandonment.

Peggy had always thought this tiny but distinct patch of ginger at the top of his head made Porky look rather rakish, and a bit like he had a small topknot of devil-may-care russet-coloured hair.

Roger glanced up to see why nobody had tittered at his joke about the oink, to see that only Peggy and Holly were still standing there with him and Porky.

Everyone else had drifted away in a silent protest as he spoke, unobserved by Roger, or by Peggy and Holly, so intent on Porky had they been. Even Angela's wheelchair barrelling away hadn't been noticed by any of those still left in the back yard.

'Oh dear,' sighed Roger. 'I didn't want to upset anyone, but it *is* the time of year for slaughtering the pigs. And having Porky was to give us some meat that isn't on the ration, after all. We have a lot of mouths here to feed, and four growing boys who need all the meat they can get. I don't want to upset anyone, Peggy, but we never got Porky to be a *pet* – he was always, in my eyes, a collection of meals on four legs.'

With a series of little snorts, at this Porky removed his ginger topknot out from under Roger's fingers, and with a grunt the pig turned around and pointedly sashayed his way out of the yard, heading for his favourite patch of mud beside the vegetable patch, his corkscrew tail jauntily aloft and his hooves beating their distinctive pattern on the path.

As if the pig had made a secret sign to the other animals, Milburn lifted his head and turned his back on what was going on in the yard and Bucky jumped down and made a swift exit down the path towards the front of the house.

'Porky is going to be collected at the end of the week,' Roger said weakly, his voice wobbling just a little, 'and he'll go to the slaughterhouse, and then to the butcher, after which we get everything back, except for a cut or two the butcher will keep as payment for the butchering.'

'Are you sure, Roger? I think there might not be much of an appetite for sausages and bacon for a while if this happens, and it would be terrible for such a sacrifice on Porky's part to go to waste if nobody wants to eat him,' said Peggy. 'Although I'm very partial to a pork banger, for instance, if I knew it was made of Porky, *I* couldn't face it. Even you would have to agree that Porky does seem very much part of the family.'

'The children love black pudding ...' Roger began.

Porky made a loud porcine noise from his hidey place around the corner as if Roger was very wrong in this assumption.

'Not a black pudding from Porky, they won't,' Peggy told Roger firmly, as if he might not have already got the point.

Roger looked down for a long while, and Peggy had to force herself not to interrupt him, and then he said quietly, 'Well, perhaps when the children are a little bigger and they won't remember Porky being such a dear little piglet quite so vividly.'

'Porky certainly was a very adorable wee chap when he arrived, wasn't he, with those little high-pitched squeaks and the way he learnt his name on the first day and would come to call?' said Peggy. 'He was easy to pick up, can you remember? And he had that miniature pale pink snout that was so sweet and so perfect-looking, and those tiny little trotters and, my, how he hated being put into that crate by the hearth each evening to keep him out of trouble!'

Roger held his hands up in defeat, and Peggy knew that Porky wouldn't be sent off with the knacker man for quite a while yet.

In fact, if she had any money going spare, which of course she didn't, she would have been quite happy betting all of it on the odds of Porky living out his natural lifespan in the large garden at the rectory.

Clearly, it wasn't helpful to the war effort if Porky wasn't slaughtered, Peggy understood, but while that was fine in theory, in practice the piglet had always had a lot of character about him, and his loss would leave a large Porky-shaped hole at the rectory that nobody and nothing would be able to fill. Peggy didn't think Tall Trees would be the only household that would be struggling to kill their pig.

'You win, Peggy; and yes, Porky was a very likeable little piglet,' said Roger. There was a pause, and then he whispered to her, 'Thank goodness the children haven't twigged that not all the chickens we eat for our Sunday roast have come directly from the butchers.'

'Well, let's not tell them that once the hens at the bottom of the garden stop laying, they're then for the cooking pot,' said Peggy.

'Yes, let's not,' agreed Roger.

To change the subject to something happier, Peggy said then, 'Roger, I have a favour to ask of you, and so will you come with me for a moment?'

He nodded, and she led him across the yard.

It was quite some time later when he and Peggy, and Holly, went into the rectory again.

Peggy's eyes were lit up with energy and enthusiasm as she told Mabel all about it.

Chapter Twenty-four

First thing the next morning, Peggy said to June Blenkinsop before she had even removed her coat and hat that they needed to have a word.

June looked a bit resigned and Peggy wondered if June had been half-expecting this.

'You know that I have enjoyed working with you here so much, don't you, June?' Peggy began.

June nodded, but as she was clearly not reassured by the faint but unusual jag to Peggy's voice; it was a suspicious nod.

'You were my first friend in Harrogate, June, and I can never thank you enough for that,' said Peggy. 'I hope that you know that I have been incredibly impressed with the way you have turned your very nice tea shop into a really excellent eatery for those needing hot meals throughout the day; it wouldn't be the same in this town without your thriving establishment. I've learnt a tremendous amount, and I will always be extremely grateful to have been given the opportunity by you of seeing how well a talented and capable woman can run her own business,' said Peggy.

'Dammit woman, get to the point!' said June irritably. 'Is this your way of telling me that you are going to open a rival eatery?'

'Of course I'm not!'

For a moment Peggy felt quite affronted that June could even for a moment think that she would do such a thing that would so obviously step on her friend's toes.

June's expression softened slightly.

Peggy explained, 'Don't be daft, June – of course not. I'm going to open a playgroup! I had a word with Gracie last night, and she is going to come in with me on this as my assistant. It will really help us with looking after Holly and Jack in the way that we would want them to be looked after, and we can help other mothers with small children who need to work, and hopefully it will earn us some profit too.

'There's a large bit of the garage going begging that Roger never uses at Tall Trees – it's huge really, and part of the old stable and coach block, and it wouldn't be too difficult to convert it into somewhere we could work with. There's a burner in it already that used to heat it when part of it was a tack room way back when the block was divided into stables and a place for the coaches, there's a proper quite low ceiling too as mine and Holly's old bedroom were above part of that, and we can clean the windows and insulate the walls without too much trouble.

'It's perfect for what we'd require, as nobody need traipse through Tall Trees as they can go around the side. And there is even a lavatory nearby that we could convert into something the little ones could use, and an annexe where I could put some cots for naptime. And it means that Holly won't be a problem causing you a headache here any longer, and in the spring the bigger kiddies who come to the playgroup can do things like collect eggs from the chickens and have a vegetable plot, and there'll be Milburn and Porky and so I'm sure they'll enjoy all the attention. Milburn and Porky enjoy the attention, I mean, and not the kiddies – but now I think on it both pony and pig can really shower the attention the other way if they think a snack might come. And if there's an air raid the icehouse will be plenty big enough for everyone. I've still got to think about meals and so forth but I am sure I can make it work.'

'Peggy, it sounds lovely, but I admit that I feel devastated,' said June as Peggy ran out of steam and had to take a big and audible breath as she had spoken all of this very quickly, she was so excited at the change her life was about to take.

'That's the honest truth,' June went on. 'Devastated for me of course, as it has been wonderful having you here. But I do understand that this is a good opportunity for you, and so I am going to do my level best to be thrilled for you – I'll have to work very hard on that, as it will be a real wrench losing you. But thrilled I will be, I promise! And with your teaching experience, you are perfect for running this, and I know you've done a first aid course, and so you are going to do very well, I just know it. Now, why are *you* crying?' asked June.

'I don't want to go now after all your kind words, you are so, er, er, *lovely*,' blubbed Peggy. 'I don't deserve you saying such nice things, June.'

'Give over, Peggy, and stop making such a fuss, else I won't offer you a teacake and a second cuppa to celebrate, and you know you wouldn't like that,' June said vigorously.

'Where *is* my hanky?' said Peggy as she patted her various pockets in vain, although she did her best to smile gratefully at her friend through her tears.

It was true what they said, she thought as she accepted June's neatly pressed and folded handkerchief and dabbed her face, that parting really was such sweet sorrow, and with that thought Peggy discovered that she had started to tear up all over again.

Chapter Twenty-five

Peggy worked another three weeks for June, in order to make sure that there was time for her friend to find a replacement for her at the café, as June wasn't going to be able to manage long-term on her own.

Peggy couldn't bear the thought of leaving her pal in the lurch, and in any case she wanted to show the new employee the ropes of keeping the busy café's books, how to manage the ordering of the stock and take the money at the till, and so forth.

Mabel helped out by looking after Holly while Peggy was over at the café, which was a relief as it stopped Peggy worrying about Holly getting into a pickle, as these days she was into everything and unless she was actually asleep she needed watching or playing with all the time.

Luckily Mabel seemed happy to step into the breach, although she always seemed very relieved to hand Holly back to Peggy at teatime. One day Peggy joked, 'You'll get your reward in Heaven, I'm sure', and Mabel replied, 'I feel that particular reward might be coming sooner rather than later, she keeps me on my toes so much.'

Peggy laughed, saying, 'I know what you mean. Just think

what it will be like if we get as many as twelve little ones in who are this age ...'

'Heavens to Betsy!' exclaimed Mabel with a look of mock horror, and she fanned her hand quickly as if beating extra air in the direction of her face. Then she laughed to let Peggy know she didn't mean it. In fact Peggy suspected that Mabel was rather looking forward to having lots of small children enjoying themselves at Tall Trees.

And during the evenings and at weekends Peggy found, to her surprise, that she was quite a dab hand at converting the space into what she wanted. She could knock in nails straight and true, and she wasn't bad at sawing pieces or wood to length either.

Of course, all of this could only happen once Peggy had bribed one or other of the children to watch Holly for her as she worked. This was usually the promise that whichever babysitter it was who looked after Holly could scavenge for anything they wanted from among all the ancient things that had been piled into the coach block that Peggy was sorting through, and they could then keep whatever treasures they found for themselves, or else put them towards the war effort as nearly everything could be repurposed these days.

For what seemed like an interminably long time, the work was back-breaking, and consisted mainly of Peggy hauling out old furniture and implements from one side of the space to another to make way for the renovations she had planned – the area had clearly been a dumping ground for all sorts of things for many years – and in her tidying out a smaller outbuilding to house Milburn's trap.

Once the first half of the space had been cleared, there turned out to be a lot of planks of wood stacked up, goodness knows where from. And to Peggy's relief Larry proved very skilled at teasing out the rusty nails with a claw hammer, so that each plank could once again be serviceable.

Peggy was delighted at this unexpected find as she thought these planks would be ideal as flooring that she could put down over a network of thin wooden struts she could place over the bricks already there, and once she had filled the gaps between the struts with old newspapers for insulation, then she could lay the planks on top to create a level floor.

Roger had asked his parishioners if anyone had rugs or carpets they no longer needed and this gleaned a good selection. Someone had a lot of unwanted linoleum that Peggy decided to place between the planks and the carpet to try and stop any rising damp.

Peggy thought it might look a bit bizarre underfoot when it was all done as the disparate patterns of the carpets might jar, but she doubted that the tiny children themselves would care a jot as they crawled or toddled around on it.

A parishioner had even said Peggy could have her old carpet sweeper, and so that meant it shouldn't be too difficult for Peggy (or better, Gracie) to clean up all the bits of dirt and fluff at the end of each day.

Peggy found that getting the premises ready was hard physical work and she was very tired each night by the time she went to bed as she wasn't used to such graft.

But there were a few unexpected upsides: the waistbands of her skirts were definitely a little looser than they had been, and Peggy discovered that the more she dragged, pulled and lugged things around the stronger she became.

The children were thrilled with the haul of old kettles and

badly dented saucepans that was uncovered, and they helped load these onto a lorry when it came to collect this precious scrap metal that also included all the unusable bent nails Larry had removed from the planks.

The discovery of an old and discarded darts board was highly prized, and it wasn't long before the boys had hung it in their dormitory; soon a rather nice mirror turned up and was bagged by Connie and Angela for their room.

June threw a wonderful goodbye tea for Peggy at the café on her last day. It could only last an hour because it had to be after school so that the children could be there, but before June needed to have the space for workers having a hot meal on their way home.

Everyone Peggy knew and cared about in Harrogate came, which touched her immensely, especially when they all belted out a rousing rendition of 'For She's a Jolly Good Fellow'.

Well, everyone Peggy cared about in Harrogate, bar one: James.

As she buried her face in the stack of nappies made from old towels – this was her leaving gift, as June had asked her regulars if they could each make a nappy from something old they had at home, or beg, borrow or steal Peggy a nappy that would come in useful for her playgroup – Peggy felt touched to her core at such kindness.

But she couldn't help feeling a distinct pang at James's absence, and she didn't have the courage to ask June whether she had spoken to him about the tea party and he had decided not to come.

As the October nights turned chill, fourteen-year-old Princess Elizabeth made a special radio speech on the BBC aimed at the 'children of the Commonwealth', with the younger Princess Margaret joining in at the end to say goodbye, which the younger listeners at Tall Trees lapped up as they sat in the parlour cradling cups of warm milk.

Peggy joined the children to listen, jiggling Holly on her knee as she wished Barbara and Ted were there too as it did feel like one of those occasions remembered long after the event and one that would have been nice to share as a family.

The war seemed to have been going on for what felt almost like forever now, and Peggy wondered how many other times there would be when they were all forced to remain apart when they should have been together, and she couldn't help shaking her head at the frustration of it all.

Speaking from Windsor Castle, Princess Elizabeth began, 'In wishing you all "good evening" I feel I am speaking to friends and companions who have shared with my sister and myself many a happy *Children's Hour*. Thousands of you in this country have had to leave your homes and be separated from your fathers and mothers. My sister Margaret Rose and I feel so much for you as we know from experience what it means to be away from those we love most of all. To you, living in new surroundings, we send a message of true sympathy and at the same time we would like to thank the kind people who have welcomed you into their homes in the country.'

'It is as if she is speaking just to *us*, and she knows what we are going through,' whispered Connie, her voice lowered in awe.

'I expect Mr Churchill wanted her to boost our morale now that the bombs have started to fall, and he thought that having a child speak on the wireless directly to other children would do the trick,' Aiden replied, looking directly at Connie.

Peggy thought Aiden's words made him sound wise beyond his years as this almost certainly would have been the suggestion made by somebody in the corridors of power. Then she realised that this was the first time she had heard Aiden say something directly to Connie for quite some time. Maybe things were thawing a little between them. Peggy hoped that was the case.

'Ssssh,' hissed Angela. 'Don't interrupt, you two. I want to hear every word the Princess is saying.'

The children continued to listen with rapt attention to the well-modulated voice which sounded almost as if she was right in the room with them all, and even Peggy felt her temples throb with emotion when Princess Elizabeth began to draw her speech to a close with, 'And when peace comes, remember it will be for us, the children of today, to make the world of tomorrow a better and happier place.'

Peggy stared down at Holly, who was gaily waving a crust of bread around as she burbled some baby speak, and Peggy thought that, yes, one day Holly and her generation would be in charge of the country, and she hoped with all her heart that the children sitting around before her would help to make the whole world a better and happier place than what they were all living through at that moment.

Quietly and unobtrusively so that nobody else in the room would notice, Peggy crossed her fingers and made a private wish that when the time came for her generation to pass the baton of responsibility down to the next age group, the country would still be free, and in as healthy a state as possible, with people in work and the economy thriving.

It was by no means certain that this would be the case of course, Peggy knew, but she vowed to herself just as Holly tossed her bread crust to the floor and chuckled at her audacious naughtiness, that if she, Peggy, had anything to do with it, then she was going to try really hard to help create a good future world for Holly and Connie and Jessie.

In fact, the very best world possible, Peggy declared to herself.

As *Children's Hour* ended and the children chattered to each other about the Princess's broadcast and her making a special mention of those who had been evacuated, an almost overcome Peggy clasped her little girl tightly to her chest, and then she leaned down and gently kissed Holly on the top of her head.

How blessed she was to have Holly, Peggy thought, and how lucky the both of them were to be able to live in a home filled with warmth and kindness as Tall Trees always was.

What Peggy and Holly, or indeed anybody else at Tall Trees, were unaware of was that James was standing in the back yard hidden in the half-light of dusk, as he gazed through the window at Peggy and Holly.

She looked lovely in James's opinion, appearing comely, loving and wholesome, all at the same time. As well as … well, strong, was the only description that sprung to James's mind of how she also seemed.

At any rate it was a fearsome combination of qualities, one the young doctor didn't feel equal to.

And the longer James peered across the yard and through the kitchen window, the less worthy he felt of Peggy.

He knew he had been unutterably rude and that he should have been in touch with Peggy long before now, and he was thoroughly ashamed, especially as he had no excuse for his behaviour other than feeling totally out of his depth.

So ashamed was James in fact, that try as he might, he just couldn't pluck up the courage to knock at the door and ask to speak to Peggy, even though that was precisely why he was standing there, feeling such a hopeless fool.

Still, it was a long time before he had had his fill of looking at Peggy and her daughter, and he tried hard to memorise every detail of her, feeling he might never be up to the task of bridging what felt to him like an impossible gulf between them.

James knew this was a gulf that was of his own unnecessary making, considering Peggy had offered him an olive branch with the letter she had written, despite her saying that he shouldn't reply, which he'd never believed for an instant.

He knew as well that he would never properly respect himself if he didn't do something to try and make things right between them.

The problem was what was it that he should do?

James had no idea, other than he didn't want to look a total twerp if Peggy rounded on him in anger and told him to get lost. He was already behaving in such a juvenile way, he knew, as he should have done something before now to make things better between them, but that didn't mean that he was ready to appear an _utter_ twerp in Peggy's eyes, and none of this sat comfortably. Not at all.

218

Chapter Twenty-six

Milburn was now very nearly ready to have his shoes put on again, and to be ridden and put in the trap.

But to give the pony a treat after his long summer of the children employing him in their drive to collect spare paper for the war effort, and of course because of his injuries sustained after Bill and James's fight, first Roger arranged for Milburn to have a fortnight's holiday before he returned to normal duties.

He was going to be turned out in a field alongside some other horses that belonged to a farmer in Roger's congregation.

Before Milburn left for his well-earned break, the children took measurements of his girth so that they could check again when he returned home to see if he put on weight when he was grazing all day.

It was a hard outcome for them to guess as Milburn was greedy, but the grass at this time of year held little nutritional value and Aiden pointed out that he might expend lots of energy if the other horses in the field encouraged the pony to gallop around. And then Jessie had a thought that because the grass was losing nutritional value Milburn wouldn't put on as much weight as he would do if he were going out on spring grass, although that would never happen as they all knew the dangers of greedy ponies overeating too much rich pasture and causing the agonising foot condition laminitis. And so it went on.

Peggy didn't listen much to these discussions as she was busy planning ahead. As far as she was concerned the pony's temporary absence meant that Milburn's stable could be sanitised at the same time as she was sorting out and disinfecting the space at the other end of the coach block, and thus would be an economic and efficient use of the lye and disinfectant that she needed to use anyway.

There was a small stall next to Milburn's stable that had been used for bales of straw, but one day Peggy said to Roger, 'You know where we keep the straw, Roger?'

He nodded cautiously.

'How about we move what's left of it to that other poky room at the end of the row, after I've given it a clean, of course, and then the children could make a proper winter home for Porky? It's going to be too cold for him out in the garden in a few weeks, and it will give the children something positive to do together. Now that Porky isn't going anywhere. For a while.'

Porky hadn't needed his own sleeping arrangements in the cold weather before. He had been only a tiny piglet when he had arrived, and as he had been easy to house-train, he had spent his earliest months inside Tall Trees where he'd more or less treated the whole the ground floor as his private fiefdom, although if he was tired his favourite place had always been as near to the Rayburn as he could squeeze himself. Over the summer, once the warm weather had arrived and the vegetable beds had been securely fenced off so that he couldn't nibble the produce, he had graduated to spending his nights shut out in the garden, wandering at will.

The nights would soon be frosty, and too chilly for the pig to be outside as he only had scanty patches of sparse fur.

However, although Porky was far too big now to come back inside the rectory, he steadfastly refused to acknowledge this. It meant that everyone had to make very sure the back door was shut at all times as otherwise Porky would try and barge in, despite everyone telling him no. Peggy smiled as she thought of this, and then at how the children would be thrilled that Porky was being given an official bedroom at Tall Trees; they would understand immediately that it meant he wasn't going to be shipped off for slaughter any time soon. The thought of the children's happy faces was a good one, and Peggy felt a pleasantly warm, tickly feeling in the centre of her chest in response.

'Okay, Peggy,' agreed Roger wearily, 'against my better judgement and all that ... Honestly, that pig lives the life of Riley!'

There was only the tiniest noise in answer from Porky's direction; he was trying his best to be unobtrusive.

Peggy thought it sounded like a snort of triumph, but she made sure Roger didn't see her sneak a second smile in the direction of the cheeky piglet.

Chapter Twenty-seven

At school, events suddenly took an unexpected turn. Connie went down with a severe case of tonsillitis that meant she was confined to bed, and without her to concentrate on, Dave suddenly began to pay attention – and not in a good way – to Aiden and Jessie again, if his long and pointed looks in their direction at breaktimes were anything to go by.

Aiden appeared calmer about this than Jessie, who felt sick to his boots. But this probably wasn't by very much, Jessie thought, when he noticed that suddenly Aiden had started to bite his nails.

Annoyingly, the school turfed everyone outside at break and dinnertimes unless it was actually raining, or really cold.

Jessie huddled close to the school building one lunchtime in what felt like a cruel and whipping wind as he hoped that they would be allowed back inside soon. His legs were goose-pimpled below the hem of his short trousers and his fingers were that chilly purple that's the stage before blue.

But when he was caught sneaking a longing look at the school's entrance, which would be the first step of the way to his none-too-warm classroom (but underheated as it was, it was still better than this), Jessie was ordered by a schoolmaster to move away.

The master added that if Jessie were feeling chilly, then he could run around to warm up, as the weather was merely a bit parky and he really should be more determined about using mind over matter in order not to feel cold.

A less polite child than Jessie might have begged to differ, but Jessie was too timid to say anything, and he resigned himself to moving as far away as he could go, where he could stand shivering over by the far wall with Aiden beside him until the bell went and they could go inside again.

In Connie's absence, Dave saw his opportunity, and he seized it quickly.

He nodded towards the other four lads, who fell in behind him, and then Dave spearheaded the phalanx of the evacuees from Hull as they marched showily across the school yard, until they stood right in front of Jessie and his loyal pal Aiden.

Jessie wasn't sure what to do, as all he could see was Dave and the others' arms crossed threateningly in front of their chests, and the threatening distance between their planted legs splayed far apart as they stood stock-still, apparently not affected by the sharp gusts of wind.

Jessie realised immediately that he and Aiden had very little option for escape as their backs were, quite literally, up against the wall.

Dave and the others shuffled forward a bit, still silent. And then they shuffled forward a bit more.

Dave didn't stop coming until he stood toe to toe with Aiden. The price of the Hull lads seeing Aiden's arm around Connie's shoulder looked like it might be high, judging by the glint of dislike in Dave's eyes.

At first, Jessie felt an embarrassing rush of relief at not

being Dave's prime target, and then he felt really guilty about feeling pleased that his friend might be in for a battering and not himself.

Although he knew he might get caught in the slipstream, whatever Dave was working up to looked as if it was to do with Connie, Jessie was certain.

Aiden's eyes never wavered as he stared unblinkingly back at his adversary, and so Jessie thought it clear that Aiden thought similarly.

He was impressed with the heroic attitude with which Aiden held his ground.

'After school Friday, behind t' tennis courts. Me an' you,' drawled Dave in a menacing voice, as he jabbed his forefinger hard into Aiden's chest.

Aiden stood up straight in a brave effort at not flinching, and although he stood firm it was very obvious that he wasn't as tall or as heavy as Dave.

'After school Friday,' Aiden agreed, his voice level, which impressed Jessie no end, as he knew he couldn't have been so calm were he in Aiden's shoes. It was very like Aiden to agree to something like this, rather than shouting at Dave to 'shove off' or to call a teacher as he himself probably would, Jessie thought.

'Now, now, boys, what's all this about?' said an elderly schoolmaster who'd wandered over to the lads. He had been brought out of retirement for the duration, and Jessie thought his lessons were extremely old-fashioned, but he had obviously noticed that something was going on that he should look into.

'Nothing, sir,' said Aiden promptly.

'Nuttin',' echoed Dave, and only added the required 'sir' after a weighty pause.

The bell for afternoon lessons went, and the schoolmaster said, 'Look lively then, lads. But no running.'

As they walked as quickly as they could to their next lesson, Jessie said, 'Saved by the bell, eh?'

Aiden didn't believe even a withering look in Jessie's direction was a worthy reply to judge by his very glum expression.

Jessie spent the rest of the school day thinking about Friday afternoon. He had a feeling of dread about the whole business.

Without saying as much, Dave had made it very clear that he and Aiden were to fight for Connie's affections, Connie not being at school having given the boys the opportunity to fuel the latent animosity between them.

'Do you think you need to set out rules of engagement, Aiden?' whispered Jessie when they were supposed to be learning some French verbs. He was worried that without official rules, then there would be nothing to stop Dave doing something very rash and dangerous, such as wielding a knife in the scrap, if he wanted.

When the Hull boys had attacked Jessie they had been brutal, and that was even without any weapons, and the thought of this filled Jessie with dread.

'Nah,' said Aiden. 'I'm going to see if I can speak to my cousin Kieran, who used to be a boxer, and then I'm going to do just what he says. After which I'm going to put that Dave in his place. He's messing with the wrong chap, bringing a fight to me.'

Jessie thought Aiden's defiant words sounded brave but also foolhardy, and while he doubted that Aiden actually believed them, he began to wonder if he should inform a teacher or one of the grown-ups at Tall Trees about what was due to happen. Peggy would be furious if he didn't tell her, Jessie knew, and so would Barbara and Ted if Peggy squealed on him for keeping quiet.

But if he didn't keep his mouth zipped and was then found out for having ratted on the boys' planned fight, it would be a disaster, as he would never be left alone after that. And for a moment, Jessie had an acute recollection as he relived lying in the alley on that summer's day, with the kicks and thumps of the rival Hull gang kicking and bruising him, and him slipping in and out of consciousness.

It wasn't a nice memory in any respect, and for a moment Jessie thought how much simpler his and Connie's life would be if they had never had to leave Bermondsey in the first place, if Connie hadn't been placed in 1E and he hadn't had to go to James for help as that was breaking the pal code and, given Jessie's luck, was bound to come out at some time.

If these complexities were a sign of how grown-up life was going to go for him, frankly he'd rather stay as a child for the rest of his days, Jessie thought despondently.

Chapter Twenty-eight

Later in the week Peggy was walking slowly down the road near the shops with Holly toddling beside her as she manhandled an empty pushchair which a customer at June's had lent her, when who should she bump into but James.

She would have chosen another route had she known. But although she had been telling herself repeatedly not to think about James (and, by association, the pretty nurse), and actually she had been relatively successful about this in recent weeks, now that she faced him unexpectedly, it was inevitable that Peggy's heart did a somersault, and then a second, slightly smaller one.

He looked equally shocked to see her, and then a bit relieved, which made Peggy wonder if he did in fact want to speak to her.

But James had an inscrutable expression, although he managed a bleated 'Hello' which, frustratingly, was a sight more than Peggy did.

She pulled herself together, and forced out the sort of grin where the giver isn't quite sure if it will come across as a smile or a scowl, as there was no point in her being sniffy about the fact that James hadn't had the good manners of replying to her letter, despite her expressly telling him that she didn't need an answer (and what a mistake that comment was proving to be, Peggy thought as she felt her neck stiffen in sympathy with her thoughts). A separate urgent churn she felt deep inside her guts proved how much his inactivity rankled now that he stood before her.

For a moment Peggy experienced once more, with a quiver of horror, the indignity of having to push Holly's heavy perambulator down the long road away from the temporary hospital after she had given him the letter she'd written in the wake of the fight with Bill, feeling James and the nurse might be looking at her, and perhaps even sharing a chuckle about her, as she stomped furiously away. The thought that they might *not* have been looking had felt almost as bad, as it would suggest that on a whim, James had merely transferred his attentions to another, and that they had never been more than trivial, as far as she had been concerned.

'Ah. Um. Er, hello, James,' Peggy managed, once she had driven her thoughts away from this unpleasant territory, and reminded herself that she should hold her head up high and not feel embarrassed that she thought herself worthy of a second stab at happiness, should love ever come calling again. This wasn't as spine-straightening a thought as Peggy hoped as there was a little bit of her deep inside that thought herself a fool for being so romantic, especially given her less than impressive track record.

There was a pause, and then Peggy was able to ask, with only the smallest of stutters, 'How are you?'

James ignored what she had just said.

Instead he said in his disarming manner, 'Peggy, please let me apologise profusely. I am just *so* sorry that I have been incredibly rude by not replying to your letter. It's been very busy as we had some casualties from the bombings elsewhere sent here, although I know that is no excuse. I have been unforgivable.'

Peggy nodded, but it wasn't so much that she was agreeing with James that his behaviour towards her had been shabby. It was the reminder of what a very engrossing and busy job he had, in itself a perfectly adequate reason for sloppy etiquette these days.

The wind felt taken rather from Peggy's sails, and then she hoped James hadn't thought her nods were an admonishment.

It was hard to tell, as James continued in what seemed like his normal voice, 'But it would be disingenuous of me if I didn't admit also that really I just couldn't think how to reply to you. Everything seemed wrong, and so in the end I took the easy way out, which was to do nothing, always promising that I would work out what to do tomorrow. And the more time passed, the worse I felt. I wanted to speak to you when I saw you in the café from the other side of the street, and I made it over to the rectory one evening – but neither time could I find the courage to make the first move and actually speak to you face to face. You looked so self-sufficient and capable, and I felt such an ass in comparison. And, harrumph, well, you know the rest ...'

'James, please don't waste another moment thinking further on this. I found your silence eloquent in a way that any letter could never be. And I did suggest that you weren't to reply, after all,' Peggy said, even though silently she finished this statement to herself with the imagined comment, 'Although I didn't really mean that, you oaf.'

229

James gave a sniff of acceptance he had been caught wanting, and then he said, 'You are polite not to be more horrid to me, when both of us know I should have been in touch. Anyway, how have you been, Peggy?' Without waiting for an answer, he looked at Holly, and added, 'I see this little lady has been eating all her greens as a good girl should, as she is so much bigger, and hale and hearty. And she is well and truly walking now ...'

Peggy thought James must feel nervous to be pointing out that Holly was walking, as it was obvious that as her mother, Peggy wouldn't need reminding of the fact. She felt herself soften a little at his obvious awkwardness.

'She has been eating up her food, and she is into all sorts of mischief given half a chance,' said Peggy. 'Meanwhile my biggest news is that I am no longer working with June – it all ended very amicably, and she threw me a lovely tea party at the café to which everyone at Tall Trees came, and a lot of June's regular customers too.'

James looked, Peggy thought, a tad wistful at this, perhaps as if he wished he'd been there, but Peggy still didn't know whether he had been asked and had decided not to come, if so possibly a decision he was now regretting. It was probably sensible that she didn't enquire further though.

She ploughed on, 'June and I became anxious about Holly being at the café once she was up and about, and I knew I needed to make better provisions for her. And so I thought that a way of doing this might be if I ran a playgroup for under-threes, and then it would be useful for local mothers who need to work. The more I thought about it, the more I thought that some of the space in the old coach house at Tall Trees might be suitable, and luckily Roger and Mabel agreed. And Gracie is going to help me, as she can have Jack there and earn herself some money. I'd like to open it before Christmas, but I think it might have to be in the new year as everything takes such an age to organise. By the way, did you know that Gracie and Kelvin Kell have got married?'

'I know! I had heard about this, and so the Harrogate grapevine hasn't been found wanting. But Gracie is very young for such a big step, isn't she?' said James.

'Gracie is unlikely to make a worse hash of being married than me and Bill, and so good luck to them, I say.'

James nodded on cue, and Peggy felt herself relax, very slightly. 'I am glad you have decided on something to do in Harrogate, and aren't planning to leave quite yet,' he said.

Peggy wasn't sure she'd heard him correctly.

But then she thought perhaps she had, as James turned around and walked slowly at Peggy's shoulder and Holly toddled alongside, clutching one of her mother's fingers, as Peggy and James's conversation once more took on the familiar companionable bent with which they had talked to each other prior to Bill's unexpected arrival on the scene.

As they strolled along side by side, James asked Peggy a few questions about the playgroup, and how the rooms would be fitted out.

And then, after they had chatted quite a while and Holly had begun to grizzle, which was the sign that she was getting tired of being asked to walk quite such a long way, James stopped and turned to face Peggy as he asked, 'Did Jessie tell you that the other day he came to see me at the hospital?'

'No, he never breathed a word. Whatever did he want?'

Peggy felt a small prod of shock as she swung Holly up and on to her hip, and she hoped that she hadn't given any sign to James that her heart had made an uncomfortable lurch again, as just when they were having a pleasant conversation it would be too bad if it then became awkward between them again if Jessie had clumsily been trying to play matchmaker.

'It was a while back, and I've been thinking about it since. Jessie was very worried about Connie, actually, and her being in the lowest stream at school. He kept saying she seems so bright, but she won't apply herself to her lessons, and he wondered if I had advice to give,' said James.

'Bless him. Dear Jessie, that's so like him to think of others; he really is a nice, caring boy,' said Peggy, who then contrarily felt a little sad that Jessie *hadn't* been playing matchmaker.

She rallied, and went on, 'But I am worried about Connie too, I admit. She's still as bright as a button, but only if school and schoolwork aren't on the agenda.

'And she's upsetting the status quo amongst the children by seeming far too keen now on the Hull lot, and especially the one called Dave who I think may have been the ringleader when Jessie was beaten up. Aside from upsetting her brother, this has put Aiden's nose badly out of joint, and so it's not all been sweetness and light as far as the children are concerned these past few weeks. And Connie is proving very temperamental and difficult to talk to about it. She's got tonsillitis though, but I don't think she'd be saying anything if she hadn't. I'm feeling very at sea in what to say to her.'

James looked at his watch, and said, 'I'm sorry, but I am going to have to go, Peggy, as there is somewhere I need to be.'

Peggy hoped this 'somewhere' wasn't to do with the blonde nurse.

James added, 'But in fact, although I wasn't yet quite brave enough yet actually to do anything about it, I had been working up to taking the bull by the horns and suggesting to you that in any case maybe I should have a quiet word with Connie about her schoolwork? I was thinking that perhaps her eyes should be tested, or that someone impartial should investigate a little about why she is struggling at school. Would you like me to do that?'

'Oh James, that is thoughtful of you. Yes, I think that would be wonderful. If you have the time, and the energy, as I know how busy you are.' Peggy felt a weight of concern slipping away with James's offer.

They looked at each other, and then one grinned and immediately so did the other. These were the first proper smiles that they shared since before Bill had arrived in Harrogate spoiling for a fight.

As James walked away he allowed himself a tiny sigh of approbation for being honest with Peggy as to why he'd not been in touch. And in having the nous to use whatever was making Connie struggle to his own advantage by offering to canvass a professional opinion. Hopefully, this meant that talking to Peggy next time should be much easier.

Chapter Twenty-nine

Thursday night was sleepless for Jessie, and for Aiden too. Tall Trees had long been quiet and in darkness when Aiden hissed quietly, 'Jessie, are you awake?'

'Yes.'

'Are you sleepy?'

'No.'

'Shall we get up and go down to the kitchen?'

Jessie thought Aiden sounded in need of some moral support. 'Okay,' he said.

They each pulled on a woolly, and padded out of the bedroom in their bare feet as quietly as they could as neither boy wanted to wake Tommy or Larry.

They crept downstairs, carefully avoiding all the creaky floorboards. Once they were in the kitchen they didn't dare make themselves a drink or find a snack, but they pulled two chairs close to the Rayburn and put their bare feet on the warmth of its enamel as the stone flags of the floor were very cold.

'Aiden, I don't think you should fight Dave.' Jessie sounded very grave.

'I don't want to, but if I don't, then I think those boys will make the lives of all of us a misery. I think it's easier to go along with what they want. And that's not to mention Connie, and whatever she might do.'

'Do you think she knows about it?'

'I doubt it as she's not been to school because of her throat. I guess everyone else knows though, as people keep looking at me oddly. Well, I don't think Angela knows, as I expect she'd be too scared of what Connie might say to her if she knew about it and hadn't told her. Connie hasn't given me any sign that she knows though.'

'Yes, I think you're right about Angela and Connie, Aiden, as they would never be able to keep quiet if they knew, and Connie hasn't hinted to me that she knows anything. Should I tell Peggy, do you think? Or a teacher?'

'No, don't say anything, Jessie. That would only stop the fight on that day, and then it would just happen another time. Kieran has given me some coaching, and so while I don't expect to win, I do hope to put up a good show to preserve something of the Tall Trees honour. I've been thinking about it lots and I'm sure it's better just for me to get it over and done with.'

'I do think Connie has a lot to answer for,' said Jessie. 'It sounds disloyal of me, I know, but if she had kept Dave at a distance, then this wouldn't be happening.'

'I disagree. It was only ever going to be a matter of time before that Hull lot pulled something like this. Connie is just the excuse for it to happen, with the added benefit for Dave that I have to stand back from her once he's leathered me.'

'Ugh,' sighed Jessie as sympathetically as he could.

*

Next day at school, the tension ramped up during the morning to an almost unbearable level.

It was obvious that virtually all the pupils knew about the planned fisticuffs, and several of the fifth-formers were openly totting up the odds and taking bets.

Jessie felt he should have a bet on his pal for loyalty's sake, but he didn't as he couldn't afford to lose the stake.

In fact the pre-fight furore seemed to reach such fever pitch by the time that lunchtime ended that Jessie could hardly believe that the teachers remained oblivious, as everywhere he looked there seemed to be pupils standing around in clusters, casting appraising glances at either Dave or Aiden.

But apparently the teachers hadn't twigged what was going on, as over the rest of the afternoon not a single master or mistress did anything to prevent the fight.

With a horrible inevitability, after the final bell had rung, there was a drift of pupils to the designated spot where the fight would take place.

Trying to ignore his rapidly beating heart and roiling stomach, Jessie accompanied Aiden, who was now pale and monosyllabic.

They turned the corner and Jessie could see practically the whole school, aside from the teachers, had already gathered in a loose circle in the time-honoured way that pre-arranged fights between schoolboys take place.

The Hull boys were gathered on one side of the space, and once Tommy and the others from Tall Trees had joined them (aside from Angela in her wheelchair), Aiden and his pals took up a spot in a group on the other.

Every time Jessie thought the fight was about to begin,

one of the fifth-formers would say time was needed for more betting, and so there would be yet another delay.

Eventually, though, all bets were laid, and the crowd fell silent.

The fighters removed their jumpers, which they gave to their seconds, and they rolled up their sleeves.

Softly the crowd began to chant 'Fight! Fight!', with each repetition becoming a little louder.

At last, as if there had been an unseen signal between them, Aiden and Dave moved close to each other, and as they raised their clenched fists with both boys keeping their thumbs on top, they began to circle in unison first one way and then the other, neither being keen to make a first move other than an occasional parry from which the other would skip back. Jessie couldn't help but think that for all the world they looked as if they were taking part in some macabre parody of a country dance.

Then there was a shout from someone in the crowd of 'Get on with it, yer lummox!', as others began to call 'go on!' and 'sock him!', with even Jessie, Larry and Tommy joining in the melee of shouting and air-punching amongst those watching.

And suddenly Aiden sprang forward and ducked nimbly under Dave's pugilistically positioned arms, to punch the Hull aggressor squarely on the nose before darting back to beyond the reach of his opponent.

Aiden may have been smaller than Dave, but this meant that he had a huge advantage in a nippiness to his movement that the wider and heftier lad clearly couldn't match, Jessie realised, while over the past couple of days Aiden's boxer cousin Kieran had clearly schooled Aiden very effectively in how to land a painful punch on somebody's hooter.

Jessie flinched as there had been an audible crack on the impact of Aiden's fist, and a sudden splatter of Dave's blood that pebble-dashed the shirts of both boys.

Dave looked stunned and shocked at what had just happened, and he raised a hand to his nose and then frowned as he examined the blood on his fingers.

But before he could respond there was a commanding yell of 'OI, YOU TWO!!'

And with a windmill of arms and legs, harum-scarum hair and flashing eyes, Connie flung herself between the two boys, and quick as a flash she sucker-punched each of them hard in the soft part of their bellies just beneath their ribcages, first Dave and then an even more surprised Aiden, causing them both to double over immediately in what looked like immense pain.

Connie was clearly furious with both of them, and as people watching began to go 'Ooooooooowaaah!' in the long-accepted manner of signalling that each lad had just been bested by a *girl*, she turned to stare confrontationally at the crowd as if urging anyone else foolhardy enough to come forward and have a go.

So ferocious did she look that everyone fell silent, even the fifth-formers.

Jessie wondered for a moment how his sister had even come to be there, let alone be brave enough to break up the fight, since she was supposed to be recuperating at home from her tonsillitis.

But before Jessie could make sense of it all, three schoolmasters pushed roughly through the crowd, and Dave, Aiden and Connie were grabbed and then unceremoniously hauled off back towards the school buildings, the boys going quietly, while Connie screamed at the top of her voice, 'Get your damn hands *off* me!'

Other teachers arrived en masse, and then nobody was allowed to leave until a list had been compiled of everybody there, and those running the tote had been made to give everyone who had placed bets their money back, although there were a few brave souls who had bet on Aiden and who tried to argue that as Aiden had drawn blood and Dave hadn't done anything, then they should receive their payout.

'Detention!' barked several teachers crossly to those calling out, and then to those who had been taking the bets, which meant more time wasted on a second list being made of everyone who had been given a detention. It was quite a long list.

And in this way order was more or less restored; Jessie thought probably a quarter of those present had ended up with detentions, although fortunately he, Larry and Tommy had had the sense to keep quiet once the teachers were there, and so they had avoided this.

Still, it was a while before everyone was told to go home, with there to be no loitering outside the school gates and no other fights.

Connie and Aiden were nowhere to be seen as Jessie and his pals slowly made their way back to Tall Trees, although Angela was waiting for the boys by the school gates.

As they headed home, she explained that it was down to her that the fight had been stopped before too much damage had happened.

Apparently, she had heard two fourth-year girls talking about the fight when she had been in a cubicle in the lavatory at afternoon break, and once she had worked out what was planned, she realised that Aiden was in trouble.

'I didn't know what to do, other than I had to try to stop it, even if Aiden and Connie hated me afterwards for all time,' Angela said, hamming it up just a little.

'You were very brave,' said Tommy admiringly, and Angela looked up at him appreciatively, clearly enjoying being the centre of attention in a way that was for once nothing to do with her being in a wheelchair.

'My last period was domestic science, and so I put my hand up to ask to go to the school nurse,' Angela continued. 'It's one of the few advantages of being in a wheelchair as nobody will ever question me if I say I need to see the nurse. I couldn't think who else I could tell without everyone watching me, or who would act immediately.'

'I think you told exactly the right person,' said Tommy.

Jessie thought Tommy was verging on the smarmy now, and he and Larry shared a look of disgusted agreement in this.

Angela pinkened, and then she added, 'The nurse listened very carefully, and then she took me to the headmaster, and at once he telephoned Tall Trees and sent a teacher around to the family Dave is billeted with as they don't have a telephone. Then the bell went for us all to go home, and the nurse and the head got as many teachers together as possible, and I waited near the school gates for you all as the ground was too rough for me to manage it in my chair. I saw Connie run in through the gates when she arrived so I guess she overheard the call to Roger, and I saw her, Aiden and Dave being dragged inside school again even though it was the end of the day. The head-master's face was very red.'

'I bet it was,' said Jessie, and he nodded his approval of what Angela had done as she had indeed been very resourceful.

'You know the rest,' said Angela. 'Maybe Connie answered the telephone at Tall Trees and pretended to be Peggy – but whatever happened, the moment Connie found out about the fight, she must have got out of her nightie and then run all the way to school like the very wind to sort it out.'

'It's a shame Connie didn't arrive a little bit later,' said Larry, 'as I would have liked to see them go on scrapping for a bit longer, as Dave could have come back and taken the scrap on.'

'But they could have hurt themselves if that had happened!' said Angela. 'What about if Aiden or Dave of them had a head injury like I did? And ended up in a wheelchair, or in hospital like Jessie and me did. Did any of you think of that?'

Larry and Tommy had the grace to look shamefaced while Jessie thought how, yes, he had definitely considered that possibility – and much worse besides, as likely outcomes.

But to stop it all getting very serious, what Jessie said to the others was, 'Well, that'll be the only time in her life that Connie ever runs to school wanting to get there as quickly as she can.'

His chums roared at his joke, even though Jessie knew it wasn't as funny as they were making out, although it did make him feel better as he laughed along with them.

Later, Jessie wondered if in fact Tommy and Larry and Angela had secretly been almost as worried as he had been, and so their laughter had been more a way of letting off steam after the event than in finding him funny.

But before Jessie could ponder further on that, naturally Peggy, Roger and Mabel had their say.

Chapter Thirty

Peggy didn't think she'd ever felt quite so angry. And to judge the shocked and subdued looks on the children's faces, she could tell that they had never seen her so enraged.

By the time Jessie and the others made it home, the headmaster had been on the telephone to Tall Trees once more, and this time he had spoken to an astounded Roger, who told Peggy what had happened. The pair then drove over to Aiden's house and picked up Aiden's father, and then they went to the school to collect Connie and Aiden. Connie had indeed pretended to be Peggy, when the headmaster telephoned.

'I don't care what the reasons behind the fight were,' said Peggy, once all the children had been given some milk to drink and were seated at the kitchen table.

Connie opened her mouth to say something, but Peggy yelled, 'Be quiet, Connie!'

Peggy noticed that Connie looked very pale still, and definitely not one hundred per cent. But she was too livid to suggest, as she ordinarily would have, that perhaps Connie had better go back to bed for a rest, and Peggy would bring her up a hot drink.

Connie looked down sulkily, as Holly, who was in Peggy's arms, began to cry.

'I didn't think you were so stupid, Aiden, and as for you, Connie, well, words fail me,' Peggy continued, refusing to pay attention to Holly, which only made her daughter bawl the more. 'You just wait until Barbara and Ted hear about this, my girl. We've all got to go back to school on Monday morning, and have a meeting with the headmaster. Dave will be there too, and an adult from his billet. The headmaster is going to decide over the weekend whether any of you deserve to stay in the school. He may well expel all three of you.'

Aiden looked horrified, and very chastened, and Connie didn't look much better.

'Aiden, Roger and Mabel are thinking that maybe you should go back to your parents to live as it's only down the road and having you here is more a favour than you needing it because of being evacuated,' said Peggy, who was now marching up and down the kitchen as she fumed in temper. 'I know they won't be pleased as it will be a tight squash for them with their evacuees, but then it's not fair on Roger and Mabel either, having to deal with this, is it?'

'No!' screamed Connie. Clearly not having Aiden around every day was suddenly a horrible thought for her. He had been allowed to lodge at Tall Trees so that his parents could make a bit of government-subsidised money to eke out their meagre income by having two five-year-old evacuee brothers sleep in his bedroom.

Not wanting to be sent home in disgrace, Aiden looked to be swallowing back tears. But then Jessie noticed him and Connie glance at each other, at which point Connie began to say repeatedly to Peggy that she was sorry, which she squeaked out between gasping breaths of panic so vehement that her whole body trembled.

Despite Connie's obvious despair, Peggy's face remained stony.

Mabel and Roger had been in Roger's study along with Aiden's father, with the door firmly shut so that their discussions could be in private.

The three of them came in, all nearly as cross as Peggy, and so while Peggy went into the study to phone the Jolly in the hope that Barbara or Ted might not be volunteering that night and perhaps somebody in the public house could fetch either one of them to the phone, Roger and Mabel and Aiden's father made their feelings very clear.

They asked Tommy, Larry, Angela and Jessie to leave the kitchen, and they shut the door, although from what the excluded children could hear as they craned to listen from the passageway, it was clear from the raised voices that Connie and Aiden were getting a furious dressing-down.

At one point Connie's voice reached a crescendo, quickly followed by Aiden's, but it was clear that the adults were doing most of the talking.

'This is worse than what happened when we all got into trouble about the apples in the orchard last year,' Jessie hissed to Tommy as they stood next to each other in the corridor. That particular day had ended with the police bringing them home in a police car, and there had been ructions back at Tall Trees as the children had inadvertently blundered into an experimental crop a government department had been growing and there had been the threat of legal action, as anything against the Government could be deemed as treason in times of war.

'I was just thinkin' o' that,' said Tommy. 'I thought that were t' worst that could 'appen.'

'Me too,' agreed Jessie.

And Larry, in the dim light of the hallway, nodded before he lifted his lip to show the black gap where a tooth should be. It had been knocked out that day.

But one look at Peggy as she had stalked back past them to return to the kitchen, and it was plain for all to see that she was still even more angry than she had been after the orchard incident. The furious set of her jaw told them she was massively disappointed in every single one of them, as how could it be that only Angela had had the good sense to raise the alarm, and even she had only managed to do that in the nick of time? And as for Connie and Aiden's behaviour, well, words nearly failed Peggy.

All Jessie could hope was that Dave was being admonished with equal vigour somewhere else in Harrogate.

It wasn't Peggy's day as later that evening she was helping Mabel sort some clothes in the church hall for a bring-and-buy sale at the weekend for the war effort, and she overheard two women helpers gossiping.

'I reckon the rector's goin' to take some flak if 'e ends up with a woman divorcee under 'is roof. 'E must think it's *shameful*,' one said conspiratorially, definitely emphasising her final word.

'Yer right there. It's against all teachin' and *I* won't approve,' replied the other. 'She must be no better than she should be.'

With a foul sinking sensation deep within her Peggy knew without a shred of doubt that these two women were brazenly talking about *her*, and the fact that as a church minister, Roger would be placed in an awkward position having Peggy live at Tall Trees should she go on to become, in the legal sense, a single woman.

Somehow the news was out that she wanted a divorce, but Peggy understood that was only to be expected.

Secrets were hard to keep at the best of times and the rectory was a hub in the community, and so anything that happened there was considered fair game by all and sundry.

Suddenly, just for an instant, she wished she'd kept her cards closer to her chest. But then she told herself not to be so daft. While it was regrettable that it hadn't worked out long-term between her and Bill, she had nothing to be embarrassed about. It wasn't she who had broken her marriage vows.

Peggy knew that after the way Bill had behaved the night of the fight, that Roger – even if rather herded into this by Mabel – was broadly supportive of Peggy staying at Tall Trees. He abhorred violence and – as he described them – 'small-minded attitudes'. And he preached regularly that the more vulnerable people in society needed protection, and Peggy understood because he'd told her so that if he asked her and Holly to leave, what signal would that then give to his congregation and the instructions he gave them from the pulpit that they all took care of one another?

Already frazzled by her dealings with the children only an hour or so earlier, Peggy wasn't in the mood to take what these women were saying lying down.

She stood up from where she had been crouching down sorting shoes, presumably hidden from the gossiping parishioners by a rail of coats.

'Excuse me!' she said firmly as she looked challengingly at the women. 'Is there something you want to say directly to my face, or are comments like that for only behind my back?'

The look of shock on both of the women's faces was priceless, Peggy thought. They clearly had had no idea that she was there.

Wordlessly they picked up their handbags and their coats, and hightailed it out of the church hall.

Mabel, who had been in the kitchen, looked on in surprise as they scooted past. 'Whatever's up wi' them?' she said to Peggy.

'They've just been reminded of the perils of scurrilous talk,' said Peggy.

Mabel frowned as she obviously still felt at sea as to what precisely had just occurred.

But Peggy's uncharacteristically expressionless face told Mabel that now probably wasn't the moment to probe further into what might have gone on.

As far as Peggy was concerned, today wasn't the day to test her patience. Especially as she was wise enough to understand fully already that what she intended to do as regards her and Bill wasn't going to be applauded across the board, and that nearly everyone who knew her would have an opinion one way or another as to whether she was doing the right thing.

Naturally a private person, Peggy felt dejected and peeved. But instead of allowing herself to walk away in shame, she reached into her handbag, found her crimson lipstick and visited the lavatories to apply it.

Mabel nodded in what Peggy hoped was approval when she came back into the church hall where all the jumble was.

But Peggy didn't respond.

She was too busy thinking that if some thought her a scarlet woman, she would own it, but only on her own terms. And with that she allowed herself a little pout of defiance, as if all the better to accent her vermilion mouth.

Chapter Thirty-one

After all the shouting had died down for the evening and Tall Trees began to revert back to its usual happier atmosphere, Aiden was sent home in disgrace with his father for at least a night or two, and an equally shamed Connie was told to go to bed ignominiously early and that she should sleep in Gracie's old bed on the attic floor across from Peggy and Holly's bedroom rather than in with Angela, so that Peggy could 'keep an eye on her'.

Peggy softened by taking her niece a glass of hot milk as she was definitely looking peaky still. But Connie knew that Barbara would be telephoning back at nine o'clock in the morning, and really Peggy didn't want Connie talking to the other children before then, and that meant not even Jessie. This wouldn't be because Peggy believed the children would help Connie cook up a story whereby she had less of a central role to play, but more because her aunt thought that Connie would benefit by having a little time on her own so that she could consider what had happened without everyone else chipping in with their two penn'orth.

Connie agreed with this to an extent as she did want to spend a little time thinking quietly about what had happened.

But this was only until she realised that never before had she and Jessie been prevented from speaking with each other. It almost felt as if a part of her had been cut off, and she didn't like it at all.

And so Saturday morning turned out not to be much of an improvement on Friday evening, at least for Connie and Jessie as Peggy made sure they didn't spend any time together prior to their parents telephoning.

Barbara and Ted spoke in turn to both the twins, the conversation with Connie lasting a lot longer, even though Connie only ever said back a subdued yes or no to whatever it was that was coming down the telephone line from Bermondsey.

Jessie listened to Connie's one-sided conversation with their parents as he stood in the passage outside the study so that his sister had some semblance of privacy for her conversation, and after Connie had said goodbye she scurried past him looking down so that he couldn't see her face, before she ran straight outside to the back yard.

Jessie's time on the telephone felt much shorter than usual and he thought both parents sounded uncharacteristically abrupt and quite wretched, if he were honest, which gave him a small clench of worry in the bottom of his tummy. 'I'll try harder,' he tearfully promised Barbara and then Ted, once they had finished telling him how mad they were with him and Connie for bringing the family into disrepute and how Jessie should have raised the alarm with a grown-up before things got so serious.

'See that you do,' was the gruff answer from Ted, who then hung up without his normal 'cheerio son'.

Before Jessie could work himself into a tizzy about his

parents being so curt with him, Peggy asked Jessie to come with her to look for Connie.

They found her sitting dejectedly on a patch of grass with her arms around Porky, who was standing beside Connie with a deliriously contented look on his face as she burrowed her face into his shoulder. In fact Porky looked so made up that Peggy thought it almost appeared as if he were smiling, although this was more because of the angle she was gazing at him. Still, girl and pig looked very sweet together.

Peggy told the twins they were to help her outside for the day, and neither child dared to give into the smallest grumble of dissatisfaction about this, even though it was cold and threatening to be drizzly, and Jessie had quite a lot of homework that he would be rather getting on with, and Connie was normally very vocal about how much she hated to do work in the yard, unless it was feeding or grooming Milburn.

Connie looked at her brother, and said, 'I'm sorry, Jessie. I thought – well, some of me thought – that if I made pals with the Hull boys, then it would mean you and Aiden would be looked after, and so I would have made you each safe.'

Jessie suspected this wasn't the whole truth, as he was convinced his sister had revelled in being the centre of all that was going on, and was an agent in stoking the Hull contingent's actions against the Tall Trees children. But it was the first time Connie had ever said sorry to him for anything, and so although it was more half-hearted than Jessie would have managed should the boot be on the other foot, he shrugged in acceptance of his sister's apology, and then both twins looked at the ground with serious expressions.

Peggy watched without comment. It felt a fragile exchange and she deemed it best if she stepped aside to let them get on with it.

'Come on then,' Peggy broke the silence at last. 'We've work to do.'

Without a word, or looking at each other, they followed Peggy back to the coach house, and morosely took the sandpaper she pointed at, and then got down to smoothing all the rough edges off the door and doorframes.

It was only later that Jessie started to wonder why he was being punished as much as his sister, who had actually punched both Aiden and Dave, and then had shouted at the teachers marching her off the field.

'Why do you think, Jessie?' said Peggy in a weary voice when at last he plucked up the courage to ask his aunt. 'Maybe because you knew about the upcoming fight, and yet you did nothing to stop it, knowing how me, and your parents, and Roger and Mabel would feel about such a thing?'

Jessie realised that Peggy had a point.

James arrived at Tall Trees after lunch, luckily when everyone other than Peggy and the twins was out, and in the kitchen Peggy quickly filled him in on what had happened at school the day before while the twins continued their work on the various cleaning tasks Peggy had set them.

'So, events have escalated to crisis point, but I think that possibly it is a good idea if you do have a word with Connie today,' she finished.

Peggy settled James in Roger's study with the ubiquitous cup of tea, and then went to collect her niece.

After he shut the study door behind Connie and they had both made themselves comfortable, James said in as reasonable a voice as he could muster, 'Connie, from what Peggy tells me, it doesn't sound as if it's been going so well lately as far as you are concerned.'

She stared at him defiantly, and for an instant James was taken aback by the fierce look in her eyes and how it seemed as if the woman she would become was only lurking just around the corner, almost as if she could burst through Connie's visage at any moment.

But then Connie expelled a long breath, and she seemed to shrink slightly until she looked very much the eleven-year-old child she was.

'You're right. It's not going at all well.' Her voice was still raspy from the tonsillitis, and so James thought that she must have been quite poorly.

'Why do you think that is?' James asked gently.

'I just hate it at school. I always have, and I always will.'

'That's a bit defeatist, no? And being defeatist isn't very much like the Connie I know.'

'It's only the truth.'

James thought that Connie sounded as if she believed that already her new school and her time in it added up to a total lost cause as far as she was concerned.

'The thing is, Connie, you have to go to school, and you know this. There is simply no way you can avoid it. And this means that you have two choices – you can make this easy on yourself, or you can make it difficult. To me it sounds as if

252

you have chosen the difficult path, but it is never too late to change. It doesn't have to be all or nothing, you know.'

Balefully, she looked at James.

'What do you think that you do well at school?' he asked, changing tack slightly. 'It might be other things besides lessons that you are good at, remember.'

'Nothing.'

'That's not true, is it? Shall I tell you the things that I've seen you do well?'

Connie thought seriously about this, and then she nodded.

'Well, you make friends easily, and you are a natural leader, and neither of those characteristics are to be under-estimated,' said James. 'You are brilliant at thinking up ideas, too, and excellent at organising things. Don't you feel all of those quali-ties are wonderful to be good at?'

'Not when it's only anything to do with reading or writing that impresses the teachers and everybody else.'

James waited, and then Connie added, 'And anyone can make friends and think up ideas and make them happen.'

'Really, Connie, is that what you honestly think? Are you sure?'

Her brow crinkled as she puzzled over James's words. He thought she looked like she hadn't considered anything she was naturally good at to be a skill as such.

After a while he added, 'I feel a lot of people would love to make friends as easily as you, and to have your knack of getting people behind you, Connie, or to be as brave as you. Not many people – children, or adults – would have broken up the fight between Aiden and that other boy as quickly as, by all accounts, you did, or with such authority, even if you chose perhaps the wrong way of doing this. And I promise you that when you are grown-up, you will be able to do great and wonderful things with all of those abilities I've described, as there are many places and occupations out in the adult world where those qualities will be highly valued, and where you will excel.'

Connie looked dubious.

'But if you have a special gift, you must treat people kindly with it, don't you think?'

Connie gave a suspicious nod.

'It was obvious that Aiden was your, er, special friend over the summer; and you have always been as thick as thieves with Jessie, which is natural seeing as he is your twin. But I hear that since you have been at this new school you've spent a lot of time with, um, Dave is it, and you have refused to talk to anyone about this decision – as spending time this way must have been a decision on your part, no? – and this meant that Aiden was upset when you didn't want to spend time with him, and Jessie too because of what happened in the summer when Dave hurt him, as you must have known they would be upset when you decided to ignore them for Dave. Is there anything that you want to tell me about any of that?'

'Nope.'

James wasn't going to let Connie avoid the issue with her usual bluster. 'Well, would you say that you behaved kindly?'

Connie refused to offer an opinion, but James held the silence.

Eventually she buckled, although it had been a close-run thing as James had been just about to give up. Connie didn't need to know that though.

'We had such fun over the summer, see,' she explained. 'We were the TT Muskets, and we took a blood oath to one another. We made plans and had a riot, and I loved leading us, and I never took it seriously with those other lads, which they couldn't work out how to deal with. Well, it was fun until Jessie was beaten up and had to go to hospital that is, as then it all got a bit serious and that wasn't long before the holidays ended. But for nearly all the summer I *loved* us having a gang, and taking on the Hull boys. Then suddenly it was all over, and the Muskets were disbanded, and it was us all going a new school.'

Connie was well into her stride now. 'And it was then as if we had to be grown-up, and I didn't like the feeling as I didn't feel ready. Immediately I was split up from the others from Tall Trees and put in the lowest class, and that made me look stupid, which I don't think I am, although everyone else does. I didn't have anyone to talk to either, and I didn't like that. I see now that on the first morning we went through the gates I had too much confidence about the new school and how well I'd do there, but I don't think I deserved *that* afterwards.'

James realised the 'that' was being put in form 1E.

'And,' Connie said, 'soon Dave and another two Hull boys were put into my class, and at first I thought it would be fun to make them my pals, seeing as how they had been my enemies and I wanted to see if I could turn that around. But they were two years older and so I had to work a bit more on this than I expected, which meant I hadn't much time for Jessie and Aiden. And then Dave and I took to spending time together, as he turned out to be nicer than I expected, and then he, well, um, and I ...'

She sighed, and James thought that perhaps some sort of boundary had been crossed between the youngsters, although he couldn't be sure, and even if he had been, he would have been hard put to say whether Dave or Connie would have instigated it.

Connie gave a little laugh to herself that James sounded a touch precocious, although whatever had happened, while almost outside of what Peggy would think acceptable for someone of Connie's age, didn't seem to be too troubling in the slightest as far as she was concerned.

It was a tricky dilemma as he wanted to do the best for Connie at the same time as he didn't want to let Peggy down, and of course Connie and Dave were only eleven and thirteen and so he didn't think anything that had occurred could have gone too far.

Perhaps it would be for the best, James decided, that unless it came up again during their conversation a bit later, that he didn't mention anything to Peggy, at least not today. Connie was opening up to him now, but it wouldn't take much for her to clam up again, and if he said something about their discussion that got Peggy back on the warpath, then he doubted Connie would confide in him ever again.

She was a complex child, and it was probably a good thing if she had at least one adult in her life who wouldn't automatically go running to Peggy if she had overstepped the mark, James reasoned.

'Then Peggy tried to interfere with who I was friends with, and although I didn't want to make Aiden and Jessie cross about spending time with Dave, somehow I couldn't make Dave cross either as he was that bit older and always seemed a step ahead of Aiden and Jessie, and anyway I had to sit next to him in class. Then I was ill, and Dave was stupid and wanted to fight Aiden, and Aiden was dumb enough to agree, and everybody was too dim to dare to say anything to me. And, well, er, you know the rest.'

'So, Connie, thinking about all of that, do you believe you treated everyone kindly and with respect?' said James.

Connie shook her head, but she wouldn't look the doctor in the eye.

'But you would agree that you managed to stir up quite a lot of things at the new school, and in a short time?'

She nodded.

'Looking back, do you think there might have been a better way of doing things?'

Another nod, albeit something of a reluctant one.

'Nevertheless, Connie, while the result of all of this wasn't good, the fact you managed to make such an impact quite so quickly suggests you *do* have many qualities that others would be envious of, as not everyone could have caused as many ripples as you have, wouldn't you say?'

Connie shrugged.

'You see if I'm not right, Connie, in time that is. As you'd do well to remember that these are all skills that come properly into their own only when you are a grown-up, and they will be wonderful for you to explore further several years down the line from now, when you are going out into the working world and are maybe thinking of having your own family. But now, at this point of your life, it's really important that you understand you have to make up your mind how you will spend your time at school. You're a smart girl, we've agreed, and so how do you think you might you do that?'

'Smart? I don't think so! I'm with all the dunces in 1E, remember.'

James refused to be drawn by her sarkiness, but carried on in his calm way, trying to steer the conversation but making sure to leave a lot of the working out of what he actually meant she should do to Connie, as he felt it was important that to some extent she came to her own conclusions so that she could feel at least a little in charge of her own destiny – and in order that she would understand that there were always many decisions to be taken, but the knack would be for her to analyse the situation and then try to choose the right one, and then take the responsibility for having chosen that decision.

He asked, 'Why do you feel that you are in 1E? What, exactly, is it that you find so difficult at school?'

There was a silence.

And then as Connie stared at the rug on the floor, she admitted in a voice so scared and mouse-like that James had to lean forward to catch her faint words, 'It's the reading and writing. The letters seem to jump on the page, and be in the wrong order when I write them down. I understand the teacher, but when I come to do what I'm asked to in writing, I just can't. And reading is no better – the meaning is there, and then it's gone. My eyesight is the best in the house, before you ask me about that.'

'Those jumping words must be horrible for you,' said James, and Connie nodded miserably before he added, 'But I do know that often people who have trouble with reading and writing have extremely good memories, and so how well do you remember things compared, say, to Jessie and the others?'

'Oh, I'm good at *that*,' said Connie dismissively, as if James was really stupid even having to ask that question. 'Much better than all the others if I don't have to write anything down, even better than Jessie and Aiden, who are real brainboxes, and I remember everything for ages afterwards. But I never put my hand up in class as what's the point when everyone and all the teachers have already decided that I'm dim.'

'Well, you can't control how others think about you, but you can control how *you* think about yourself and how you behave to show this to other people, Connie, and so please do remember that. And if I were in your position, I think I'd concentrate very hard on listening to what the teacher was saying at all times, and I'd make damn sure that I could remember it,' said James. 'And then when a teacher asks a question, I'd put my hand up to answer, and if I did this often enough then it wouldn't be long before *nobody* believed I was stupid. I'd make myself put my hand up all the time, as I would know that because it was difficult for me to write things down, then this makes it extra hard for a teacher to know if I were clever or not if also I never said anything in class. But if I was always answering a question, then I would be sure that would be a good way for me to demonstrate that I'd understood and had learnt what the teacher was saying. That's what I'd do, Connie.'

'It can't be that simple,' said Connie, looking properly engaged with the conversation for the first time.

'I don't think what I'm saying is simple, as it's bound to be a series of stages, which actually is the same for everyone at school. But this first bit of you putting your hand up is easy to do, and so it's what I'd try first,' said James.

'Really?'

259

James made himself sound as convinced as possible as he replied, 'Really; most definitely, truly absolutely, *really*, Connie.'

Peggy walked James to the gate. He didn't have the heart to tell her that she had cobwebs in her hair, and several smudges of dirt on her face as he felt she'd be embarrassed. He thought she looked very fine, even with the cobwebs and the smudges.

'From the way she describes it, I think what Connie suffers from is something called congenital word-blindness. This means that what she sees written down, whether somebody else has written it or she has, becomes jumbled up for her in what she sees on the paper or on the blackboard. It's not her fault, and sadly there is no cure,' James explained. 'I wondered if this was the case, and so I did some reading up, and although I'm no expert, Connie's own description of what she finds difficult about reading and writing shows some of the classic symptoms.'

'Hmmm,' muttered Peggy thoughtfully. 'I've noticed that when she writes on a clean piece of paper she might begin in an odd place, maybe over at the right-hand side or close to the bottom.'

'I don't know, but that could be part of it,' said James. 'As I say, I'm no expert and I don't think there is any treatment as such, but you should mention it to the school all the same – some establishments allow children like Connie a little leeway in examinations, such as extra time, and it might be taken into account in her school reports. I can see if I can find somebody to give a second opinion if that is helpful. There doesn't seem anything wrong with her logic or intelligence, and she was one step ahead of me over the quality of her eyesight at any rate.'

'Sounds like Connie,' said Peggy.

James added, 'I did say that one of the things she might find useful would be to really listen to the teacher, and then always to put her hand up if she knows the answer. I'm sure that if she has her confidence built up a bit in this respect, then that can only ever be a good thing.'

Peggy shook her head, and added, 'I've said that to her too, time and time again, about really listening, and that she should engage more with her teachers. But she's never followed that advice.'

'I suppose people only really hear what they are ready to hear. Perhaps Connie is ready to hear right now what you've been saying to her all along, but I just got in a bit earlier in saying it to her today,' said James.

They looked at each other for a moment in what to Peggy seemed like a significant manner.

'Yes, people only hear what they are ready to hear,' she echoed, and as Peggy spoke, she wondered if he was thinking that, as she was, this simple statement applied almost as much to the situation between herself and James, as to what was going on with poor Connie.

Chapter Thirty-two

It wasn't long before troubling news came through, although irritatingly just when Peggy was tossing a coin to see which children would have the honour of the first bath.

Once a week on bath night, Connie and Angela would take it in turns in the bath, washing their hair on alternate weeks to each other. The bath would then be emptied, and refilled and the boys would have their turn, although they dunked their short hair most times in the bath water and never gave it a specific wash.

Roger was removing his outdoor shoes in the hallway following Evensong when there was a knock at the back door, and the farmer who had the holidaying Milburn grazing in his field with his carthorses, put his head around the door to announce, 'Pony's gone.'

'What do you mean, gone?' said Mabel.

'Gone. I went to bring t' mares in for the night, an' there were no sign of t' pony,' he said. 'But t'were this pinned t' gate.'

Tommy was just wandering through the kitchen in case of any food going begging – there wasn't – and he grabbed what the farmer was holding out.

It was a ransom note.

Fight rematch else pony gets it. Plus sweet ration for five for one month.

'Roger! Peggy!' screeched Mabel. And with that Roger and Peggy, and the children, all thundered into the kitchen in panic to learn that Milburn had been kidnapped.

The twins looked at each other askance, and Jessie was pleased to note that a shamefaced Connie seemed as bowled over by the shock news as the rest of them were. It was obvious that while Connie had enjoyed flirting with the danger the Hull boys represented, now it was coming home to her that to behave like this might have most unpleasant ramifications. Jessie felt vindicated for a few seconds, and then much less so as it stuck in his craw to gloat when his sister was feeling bad.

Whatever, with Mabel's announcement, nobody could now deny that the events of Friday afternoon had now escalated into something quite nasty.

The next morning saw a very solemn mood at Tall Trees, partly because everyone felt worried about Milburn, partly because nobody had slept well and partly because there was going to be a meeting at the school first thing with the headmaster to discuss the events of Friday afternoon.

Of course bathtime had gone out of the window the previous evening as Mabel couldn't get any of the children near the tub, they were all so anxious, while Peggy and Roger had to use precious petrol to drive around looking for Milburn in all the obvious places.

But it was dark and they couldn't see much, and there was never Milburn's familiar whinny when they called him and noisily shook some cut-up windfall apples about in a bucket, and so they had to return home empty-handed.

They decided that to call the police, at least on the Sunday evening, wouldn't be a good idea as it risked fuelling the flames at a very sensitive time between the Tall Trees children and the Hull boys.

'Much as I'd like to teach those little imps a stern lesson right now,' Peggy said to Roger in the car on the way home from their abortive searching mission, 'I think we should go to the meeting at the school first before we do anything official about this, and see what the headmaster has to say. I'm sure this is just a bit of childish sabre-rattling and I doubt those boys would actually go as far as harming Milburn, although I admit I am worried about him in case they have put him somewhere that is dangerous for him, or have given him something to eat that could make him ill, or not given him a drink ...'

'Peggy, don't let your thoughts get the better of you. What a damned nuisance though,' said Roger. 'We can't lie to the children that Milburn will be all right, as we don't know that for certain. But we need to keep them as calm as possible, and insist that this doesn't mean a vendetta between the two groups can go on, or be ratcheted up to a new level. This silly business between them needs stamping out, and everyone make an effort to get on well. And as soon as possible.'

'Poor Milburn.'

Roger slammed on the brakes, and looked at Peggy. He slapped a hand to his forehead.

'Actually, Peggy, I've just had an idea. I need to make a couple of telephone calls, but it might just work.'

She asked Roger what he meant, but he refused to be drawn.

'Headmaster, before we begin the meeting proper,' said Peggy the next morning as quite a large group of people gathered in his office, although not Connie or Aiden or Dave, who were waiting in a nearby classroom under the strict eye of the head boy until the headmaster sent for them, 'I think you should be aware that there have been two developments. And also that Roger would like to make a suggestion.'

Roger, Mabel, Peggy and Aiden's father had agreed beforehand that it was going to be much quicker if one adult did the bulk of the speaking on behalf of the Tall Trees contingent, and as a former schoolteacher, Peggy was used to how schools worked, and so she had been pushed into the position of spokesperson.

Quickly, Peggy filled the headmaster in on the kidnapping of Milburn and showed him the ransom note.

And then she said the second development was that James had spoken with Connie at the weekend, and although he was a medical doctor trained in the field of general surgery, he thought it highly likely that she was suffering from congenital word-blindness, and while this didn't at all excuse Connie's role in the fracas between Aiden and Dave, it might help explain why Connie had found it harder than the others to settle in the new school, and thus may lie at the root of all the recent trouble.

'Right,' said the headmaster after Peggy had finished, and he had pondered for a while about what she had said. 'I have given the matter due consideration and I think that Aiden, Connie and David should be given formal warnings but not asked to leave the school. This is largely down to their young age. I am minded that Connie and David should be separated in class, however, and so I propose that Connie should be moved to 1D, where she would be in the same class as Larry, Angela and Tommy, which hopefully will help her settle. And I will make sure all of her teachers are aware there may be a physiological problem with her reading issues and so it might not be a case of her simply being naughty and they must spend one-to-one time with her regularly on her reading.

'Meanwhile, I am going to personally spend half an hour a day during school hours with David and his two friends from Hull, who have all now been held back two whole years, and this time with me shall be spent focusing on teaching them how to read. Their family situation in Hull is chaotic in all three cases, and so they haven't had the best start in life, but I want to give them an opportunity to better themselves, should they choose to commit to it. I will insist that the pony must be returned at once, and all threats between the groups of children end. Is this acceptable to any parents or guardians, and are there any questions? Are we able to draw a line under this unfortunate incident now?'

All the adults thought the headmaster's comment sounded very fair.

And then Roger put forward his idea.

The headmaster and the deputy head thought about it for a while, and after they had a quick confab, they said it sounded interesting and they were willing to support it. And then the headmaster proposed a few things the school could do to help.

*

'Come in, children,' said the deputy head, and the head boy was told to round up the other children from Tall Trees and Hull, after which he could go back to his lessons,

It was quite a squeeze in the headmaster's office once Connie, Aiden and Dave were there too.

The headmaster explained to the newcomers what was going to happen. There was to be no further fighting and any vendetta had to end forthwith; an unharmed Milburn had to be returned; none of the three would be expelled from the school, as would be normal once violence had come into the equation, but all of them would be put on final warnings, which meant that the slightest misdemeanour from then on could lead to any one being asked to leave immediately; Connie would be moved up a grade and her reading discussed with her form tutor and other teachers; and there would be compulsory reading tuition overseen by the headmaster for Dave, Hugh and Stuart, who were also reminded that there were to be *no* reprisals of any description for Connie being removed to a different class from them.

'Does everyone understand what I have said?' said the headmaster.

'Yes, sir,' the three children said.

'And the vendetta between all of you ends now?'

'Yes, sir.'

'And will there be no problem in returning the pony?'

'No, sir,' said Dave, a guilty twang in his voice.

'Let this be an end to the matter then, and we will mention it no more. But mark my words, any sign of bad behaviour from any one of the three of you, and you will be hauled back to my office and a much more severe punishment given,' said the headmaster very firmly.

The children said as one 'thank you, sir', and then made as if to stand up once it was obvious the headmaster had finished, but to their surprise the head then said the meeting wasn't over yet and they should remain seated.

'Reverend Braithwaite is going to talk to you now,' he explained.

For a split second Peggy wondered who the headmaster was referring to, but then she realised that this was Roger, of course, and she just wasn't used to hearing anyone say his surname.

'Right, before I begin, I want you to understand that us adults and teachers are all in agreement here,' Roger said. 'And before I explain further, we need to have the other four evacuees from Hull here, and the rest of the children from Tall Trees, and so we will wait until they join us.'

A few minutes later the new influx of pupils had managed to squeeze into the room.

'For the benefit of the newcomers, you have not been called here as regards any punishment about the events last Friday afternoon, but because there is a project afoot that concerns all of you,' explained Roger, and the children exchanged questioning looks with one another.

'It is a project that will be to everyone's advantage, and it is one that's been sanctioned by the school—' the headmaster nodded gravely as Roger spoke '—but before it can begin, Milburn is to be returned safe and sound from his horse-nap, otherwise the police will be involved, make no mistake about that. This is non-negotiable, as is the fact that all fighting between anyone in this room stops from this moment on. For good, do you hear? Are we all agreed on that?' Roger repeated for the benefit of the newcomers.

Everyone nodded, and Peggy noted that several of the Hull boys looked quite pale when Milburn was mentioned. She thought they had probably taken the pony as a joke, and to see how the Tall Trees children would respond to the threat, rather than the ransom being serious in any way.

Roger then said, 'Secondly, David – along with the other evacuees from Hull: Hugh, Stuart, Sam and Jared – and the younger residents at Tall Trees, who are Tommy, Larry, Angela, Jessie and Connie, and yes, you too Aiden, as we are happy to have you back living with us, if your parents will allow it—' Aiden's father nodded at this, and Connie and Aiden risked a quick smile at each other that they weren't going to have to live apart after all '—will all have to combine forces to work together on a single project. Working together for one objective, which will be to make the project a success …'

The children, to a person, looked dumbstruck at an adult suggesting that they combined forces.

Roger continued, 'And that project is to be a, er, panto-mime, which will be put on at the temporary hospital between Christmas and New Year for two performances to amuse the recuperating servicemen, and then in the new year it will transfer to the church hall for another two performances, this time to raise money for the war effort. So it is a serious project, and the success of it, or not, will be a matter for public scrutiny.'

There was stunned silence from all of the children.

Roger was undaunted. Peggy was impressed with how important he made the panto seem.

'There are stipulations to this, and these are non-negotiable too. These stipulations are that Connie is to write the pantomime, Aiden to direct it, and David will be stage manager. We adults will help you in every way we can, but – and this is a huge but – it is the responsibility of the three of you to make all the key decisions, and to work out from amongst those from Hull and those from Tall Trees, precisely who should do what. Every evening a classroom at school will be kept open until six o'clock for you to use under the supervision of a teacher or Mrs Delbert—' with a nod towards Peggy '—and you can have free use of the school library at breaks and lunchtimes so that you can work on this. It is up to you – are you listening, Connie, Aiden and Dave? – to get this show on the road, and to make some money from it for good causes,' said Roger. 'Failure is not an option.'

'But I've never even seen a pantomime,' wailed Dave.

'I don't know how to write one – quite literally, I don't know how to write one!' cried Connie.

'And everyone is going to argue with me,' moaned Aiden. 'And I'm never going to be able to get my way, and make people to do what I say.'

'Well,' said Peggy, 'there's a lot for all three of you to get your teeth into then, isn't there? Best crack on with it, I'd say. Some tips: pulling together is going to make life a lot easier for all of you, rather than working against each other. And do remember that you have a team of helpers in the others from Hull and from Tall Trees. Most of all, you three, throw yourself into getting this panto up and running with enthusiasm and gusto – don't any of you be half-hearted about it, or believe for a moment that it cannot happen. All of us grown-ups here think you can do this, and very successfully too.'

Dutifully the grown-ups nodded, and Peggy hoped that

nobody noticed her sneak her fingers behind her back so that she could cross her fingers about all the adults believing the children could do this.

She added, 'Finally, as special dispensation, your headmaster has agreed that Roger and I can take you to a matinee at the cinema this afternoon, where we hope you will find some inspiration. We are going to watch *The Wizard of Oz*, which might be of help to you. But before this can happen, Milburn needs to be back in his stable at Tall Trees. You have until eleven o'clock this morning for him to be returned and then have you all back in your classrooms, as at that time if Milburn isn't back, I shall telephone the police to report a horse theft.'

All the children seemed stunned still over the pantomime announcement, but they rose as one and went to deal with the Milburn question.

But as they headed down the school corridor away from the headmaster's office, the Tall Trees group kept looking at each other with puzzled brows, and Jessie noticed similar glances being shared amongst the Hull lads, who were walking ahead of them.

What a strange turn of events, and goodness knows how it would all pan out was what the questioning looks seemed to be saying.

Still, Jessie saw at once that being so perplexed did unify them all in quite a lot of ways.

He could only hope that this was something that would continue until after the dratted pantomime had been written, performed and then put away for good.

Connie caught his eye. It appeared she was thinking exactly the same thing.

Chapter Thirty-three

Peggy never needed to make the call, as at five to eleven there was a tap on the headmaster's door, and Dave entered to say that Milburn was back at Tall Trees, and everyone was in their classrooms other than him, and he would be in time if they let him go that very minute.

It was a close-run thing that left Peggy relieved as she hadn't fancied getting the police involved.

She left the school, and at midday she enjoyed a long telephone call with Barbara, when Peggy called the Jolly as they had agreed the previous evening she would do to update Barbara and Ted on how the meeting in the headmaster's office went.

'Honestly, Barbara, it was miles better than expected – I wish you could have been there to see it. Roger told the children about the pantomime, and they were all simply knocked for six. Of course they don't know, and hopefully they never will need to, that there is a back-up plan every bit of the way, and I can step in if necessary, and James has lots of people with him at the hospital who aren't well enough to go home but who are well enough to help with stage sets, or costumes, or music or whatever. But we'll let Connie and co struggle on their own a bit, and see if they can work it all out for them-selves, and delegate various jobs to one another,' said Peggy.

'Goodness,' said Barbara. 'I thought it sounded barmy last night, and I still do, and there's only about nine weeks until the first performance, which would put off most professional outfits. But if they can pull it off, what a feather in their caps!'

'I really hope they see it for the opportunity it is,' Peggy said, 'and that if it goes well, they should be able to get immersed in the schoolwork the spring term full of confidence at having achieved something that will feel stupendous to them. I definitely think it will help with the self-assurance of all the children. They are all fired up with how they can put on the pantomime and donate all the profits from the ticket sales to the war effort. Connie and Jessie have been wanting to think of something else to do for this after what they'd seen in London, especially as the paper and metal collection from the summer has had to be on hold since Milburn injured himself.'

'That's as maybe re the pantomime raising money. I mean, it'll be very welcome and that, I'm sure, but aren't you missing something out, Peggy?'

Peggy wasn't sure what her sister was driving at.

'Well, wouldn't you say there could be a benefit for you too?' said Barbara teasingly.

'I'm sure I have no idea what you mean.' Peggy knew now precisely what Barbara was saying, but her heart had leapt with this understanding, and she felt she needed to buy herself a little time to get herself back under control.

'I was thinking that perhaps you and the lovely doctor might have to spend a little time together if you need to go to him to talk about the panto skills of his patients and, as they say, one thing might lead to another?' Barbara elaborated in a manner that she could have used talking to any small child.

'The thought had never crossed my mind!' declared Peggy.

Barbara laughed. She hadn't needed to add, 'Liar!'

Peggy refused to acknowledge her sister's joshing, but nevertheless the pregnant silence told Barbara she was definitely smiling at the thought.

All of this meant that Peggy decided to postpone the opening of her playgroup until the end of January.

She felt she needed to be on hand in the meantime for the pantomime preparations in case of any emergency there, and she wanted to repay Roger and Mabel's kindness in not insisting that she and Holly, and Jessie and Connie, leave Tall Trees after causing yet another drama, and Peggy thought she could do this by making herself useful at the rectory. The festive season was always a busy one for the clergy.

And as the Blitz – as it was now routinely known, being slang for the German term for military strategy, *Blitzkrieg*, or 'lightning war' – continued with prolonged Luftwaffe assaults every night across the country, and especially in London, Peggy devoted much time writing to Barbara, as she wanted her sister to know that she was thinking of her and Ted, and was worried about them.

But letter writing tended to be done in the evenings, and so during the days Peggy threw herself into doing useful things such as dropping Holly over to Granny Nora's for Gracie to look after, which gave Peggy a chance to finish off Porky's stall, and to stand in a biting wind with Milburn at the farrier's while the pony had a spanking new set of metal shoes made and then nailed on, so that he could once again be ridden and used in the trap.

Peggy hadn't realised that a farrier would make the shoes from red-hot metal, or that after shaping, the still burning-hot shoe would be held against the pared-back hoof, causing smoke and the smelly sizzle of burning keratin, before it would be plunged into cold water to cool, after which it could be nailed on properly.

Milburn seemed none the worse after his kidnapping. (Dave and the other Hull boys never did let the cat out of the bag to the others as to where they had hidden him that Sunday night, but Peggy thought that to allow them this one small victory would mean they could save some face after their foolish idea was shown up as the silly thing it was.)

The pony seemed much less excited by his new shoes than Peggy was, she thought as she watched him close his eyes and doze while the farrier worked, and she stroked his velvet nose, telling him it was good to see him back where he belonged and ready for work once more.

Then she wondered if she needed to remind the Tall Trees children that camaraderie and finding peaceful resolutions with people you might disagree with was always going to be better than making enemies and holding on to grievances. Goodness knows why the Hull lads had taken against the Tall Trees lot, but it had happened, and although Peggy felt she had personally failed in averting the tensions that had escalated, now she felt the important thing wasn't what had already occurred but what was still to occur, and in this respect the children needed to be quite grown-up. They were all finding new types of family and homes away from home, and it was only natural there were teething troubles. It didn't mean that valuable lessons hadn't been learned along the way.

But as a gust of wind whipped her skirt against her leg and a fluffy-looking Milburn, now his woolly winter coat had come through, and nuzzled her pocket just in case she had hidden a windfall apple there (she hadn't, much to the pony's disappointment), Peggy thought that actually perhaps it was best if she didn't say anything to the children.

Moving towards adulthood meant that at some point adults needed to step back a little and let children come to their own conclusions about the best manner of doing things. While every instinct was to keep helping them all every step of the way, Peggy didn't feel that long-term this would be doing any of them a favour.

She must trust them to do the right thing, and to recognise that wartime had meant that each and every one of them now had several 'families' to which they belonged. And each of these families – whether blood relations, school classes or friends – had a lot to offer, provided each one of the children was open to it.

Peggy realised that the same was true for her and Holly too. And then with something of a jolt Peggy understood that Harrogate and Tall Trees properly felt like 'home' now, despite it not working out as she wanted with James, and that all her years living in Bermondsey, and her time there as a school teacher and as Bill's wife had somehow come to seem almost dreamlike and quite unreal.

She'd never expected that she wouldn't want to return to Bermondsey at some point, but suddenly she saw that wasn't necessarily the case any longer.

Milburn swung his head upwards and he and Peggy stared into each other's eyes. 'Tall Trees is where we belong' the pony seemed to be saying. Peggy grabbed his soft muzzle and gave him a kiss on his nose, and he responded with a deep sigh, one which Peggy hoped was of appreciation rather than irritation.

After she returned Milburn to his stable, Peggy turned to look across the yard; the lights were now on in the kitchen and the children were seated around the table looking as if they were united in their pantomime project and making money for the war effort.

Chapter Thirty-four

The first pantomime committee meeting took place after school the day following the trip to the pictures to see *The Wizard of Oz*. Jessie realised that one of the huge benefits of Roger's idea was that it meant they could definitely be indoors at breaks and lunchtimes, which was a major win during the harsh winter months whichever way one looked at it.

Aiden was put in charge of the meeting, and the first thing that he made sure of was that Jessie was elected as pantomime secretary.

'Connie, Dave and Aiden have been told what they need to do; and as secretary I can be in charge of keeping a note of our meetings and I'll draw a table to make sure everything is happening when it should. Unless anyone else wants to do this?' said Jessie.

Everyone else shook their heads as it sounded dull as ditch-water, and Jessie duly made a note of the lack of response at the back of his jotter, where he was going to write up the minutes of every meeting.

Aiden, looking at what he had scribbled during double algebra, then said, 'I think everyone needs to have jobs to do. My suggestions would be that Tommy help Dave with the sets, and Tommy can also play the piano on the performance days as he's good at that; Angela can be make-up artist and do everyone's hair, and she can also be the promoter prior to the event; Hugh can do costumes; Connie can do prompting at each performance and in rehearsals, as well as write the script everyone will learn; Jared and Sam can set up the rooms for the rehearsals and the performances, and then on the days of the pantomime they can take the money, and be the people who get all the performers when they are needed. Does that sound a plan?' asked Aiden. 'We'll need others on stage for the performances as actors, but Larry can be one of the actors, as can Stuart and Sam, and Angela.'

Nobody disagreed, although Stuart pointed out that Jared was good at cooking, and so maybe, if they could find the ingredients, he should bake some biscuits to sell at the performances. And then Angela said as it had been a good year for apples and there'd been a lot of bottling, possibly they could do some apple pies to sell on the opening night. Connie added that they could work out a drink they could sell too.

Jessie made a note of all of this.

There was then a silence, as Aiden hadn't expected everyone to be so amenable.

'Which pantomime?' prompted Jessie in a stage whisper.

'Now, the next thing is that we must decide which pantomime we are going to do,' said Aiden. 'I went to the town library and looked at old newspapers to see the pantomimes that had been put on, and the librarian told me that we can take liberties with the story in whatever we want. I've a list here of different ones, but I wondered about *Sleeping Beauty*, with Angela as Sleeping Beauty, as she can spend a lot of it asleep.'

They all laughed.

Aiden looked a tad shamefaced as he said, 'That didn't come out quite as I expected. What I meant is that it's a role that doesn't require a lot of running about.'

'Well, I probably will be asleep if I'm in charge of all the hair and make-up, and do all the posters – making it very clear we're doing this to raise lots of funds for good causes – and I can make apple something or other to sell on the door – depending on what we agree should be baked – and have a starring role as the main character ...' said Angela in a mock-grumpy way, although really she was delighted to be given so many jobs to think about, as often people thought that because she was in a wheelchair there wasn't much she could do. She had clearly decided that working on this pantomime was going to be a great chance for her to show everyone in no uncertain terms how wrong they were to think this even for a second.

Angela added firmly, 'Actually, I think we should say that the profits will go towards something useful at James's hospital, and we can tell everyone that the patients can decide what that should be. They're the ones after all who will know most what they'd like to have.'

The other children thought about this, and then Tommy said, 'That's a good idea, Angela, you keep them coming ...'

And so Angela did, and then everyone added something they had thought of, and so, almost without the children realising it, the tentative first steps to putting on their pantomime had been taken.

*

The weeks slipped by, and the children were nearly always chattering cheerfully about the preparations, to the extent that they were usually extremely weary by the time they went to bed each night.

'It's good 'earing those kiddies laugh together again, isn't it?' said Mabel one evening.

'Very good,' agreed Peggy. 'I hadn't realised how quiet and subdued they'd become, or how much I missed hearing them bicker and joke with each other.'

'Long may it last,' said Mabel, and the two of them softly chinked their teacups together in agreement.

One evening a sleepy-sounding Connie asked Peggy after they had listened to the news on the wireless if she could have a moment with her to talk something over.

'Peggy, I had an idea, and I went to ask June Blenkinsop about it. She was really helpful and put me in touch with a place where retired actors and actresses live, and June took me and Aiden there after school today. A lot of the actresses had taken part in pantomimes before, and so they gave us lots of ideas. And one has trouble writing like I do, and so she said why didn't I make up the words, and Aiden or Jessie could write them down for our other actors to learn, and so that that is what I am going to do; I'll just remember what I've said. Another had some old scripts of pantomimes and I was allowed to take them away, as apparently there's always a Prince Charming, and a dame, and a principal boy who is really a girl, and so I'm going to get Jessie to think about who we should have in it, and then I can make up some current jokes,' said Connie. 'And we must have a guest celebrity, but I haven't had any ideas on that yet.'

Peggy already knew about the visit to the home for retired thespians as the previous week June had popped over to ask if it was all right if she took the children there, and Peggy had said yes, but nobody was to tell Connie that Peggy had known about and approved the visit.

'How clever of you, Connie,' said Peggy.

'I think Tommy and Dave need to visit that home too, as there is a lot about props and sets the old actors could tell them. And Angela can go as well, as some of them have even got what they called panstick make-up that we can use,' said Connie. She paused, and then she said, 'Do you remember when James got some of his patients to talk at the church hall that time?'

Peggy said she did remember. Actually she remembered this very well indeed.

'Do you think James might know of anyone who could help with building the sets?'

'I've no idea, Connie. Why don't you ask him?' Peggy knew James would definitely be able to help, but she kept this to herself.

'I will, if you think it's a good idea, ' said Connie, and Peggy smiled and nodded that she did.

And then in a rather dreamy voice Connie asked her aunt, 'Do you think I might make a good principal boy?'

'My dear girl, I can't think of anyone better suited to be your pantomime's principal boy than you!' said Peggy, and Connie smiled at her in pleasure.

A sombre mood fell over everyone in the middle of November, however, when Coventry was badly bombed in an air raid that went on for an agonising eleven hours.

There'd been an RAF attack on Munich and this answering raid of almost 500 Luftwaffe bombers was in retaliation, quickly being described in the newspapers as the single most concentrated attack on a British city so far in the war, and the first time that vicious exploding incendiaries had been used on British soil.

The cost on human life was devastating, with 554 official deaths, but with many families having loved ones tragically unaccounted for. The cathedral was burned to the ground, as was the central library and the market hall, and the sixteenth-century Palace Yard where James II had once held court, and there had been so many firestorms during the night that the next day felt very warm in the city, so great had the heat been from all the fires. The city's Daimler works had so many incendiaries fall on it that all fifteen acres of the site went up in flames.

The children were horrified by what had happened, pictures of which being splashed over all the papers, and Roger had to answer some taxing philosophical and theological questions from the children about how God could allow such things to happen.

Peggy felt that such events proved to her that there probably wasn't a God, but as she was in Roger and Mabel's household, and obviously they did believe, she chose not to share those opinions, even when directly questioned on the matter by the children.

A lighter moment in analysing the tragedy came when the boys spent a lot of time trying to work out through algebra and physics how an abandoned tram had managed to be lifted by a blast and blown clean over a house, landing in a garden with every single window still intact.

They couldn't prove the mathematics, although when Larry wondered if this was the sign of a bona fide miracle in the technical sense, both Roger and Peggy shared a smile of amusement when Tommy scathingly replied, 'Funny of God t' reveal a miracle by usin' t' empty tram, when 'e could've shown it more impressive by somethin' much bigger. Like a full train.'

For several weeks Peggy half expected James to get in touch now that it had thawed slightly between them, and sure enough he telephoned at long, long last.

'Peggy, I'm going to go down to Coventry for a week to help out, as they are so overwhelmed with casualties, and then I'll bring some patients back with me who we can treat here at the hospital,' he said.

'I wondered if you might go,' Peggy said. And then she hoped that her comment didn't sound as if she had been thinking of him when perhaps he would prefer that she didn't, and so she added quickly, 'I'm sure you could do an awful lot of good there, James. There'll be some horrible injuries though, won't there?'

'There will, and burns are very painful for the sufferer as well as difficult to stop infection taking hold,' he said gloomily. 'But what I want to say to you that if the children do need help with staging the panto, I've left a list with Nurse Bassett of patients and people here and who could do what, and I'm sure Nurse Bassett would be able to help out too. I know you want to leave everything to the youngsters to arrange, but if you let them know casually I'm going to be otherwise engaged but that I have a very capable second-in-command they could speak to in Nurse Bassett, I think that would be very helpful.'

Peggy frowned. 'Would Nurse Bassett be the nurse you were talking to when I dropped off the letter all those weeks ago, by any chance?' she tried to say in as casual, devil-may-care a manner as possible.

'Maybe. If it was a fair-haired nurse, it probably was. Susan is always very capable and thorough, and is a favourite with the doctors and patients,' said James. 'People do tend to remember her.'

I blimmin' bet she *is* a favourite, thought Peggy as she looked down to inspect her hand that wasn't holding the telephone receiver. But I bet too that those doctors haven't noticed how incredibly stubby her fingers are, was her next thought and she had to tell herself off then for being spiteful, as spite was a nasty quality, Peggy always felt. However, her next thought was how incredibly annoying it was that James had slipped in that 'Susan' in a matey tone. A *very* matey tone …

What was particularly galling to Peggy about Nurse 'call me Susan, Connie dear' Bassett at the hospital was that, according to Connie, she was really helpful and able to persuade even the most recalcitrant patient to help with the panto, as well as proving to be an absolute mine of information that Connie could call upon. It seemed as if nothing was too much trouble for Nurse Bassett, as far as Connie was concerned.

And Connie was bowled over by how exceptionally beautiful Susan was too (Peggy knew this already, but Connie was determined to point this out anew what felt like every single time the dratted nurse was mentioned, which seemed an unbearable number of times). Of course Nurse Bassett was always happy to give Connie tips about how to style her hair, and to let Connie try on her lipstick.

It was Susan who pointed Connie, Aiden and Dave in the right direction to plunder various skills from servicemen at the hospital – who, Peggy could see, all had clearly been primed by James – and so very quickly the children had appointed undermanagers for lighting, props and set-building culled from the large pool of talent at the hospital.

Susan, was, it turned out, really a midwife, but she was doing general nursing at the hospital, along with her nurse friend Nina, she told Connie. And she must have spoken about midwifery in a very inspiring way as suddenly all Connie could talk about, when she wasn't transfixed by stuff to do with the pantomime, which to be fair wasn't very often, was how wonderful it must be to be a nurse and, specifically, a midwife. And perhaps this was what Connie should do too when it came to her leaving school.

Connie took to spending time with Holly, studying her development and occasionally pointing out to Peggy when Holly was advanced in something (walking) or behind (teething apparently, and also talking), all according to Susan's intimations as to when children ordinarily did things.

It was hard not to grit her teeth at these times, but Peggy knew too that really she should thank the nurse for managing to enthuse Connie about life after school in a way nobody had managed to previously. And especially so, as the welcome side effect as far as Peggy was concerned, was a little more time to herself to spend on preparations for opening the playgroup, as now Connie virtually snatched Holly away at every opportunity and quite often took her over to see Susan.

Peggy found it tiring though keeping a cheerful countenance every time Connie came back from the hospital with yet more stories of how wonderful Susan was, and Nina too, and she began to long for the time when the pantomime would have been put to bed.

But until then, very quickly Peggy's cheeks would be aching from the effort of smiling at Connie's open admiration of the nurse, and usually it wasn't long before she would have to resort to thinking about the nurse's fingers, as this was the only weak point that, by all accounts, she possessed.

It was all extremely irritating.

Chapter Thirty-five

James returned from Coventry, Peggy heard on the grape-vine – well, Connie was the source, having been kept up to date on all of James's movements, apparently, by Susan – and meanwhile the children moved to the rehearsals stage of getting the pantomime ready.

There was a lot of whispering and laughing, which only Roger seemed privy to, and more than once Peggy felt quite tetchy.

She knew she was probably tired.

She'd almost single-handedly refloored the space in the coach house for the playgroup, and she had insulated the walls, stuffing old straw and whatever she could find inside the internal cladding. She'd painted parts of the room, and so now it needed a small reception area building where coats could be hung and that would have the added advantage of being a two-door foyer, in order to stop any little ones sneaking out unattended.

The windows needed reconditioning to provide an opening for a fire exit, and Roger had insisted that some small toilet pans must be installed in the large outside lavatory in the yard and tiny handbasins. And in the run-up to the festive season,

Peggy's repurposing reached a point where nothing further would happen now until into the new year when the work could be completed by professional plumbers and electricians.

Then Peggy would finish the decorating, and finally she could fit out the room with small tables and chairs and so on that she was busy begging, borrowing or stealing from wherever she could, all painted a bright yellow, which was a sunny colour and, fortuitously, came from six huge tins of paint that one of June's customers had sent over.

Still, as Christmas neared, and also Holly's first birthday, Peggy felt strangely removed from the world, being simultaneously a bit dreamy yet verging on the irritable.

The children were as good as gold though, and it seemed sweetness and light continued to prevail between the group from Tall Trees and those from Hull, and Peggy had to concede that Roger looked to have lifted a rabbit out of the hat with his bizarre plan for making the children pull together.

One evening the Hull boys were invited over to Tall Trees for a supper of jacket potatoes, and Mabel played the piano as the children practised their carol singing. The plan was them to go out to various parts of Harrogate to sing carols, as a way of raising some money and of publicising the upcoming pantomime.

Peggy and Roger listened from the hall as Mabel bashed away on the piano and the children belted out the carols as best they could.

'Not necessarily the sounds of heaven,' said Roger, giving a rueful smile.

'But much lovelier than the sound of children arguing and egging each other on to fight,' said Peggy.

'Agreed,' said Roger. 'And thanks be to heaven.'

Peggy laughed. 'Amen to that.'

Very late on Christmas Eve, Peggy received two telephone calls, neither of which she was expecting.

The first one knocked her for six.

'Peggy, it's Bill here. I've telephoned to wish Holly a happy birthday, an' to wish you both a merry Christmas.'

'Oh, Bill, what a surprise, but you know that Holly has been in bed for a couple of hours now and is asleep.' Peggy gulped, unsure of what else to say.

It was quite late, and so Peggy wondered if Bill had been in a public house to build up some Dutch courage before speaking to her.

If so, she really didn't need this when she was already feeling quite emotional at the memories of Holly's tricky descent into the world twelve months earlier.

'Don't worry, Peg,' he said, as if reading her mind. 'I expected as much. I wanted to tell you that I'm teetotal now, an' I have been since that night in Harrogate, although really I never drank that often. I was bad that night though, I admit, shamefully bad.'

'Really? Goodness. Has not drinking been difficult?'

'Surprisingly not,' he said, 'as I had a lot to think about and I wanted a clear head for that. I started to spend time with little Peter, and that made me think about you an' me, an' Holly. Peter's a grand little lad. An' knowing him, I understand why you have been so cross with me, and Maureen's helped me to see that.'

Peggy wanted to say that Holly was a grand little girl too, but she bit those words back.

Instead she said, although her voice sounded tight, 'I expect Maureen and the baby have liked you being with them.'

'I think they have. An I've thought a lot about both of my children, an' I think you are right that I must look after them each, with proper money as the least of it.'

'Good, Bill. I don't think you'll regret it.'

There was a silence, but for once, it was a pleasantly companionable one between the pair of them.

At last Bill said, 'Peg, can you answer me honestly one thing? Do you still want a divorce?'

'In a perfect world, Bill. I'm sorry.'

'Well, Maureen and I have had something of a reconciliation as it were, and she has helped me see that if I let you go, then that would be the right thing for me to fix for you.'

Peggy wanted to laugh as she had once made a throwaway joke to Barbara – or was it June? – about perhaps relying on Maureen to persuade Bill of the value of divorce. Now, she wasn't certain who she'd said it to, but it didn't matter. Peggy hadn't expected such a throwaway flippant comment to have ended up having such a ring of truth about it, and perhaps promising her that at some point she could be free of a marriage that was no longer working.

Peggy made sure to keep her voice steady for her reply as she didn't want to jinx the seriousness of what Bill seemed to be trying to tell her. 'Are you telling me that you and Maureen are on good romantic terms right now?'

'I think I am.' Bill's tone was cautious.

'And you are happy about this, and it's what you want?'

'I am, and it is.'

'Then I'm wishing you sincere congratulations, Bill!' said Peggy, and there was a real warmth in her voice.

Bill gave a chuckle, and Peggy thought it sounded as if he couldn't quite believe his luck that his wife was letting him off so easily for his peccadillos and roving eye.

Peggy smiled to herself. This was just *so* Bill, and also utterly predictable of how she would have expected him to behave in this situation.

She thought that she would probably never know a man again as well as she knew Bill, and she had just the tiniest pang, only for an instant, as although she didn't want him now for herself, it didn't mean that he and Peggy hadn't shared a lot in the past, or that they hadn't once been very close to each other. That had to count for something, surely?

'And so we, er, I mean I, wondered if you and I should move towards something more formal, with me taking all the blame and admitting everything, and all. And making it as painless for you as possible of course,' Bill said quickly.

'Bill, I can't think of anything I would like better,' said Peggy.

'Well then, that's sorted! Merry Christmas, Peg, and a special kiss for Holly. We can thrash everything out properly in the new year. It will take a while, with the law being what it is, but I think if you and I can work together on this, it will be for the best.'

'Hold that thought, Bill, hold that thought,' reiterated Peggy, 'and wishing Merry Christmas to you, and to Maureen and little Peter too.'

Gently Peggy placed the telephone receiver back into its cradle, and she leant back in Roger's chair thoughtfully.

She wasn't there yet with the divorce, but this felt very much as if it was a momentous step in the right direction.

In fact, it felt so good that it was as if Bill had just bestowed on her the best Christmas present in the world.

The telephone rang again, and Peggy picked it up, saying 'The Rectory' in the sort of voice that announced she expected the caller to be wanting the services of Roger.

'Peggy? It's James.'

'Oh.'

There was a silence.

'Are you still there, Peggy? Is it too late for you?'

'Yes, it's me, James. I do apologise. And of course it's not too late. I was just thinking about something else for a moment, and so you caught me on the hop rather. Where are you?'

'I've just got back to Harrogate, and I realise it's a year to the day since I delivered Holly, and so I wanted to wish you both all festive tidings, and to say a happy birthday that you can pass on to Holly.'

'As she was born on the pip of midnight, we're treating tomorrow as her birthday, as then we can roll her birthday celebration into Christmas Day teatime, not that she'll let us do this when she is a bit bigger, I don't doubt, as she'll want two days of festivities. Do join us if you can tomorrow for Christmas tea.'

'I'd love to, but I'm working all tomorrow and in fact right up until the pantomime.'

'That's a shame,' said Peggy, with her heart lurching a little downwards. 'But how thoughtful of you to telephone to pass on your greetings.'

The grandfather clock on the other side of the room gave its half past chime, and it made Peggy start.

She added, 'Please don't think me rude, James, but I promised Roger I'd escort the children to midnight Mass, and I've got to get Holly into her outdoor clothes, and so I must go. Have a good Christmas, James. And I do appreciate you telephoning.'

'Merry Christmas, Peggy.'

Chapter Thirty-six

Christmas Day and Holly's birthday tea, and then Boxing Day passed in the way that one would expect, and fortunately in a much less dramatic way than when Peggy and Holly's lives had both hung in the balance the same time the previous year, although now Peggy realised that actually she could remember very little from that time, other than how resourceful the children had been when she needed help, and how kind James's eyes had looked when she saw him staring down at her as she lay in the hospital bed and clasped her new-born babe to her breast.

A grateful parishioner with a smallholding had dropped off two chickens and lots of potatoes and three cabbages, so it meant that there was a scrumptious roast for everyone on Christmas Day, and then hearty chicken soup the next day, all without sacrificing any of the hens that lived at Tall Trees. The children were sworn to secrecy about the gift of the chickens outside of the ration, but they were so delicious that they would definitely keep schtum in case no parishioners ever gifted them again if word were to come to the attention of the authorities.

As to the deliciousness of Peggy and Holly's attempt at making mince pies, which turned out very disappointingly as the pastry was hard and the home-made filling peculiar, maybe the least said about that the better.

Still, Peggy didn't mind she had been shown up as the mediocre cook she was. Bill's telephone call put her into a permanently good mood for the whole of the festive period, helped by Jerry deciding that hostilities could be ceased for a little while in London, according to Barbara and Ted, and so the constant concern about how they were getting on down in the Smoke could be put aside for a short while.

Barbara and Ted telephoned the twins from the Jolly, full of Christmas cheer.

And later Jessie and Connie whispered to Peggy that the florins that Ted had given them when they had been sitting with him on the hill in Greenwich Park were going to be donated to the fund for the wounded servicemen at James's hospital that the ticket money from the panto was going to go towards.

'Are you sure?' said a surprised Peggy. 'I think Daddy meant you both to have that money just to spend on something that *you* wanted.'

'I know,' said Jessie.

'But how could we enjoy it when there are people who are much more deserving than us?' added Connie.

Peggy looked at them both. They looked bigger and much more grown-up than the children who had arrived in Harrogate. The last year had seen them change from young children towards a version of themselves that was wiser, more thoughtful and mature.

'Well,' said Peggy, 'as long as you remember that nobody would think the worse of you if you did even now decide to spend it all on yourselves, but if it really is your decision to donate the money to make a wounded soldier have a bit of cheer in his life, then I don't there'd be anyone prouder in London than your father.'

The twins gave a shy smile, and then Peggy added, 'And your mother too, of course; we mustn't forget Barbara!'

Holly looked wide-eyed at everything but was very good-natured throughout the festivities, although blowing out the single tiny candle on her birthday cake proved a bit too much for her as she couldn't work out the difference between blowing and sucking. Not that it mattered a jot.

And she was very patient when Peggy spent an age posing her by the fir tree draped with old but still perfectly serviceable tinsel so that she could take a photograph to send to Bill. Holly looked angelic as she sat beside the tree, staring up at the shiny tinsel with such an innocent look on her face that it was hard to believe that she would ever cry or throw a tantrum.

The camera and a roll of precious film was the present to Peggy from everyone at Tall Trees, masterminded of course by Mabel and Roger.

Peggy had been so touched when she saw it that she had been unable to say anything for quite some while. She thought it one of the nicest and most thoughtful presents she was lucky enough to ever have been given.

'You wait, Peggy, next year little 'Olly will find Christmas so exciting, you'll be run off yer feet, so make t' most o' this one,' said Mabel, as Peggy leapt forward once more to arrange a fold of Holly's skirt a bit more becomingly before she pressed the button to take the photo.

'In that case Roger and you had better hope that the war is over by then, and we're all back in Bermondsey so that you don't have to see Holly wrecking such a lovely tree,' said Peggy, darting back to the camera once more and then again to Holly, still without pressing the button.

'Well, at this rate you're still going t' be trying t' take t' same photograph an' so you'll all still be 'ere,' said Mabel with a chuckle.

Chapter Thirty-seven

The children were up early on December the twenty-ninth. *Sleeping Beauty* would have its premiere in a large empty ward at the hospital at two o'clock, with the second performance at the same time on the thirtieth.

The following week, the production would move to the church hall, but apparently the children had been so good at drumming up an audience that those later two performances were already sold out, and James had allowed the audience overspill of the general public to join the performances at the hospital, which were already going to be swelled by all the elderly actors and actresses from the home who were attending to show their support for the children's brave endeavour.

Best of all, the headmaster had bumped into Peggy when they were both doing their Christmas shopping, and he had said that he'd decided the pantomime would also have a special performance at the school once the spring term began and everyone had returned to school in January.

By nine o'clock the children had all had their breakfast and had left for the hospital, with their lunches in brown paper bags after exacting promises from Peggy and Mabel that neither of the women were to go out into the back yard.

The children had been uncharacteristically quiet as they ate breakfast, and so Peggy thought the nerves might be kicking in. She knew there had been a dress rehearsal the day before, but the children had been hard to draw out on the topic when she'd asked about it, saying that they wanted it to be a surprise.

What the children didn't know, but Peggy was excited by as she couldn't wait to see the twins' faces, was that Barbara and Ted were on the way up to Harrogate on the first train, and would soon be enjoying a beverage or two beside a log fire in a tavern in the town.

It had been arranged with James that they would sneak into the performance once the lights were lowered, so that Jessie and Connie would have a bombshell of a surprise at seeing their parents there once the hour-long performance had ended.

Roger drove Mabel, Peggy and Holly over to the hospital at one-thirty, as it was cold and Peggy had been worried about Holly becoming fractious during the show if she got chilly on the way there while being wheeled over in the pushchair, especially as Holly would make a fuss about wanting to walk, which would really try Peggy's patience, and then Holly would grizzle when she became tired after a few yards.

Having a lift was also useful because Peggy had her prized but surprisingly heavy camera in her basket, along with an emergency rock cake for Holly should she get a bit peckish or peevish while the children and everyone else were on stage. Peggy wanted to take a photo of all the cast, and if it was good enough, she planned to send it to the local newspapers to show everyone just what evacuee children could pull off, should they be so minded.

The ride by car over to the hospital was also useful as far as Peggy was concerned as there was a vanity mirror behind the flip-down shade on the passenger's side.

As Roger stood beside the car and patted his various pockets as he attempted to locate the key to start the ignition, Peggy took a second to colour her lips in her Auxiliary Red lipstick. She blew Holly a kiss, her lips parting with an audible pop, and Holly giggled and stretched a pudgy hand towards her mother's lips.

Roger did a double-take when he saw Peggy's lipsticked mouth but he didn't say anything.

His eyebrows were still raised as they drove down the road, Peggy was amused to note, and so she decided to believe that this was because the lipstick was definitely doing its job.

The moment they got to the hospital, Roger promptly disappeared as was usual for him at dos like this as there was always a queue of parishioners he wanted to speak to, or who wanted to speak to him.

It wasn't long before a very smiley Connie sidled up to her aunt and insisted that Peggy come over right away and say hello to Susan, the pretty nurse.

This was especially tiresome as Peggy had just that moment settled herself and Holly in a seat near the end of a row in as comfy a way as possible, and Peggy was perusing the programme which suggested two special guests, while Holly seemed to be on the verge of nodding off (she had been given three potatoes at lunchtime with her soup in the hope of this very outcome).

But keen not to dampen Connie's enthusiasm on what after all was such a big, nerve-wracking day for her, Peggy stood

301

up with Holly in her arms and, leaving her basket and coat on her seat to mark it as taken, followed Connie across to where Susan stood helping some patients on crutches to their seats.

Mabel came up and whispered, 'I'll take the photograph of the cast, Peggy, as you've got your hands full', and Peggy mouthed back 'thank you' and passed across the precious camera.

Peggy noticed June enter the room and instantly guess who Susan was, if her single raised eyebrow was anything to go by.

Peggy ignored her friend in an extravagant way that would tell June she was joking, and to make sure she got the point that she didn't really mean to be rude, Peggy flashed a quick smile in June's direction as she and Holly stopped beside the lovely Susan.

'Susan, this is my lovely aunt Peggy, and my cousin Holly,' Connie announced proudly.

Peggy was touched by the very nice way Connie introduced her.

If Susan recognised Peggy from the one time they had seen each other up close, back on that late summer morning, she was far too polite to give any sign of it.

Instead Susan gave her a beaming smile and then went on to say in a totally disarming way, 'So you are the wonderful woman who Connie can't stop talking about. I'm so *very* charmed to meet you, although I rather think I know everything about you already, all of which has left me in total awe.'

Susan had something extremely charming about her, Peggy had to admit as she tried not to grit her teeth.

But she told herself not to be so silly, and Peggy then found she couldn't help but grin back in response to Susan's warm greeting and say 'Likewise', although she felt her unique mix

302

of elocution lessons and south-east London gorblimeyness felt a little wanting, and was certainly no equal to the honeyed manner in which Susan spoke.

As they made polite chit-chat Peggy saw why Connie was so drawn to the young nurse. In fact, Peggy herself was bowled over by how extremely attractive Susan was close up. She was stunning, the absolute picture of prime health, with perfect skin and hair and teeth.

Peggy sneaked a look at Susan's fingers to cheer herself up a little, and to her huge chagrin saw that the nurse's digits were no stubbier than anyone else's, and were in fact distinctly more slender than Peggy's. Peggy felt a louse at being so mean.

Susan called her colleague Nina over to say hello, and both nurses then spent quite a while telling Peggy what a live wire Connie was, with Peggy nodding agreement. Then they explained that James was really busy with several tricky cases that needed urgent treatment, and it was likely he wouldn't be able to watch the panto. He had passed on apologies for the nurses to give to Peggy though, who really wasn't sure how she should respond.

Luckily she didn't have to because at that moment several hospital orderlies shepherded some injured servicemen into the room, and needed Susan and Nina to help them to their seats.

Peggy watched with admiration the care with which the two gentle and smiling nurses helped the shuffling officers, easing them down carefully so that they didn't open up healing injuries.

She carried Holly back to her own seat a few minutes later, thinking that if Susan had usurped her in James's attentions, at least Peggy knew that she had been knocked into second place by an extremely worthy opponent.

Gracie bustled in with Jack and plumped herself down beside Peggy.

'How's married life?' said Peggy.

'Wonderful. I love it.'

Peggy realised that her feelings of trepidation over what Gracie was about to do on the morning of the marriage hadn't come to fruition. She hoped it would stay that way.

Gracie was naturally a buoyant, optimistic person, and so possibly this really helped her charge through life in a positive manner. Peggy wondered if she should try to be a bit more like Gracie in her own attitude.

'And Granny Nora?' Peggy was interested to hear how Gracie was finding dealing with her.

'Granny Nora is about to be thrilled that Jack is to have a little brother or sister,' said Gracie.

'No!' Peggy almost squealed. 'Congratulations. That's wonderful news, Gracie, although I suppose this might affect you wanting to come and spend time with me running the playgroup.'

'Not a bit of it,' laughed Gracie. 'Something's got to take up my days to stop me from killing the old bat after all!'

Peggy guessed the 'old bat' was Granny Nora. 'Gracie, you are naughty! By the way, have you clocked what the food and drink the children are selling is like? I completely forgot to notice when I came in, which will be a very black mark for me if I ever get found out.'

'Have I noticed?! I polished off two biscuits and two cups of something quite strange but very pleasant as I stood right there at the stall; I'm hungry all the time and I couldn't wait to get inside here before scoffing them. Anyway, you can report back that the biscuits were very tasty, and they really hit the spot,' Gracie told her.

'This makes me wonder, Peggy – did you by any chance see the large box of toys outside by the desk where those lads are taking the money? I ran into Angela while I was eating those biscuits, and she told me that she put on the posters that donations of usable toys and other stuff for the Tall Trees Playgroup for Working Mothers would be gratefully received. And people have really gone to town in showing their support for it, to judge by what I saw.'

'Really, Gracie?' said Peggy. 'I didn't see. I had no idea.'

'Really, Peggy. And it's all down to those children.'

Peggy smiled happily. She could hardly wait to see what the kind people of Harrogate have donated to her playgroup. What had been a mere dream several months ago was fast becoming a reality, and the thought of all that it might mean for herself and Holly in terms of income and independence was intoxicating.

But before Peggy could think too much further about any of this, the lights in the room were dimmed and it was time for *Sleeping Beauty* to begin.

Peggy looked behind her, and from the corner of her eye she saw Barbara and Ted creep in and Susan escort them to two seats she had saved for them which although near the back, gave excellent views of the stage.

Unfortunately, just then baby Jack chose that moment to give a single howl at sitting in the dark when there were really interesting things he wanted to know about that weren't on the stage, and so Gracie had to hurry out to attend to him before he set Holly off and together the little ones screamed the place down.

But not before Gracie leant over and whispered to Peggy, 'I wonder if there's any of those biscuits left. I'd best go and check.' And with that Gracie made herself and Jack scarce.

This was something of a relief as although Peggy was really fond of Gracie and Jack, the reality was that two screaming toddlers wouldn't be much of an advert for her playgroup, she thought, and she was relieved that Holly hadn't stirred when Jack had made his familiar squalling sound and that her own little daughter was obligingly still dead to the world as she slept on.

Peggy chuckled to herself as she imagined Gracie polishing off any food she could find still left, and then she thought the irrepressible Gracie would quickly make herself scarce, leaving it a mystery as to who had scoffed the last of the scran.

Peggy made sure Holly's legs were covered so she wouldn't get cold, and after a quick look around to make sure that none of James's patients needed help or anything fetching for them that she could see, and that James wasn't anywhere in sight to distract her, Peggy settled back in her seat to enjoy the pantomime.

The children had excelled themselves.

Aiden had managed to bring the best out of his actors, who were a mix of children and adults, while Dave and Tommy's sets were extraordinary and with the help of James's patients looked very professional. The pantomime managed to blend *Sleeping Beauty* with rather a lot of other pantomimes, but it was all to good effect.

What really stood out though, in Peggy's humble opinion, was the script, which was far better than Peggy could have

dreamed of. Connie had come with something that was amusing – hilariously so at times – and there was plenty of 'it's
behind you!', and 'oh yes, it is – oh no, it isn't', so that there
could be lots of audience participation with everyone joining
in.

Best of all, Peggy thought, was the intricate way Connie had
managed to weave in many references to everyone's current
situation that they would all recognise, with moments of high
drama and, at time, real pathos.

There were some jokes about the hospital and the school
(including a risqué one about the rivalry between the TT
Muskets and the Hull boys that mentioned the kidnapping of
Milburn), and even was a section called Operation Pied Piper,
which everyone knew had been the Government's codename
for the first stage of the mass evacuation that Peggy and the
twins had experienced at the start of the war, but which now
was given to a plan that the players kept getting deliberately
wrong to steal sweets from the Wicked Fairy.

The audience threw themselves into participating in the
performance.

At one point Dave did some magic tricks on stage, and
Mabel had to go up there as his helper; Peggy looked for
Roger to share a smile with him, but she couldn't see him
anywhere. A few minutes later the reason for this was clear –
Roger was the Dame, and he was in his element as he hammed
up his performance no end, playing the crowd for laughs, and
joking around with the pantomime horse. There was a second
surprise in June turning up as an ugly sister, and Peggy mar-
velled how in just a few short minutes her friend had been
transformed into a grotesque but amusing caricature. A little

later Peggy laughed at the Wicked Fairy turning out to be the headmaster from their school, who flung himself into the role with more than a hint of Max Schreck's interpretation of Count Orlok in the 1922 vampire horror silent *Nosferatu*, and Peggy wondered if the sight of him might leave some of the more impressionable school pupils with nightmares when the pantomime was put on there once term had begun.

Then Peggy had the biggest surprise of the afternoon when both Milburn and Porky appeared on stage with tinsel wrapped around them in strategic places and Porky sporting a jaunty red and green felt hat that made his face look like that of an elf, balanced by a huge red bow on the tip of his corkscrew tail. Both animals were a credit to Tall Trees, being impeccably well-mannered and not at all skittish about being on stage with people laughing at them.

Peggy glanced at the programme Angela had designed and realised that 'Special Guests' *Limnurb* and *Kryop*, were of course anagrams of Milburn and Porky's names. The pantomime horse was hilarious when it pretended to take umbrage at coming across a real horse on the stage, and everyone one hooted with laughter when only reluctantly could it be persuaded off the stage, and then kept running on again to see if Milburn had left yet.

Angela was, naturally, a lovely Sleeping Beauty, and when at one point she forgot her lines, Prince Charming sprang to her rescue, with a deadpanned echo of the lines from the pantomime horse standing on the edge of the stage, which meant it seemed as if this blip had been planned all along.

And if anyone had doubted Connie's memorising abilities, such notions were cast asunder by her control of a potentially disastrous situation as she coaxed Angela back towards the script, while managing to throw in a funny ad lib or two.

Peggy suddenly found she couldn't stop the tears spilling.

She was SO proud of the children and what they had done. Somehow they had managed to work a feat of magic.

Not only was this a pantomime that fulfilled all the normal expectations of what a pantomime should be, but it was a really excellent one, being that sublime mix of the fun, light, dark, irreverent and serious.

As everyone stood to sing 'God Save the King' at Prince Charming's request to close the performance, James slipped into the seat beside Peggy where Gracie had been.

He smiled and when he saw Peggy's teary cheeks he delved into his trouser pocket and came up with a pressed clean hanky for her.

He said, 'Give her to me', and Peggy passed him a blissfully snoozing Holly, who was still knocked out, despite the rousing sounds around her.

James looked down at the sleeping child in his arms, and said, 'You'll pay for this later tonight as she'll be up and raring to go.'

'Don't I know it,' agreed Peggy. 'But don't think you'll get off scot-free either, although maybe not tonight. Apparently Jessie has done a survey of your patients about what the money raised should buy to donate to your hospital. And what the men have decided that they really want are some kegs of beer and some cigarettes, and Jessie has agreed to this.'

James shook his head in mock alarm, his hand on his brow.

'I cannot wait,' he smiled at Peggy.

There was encore after encore, and a standing ovation, the deep-voiced cheers of the wounded servicemen in the audience bringing tears afresh to Peggy's eyes, as she earnestly hoped that the happy experience of watching something so innocent as a pantomime would have done huge amounts to lift spirits across the whole audience, but especially in raising the spirits of these poor injured men who had already given so much for their country.

If the panto had made everyone forget about all the worries to do with war and rationing and all the rest for an hour of riotous fun, then the children really were to be applauded.

Connie and Aiden were carried aloft around the room by a mix of the Tall Trees children and the boys from Hull, as everyone belted out 'For She's a Jolly Good Fellow' for Connie's benefit.

And then Jessie and Connie noticed Barbara and Ted, and they ran to their parents and there was a four-way hug that looked as if it was never going to end.

'I'm sorry, but this is making me blub all over again,' said Peggy.

'Shall I get a second hanky?' said James. 'Susan always seems to have a ready supply.'

'I bet she does,' said Peggy, being unable to keep a certain spikiness from creeping into her voice.

James glanced towards Peggy with a confused look at Peggy's tetchiness, and then he cottoned on to what was causing this.

As Holly started to wake up, James leaned over and whispered in Peggy's ear, his lips so close that Peggy could feel them brush against her and electrify her skin, saying, 'Would it help you to know that Susan most definitely wouldn't be interested in *me*?'

Peggy wasn't sure what he meant, although she twigged that he'd realised she was jealous of Susan, and so she squinted at him in confusion.

'Peggy, you are hopeless,' he said, unable to keep a smile from his face. 'Nurse Bassett isn't fond of *men*, you dimwit, it's her friend Nina she likes.'

The penny dropped, and suddenly Peggy felt a whole lot happier, even though James's description of the lovely Susan's proclivities might have been found offensive in the eyes of some, although Peggy had never personally thought it so.

In her eyes, what he had said in essence about Susan was damn plumb perfect, and Peggy could completely see what Susan and Nina saw in each other. In fact they looked a match made in heaven.

Peggy inched imperceptibly closer to the doctor, and encouraged by the warm look James sent her, risked giving him a little bump on his hip with her own as she grinned sideways at him.

She had never, in her whole life, been so forward before to do something like bump her hip, and so she didn't know whether it was this brave step into the unknown, or the fact that their bodies had just touched that jolted her so.

But maybe the precise why didn't matter too much. For, quite simply, suddenly Peggy felt electrified in every cell and fibre of her being.

And it was a wonderful, wonderful feeling.

James's eyes were bright, and he opened his mouth to say something.

But Holly stole his thunder by choosing that very moment to enunciate 'Susan' distinctly.

The irony of this wasn't wasted on Peggy, and she laughed until her sides hurt.

'It's Holly's first word,' she managed to splutter.

'I hope I'm with you both when Holly says her second, Peggy,' said James in a serious voice and then he and Peggy stared deep into each other's eyes for a long moment as the sounds around them seemed to fade into the background.

And softly he nudged his hip back against Peggy's as he passed Holly back to her mother, managing to do this while somehow interlocking their fingers.

'Here's to 1941,' one of them said softly.

'1941,' the other whispered, 'I think it's going to be a good year.'

'Me too.'

Acknowledgements

I'd like to thank all the usual suspects for their help in getting this book ready to meet the world, with a special shout out to my agent Cathryn Summerhayes, and my editor at HQ Kate Mills, who has been ably aided by Becky Heeley and copy-editor Cari Rosen. I couldn't have done it without you all, and I am very grateful. Any mistakes are, of course, my own.

Read on for more about the courageous
twins in a heart-warming extract from

The Evacuee Christmas

It's autumn 1939 and London is preparing
to evacuate its young …

Chapter One

The shadows were starting to lengthen as twins Connie and Jessie made their way back home.

They felt quite grown-up these days as a week earlier it had been their tenth birthday, and their mother Barbara had iced a cake and there'd been a raucous tea party at home for family and their close friends, with party games and paper hats. The party had ended in the parlour with Barbara bashing out songs on the old piano and everyone having a good old sing-song.

What a lot of fun it had been, even though by bedtime Connie felt queasy from eating too much cake, and Jessie had a sore throat the following morning from yelling out the words to 'The Lambeth Walk' with far too much vigour.

On the twins' iced Victoria sponge Barbara had carefully piped Connie's name in cerise icing with loopy lettering and delicately traced small yellow and baby-pink flowers above it.

Then Barbara had thoroughly washed out her metal icing gun and got to work writing Jessie's name below his sister's on the lower half of the cake.

This time Barbara chose to work in boxy dark blue capitals, with a sailboat on some choppy turquoise and deep-blue waves carefully worked in contrasting-coloured icing as the decoration below his name, Jessie being very sensitive about his name and the all-too-common assumption, for people who hadn't met him but only knew him by the name 'Jessie', that he was a girl.

If she cared to think about it, which she tried not to, Barbara heartily regretted that Ted had talked her into giving their only son as his Christian name the Ross family name of Jessie which, as tradition would have it, was passed down to the firstborn male in each new generation of Rosses.

It wasn't even spelt Jesse, as it usually was if naming a boy, because – Ross family tradition again – Jessie was on the earlier birth certificates of those other Jessies and in the family Bible that lay on the sideboard in the parlour at Ted's elder brother's house, and so Jessie was how it had to be for all the future Ross generations to come.

Ted had told Barbara what an honour it was to be called Jessie, and Barbara, still weak from the exertions of the birth, had allowed herself to be talked into believing her husband.

She must have still looked a little dubious, though, as then Ted pointed out that his own elder brother Jessie was a gruff-looking giant with huge arms and legs, and nobody had ever dared tease him about his name. It was going to be just the same for their newborn son, Ted promised.

Big Jessie (as Ted's brother had become known since the birth of his nephew) was in charge of the maintenance of several riverboats on the River Thames, Ted working alongside him, and Big Jessie, with his massive bulk, could single-handedly fill virtually all of the kitchen hearth in his and his wife Val's modest terraced house that backed on to the Bermondsey street where Ted and Barbara raised their children in their own, almost identical red-brick house.

Barbara could see why nobody in their right mind would mess with Big Jessie, even though those who knew him soon discovered that his bruiser looks belied his gentle nature as he was always mild of manner and slow to anger, with a surprisingly soft voice.

Sadly, it had proved to be a whole different story for young Jessie, who had turned out exactly as Barbara had suspected he would all those years ago when she lovingly gazed down at her newborn twins, with the hale and hearty Connie (named after Barbara's mother Constance) dwarfing her more delicate-framed brother as they lay length to length with their toes almost touching and their heads away from each other in the beautifully crafted wooden crib Ted had made for the babies to sleep in.

These days, Barbara could hardly bear to see how cruelly it all played out on the grubby streets on which the Ross family lived. To say it fair broke Barbara's heart was no exaggeration.

While Connie was tall, tomboyish and could easily pass for twelve, and very possibly older, Jessie was smaller and more introverted, often looking a lot younger than he was.

Barbara hated the way Jessie would shrink away from the bigger south-east London lads when they tussled him to the ground in their roughhouse games. All the boys had their faces rubbed in the dirt by the other lads at one time or another – Barbara knew and readily accepted that that was part and parcel of a child's life in the tangle of narrow and dingy streets they knew so well – but very few people had to endure quite the punishing that Jessie did with such depressing regularity.

Connie would confront the vindictive lads on her brother's behalf, her chin stuck out defiantly as she dared them to take her on instead. If the boys didn't immediately back away from Jessie, she blasted in their direction an impressive slew of swear words that she'd learnt by dint of hanging around on the docks when she took Ted his lunch in the school holidays. (It was universally agreed amongst all the local boys that when Connie was in a strop, it was wisest to do what she wanted, or else it was simply asking for trouble.)

Meanwhile, as Connie berated all and sundry, Jessie would freeze with a cowed expression on his face, and look as if he wished he were anywhere else but there. Needless to say, it was with a ferocious regularity that he found himself at the mercy of these bigger, stronger rowdies.

Usually this duffing-up happened out of sight of any grown-ups and, ideally, Connie. But the times Barbara spied what was going on all she wanted to do was to run over and take Jessie in her arms to comfort him and promise him it would be all right, and then keep him close to her as she led him back inside their home at number five Jubilee Street. However, she knew that if she even once gave into this impulse, then kind and placid Jessie would never live it down, and he would remain the butt of everyone's poor behaviour for the rest of his childhood.

Barbara loved Connie, of course, as what mother wouldn't be proud of such a lively, proud, strong-minded daughter, with her distinctive and lustrous tawny hair, clear blue eyes and strawberry-coloured lips, and her constant stream of chatter? (Connie was well known in the Ross family for being rarely, if ever, caught short of something to say.)

Nevertheless, it was Jessie who seemed connected to the essence of Barbara's inner being, right to the very centre of her. If Barbara felt tired or anxious, it wouldn't be long before Jessie was at her side, shyly smiling up to comfort his mother with his warm, endearingly lopsided grin.

Barbara never really worried about Connie, who seemed pretty much to have been born with a slightly defiant jib to her chin, as if she already knew how to look after herself or how to get the best from just about any situation. But right from the start Jessie had been much slower to thrive and to walk, although he'd always been good with his sums and with reading, and he was very quick to pick up card games and puzzles.

If Barbara had to describe the twins, she would say that Connie was smart as a whip, but that Jessie was the real thinker of the family, with a curious mind underneath which still waters almost certainly ran very deep.

Unfortunately in Bermondsey during that dog-end of summer in 1939, the characteristics the other local children rated in one another were all to do with strength and cunning and stamina.

For the boys, being able to run faster than the girls when playing kiss chase was A Very Good Thing.

Jessie had never beaten any of the boys at running, and most of the girls could hare about faster than him too.

It was no surprise therefore, thought Barbara, that Jessie had these days to be more or less pushed out of the front door to go and play with the other children, while Connie would race to be the first of the gang outside and then she'd be amongst the last to return home in the evening.

Although only born five minutes apart, they were chalk and cheese, with Connie by far and away the best of any of the children at kiss chase, whether it be the hunting down of a likely target or the hurtling away from anyone brave enough to risk her wrath. Connie was also brilliant at two-ball, skipping, knock down ginger and hopscotch, and in fact just about any playground game anyone could suggest they play.

Jessie was better than Connie in one area – he excelled at conkers, he and Connie getting theirs from a special tree in Burgess Park that they had sworn each other to secrecy over and sealed with a blood pact, with the glossy brown conkers then being seasoned over a whole winter and spring above the kitchen range. Sadly, quite often Jessie would have to yield to bigger children who would demand with menace that his conkers be simply handed over to them, with or without the benefit of any sham game.

Ted never tried to stop Barbara being especially kind to Jessie within the privacy of their own home, provided the rest of the world had been firmly shut outside. But if – and this didn't happen very often, as Barbara already knew what would be said – she wanted to talk to her husband about Jessie and his woes, and how difficult it was for him to make proper friends, Ted would reply that he felt differently about their son than she.

'Barbara, love, it's doing 'im no favours if yer try to fight 'is battles for 'im. I was little at 'is age, an' yer jus' look a' me now' – Ted was well over six foot with tightly corded muscles on his arms and torso, and Barbara never tired of running her hands over his well-sculpted body when they were tucked up in their bed at night with the curtains drawn tight and the twins asleep – 'an' our Jessie'll be fine if we jus' 'elp 'im deal with the bullies. Connie's got the right idea, and in time 'e'll learn from 'er too. An' there'll be a time when our Jessie'll come into his own, jus' yer see if I'm not proved correct, love.'

Barbara really hoped that her husband was right. But she doubted it was going to happen any time soon. And until then she knew that inevitably sweet and open-hearted Jessie would be enduring a pretty torrid time of it.

Still, on this pleasant evening in the first week of September, as a played-out and shamefully grubby Connie and Jessie headed back towards their slightly battered blue front door in Jubilee Street, the only thing a stranger might note about them to suggest they were twins was the way their long socks had bunched in similar concertinas above their ankles, and that they had very similar grey smudges on their knees from where they had been kneeling in the dust of the yard in front of where the local dairy stabled the horses that would pull the milk carts with their daily deliveries to streets around Bermondsey and Peckham.

As the twins walked side by side, their shoulders occasionally bumping and two sets of jacks making clinking sounds as they jumbled against each other in the pockets of Jessie's grey twill shorts, the children agreed that their tea felt as if it had been a very long time ago. Although the bread and beef dripping yummily sprinkled with salt and pepper that they'd snaffled down before going out to play had been lovely, and despite Barbara having seemed quiet and snappy, which was very unlike her, by now they were starving again and so they were hoping that they'd be allowed to have seconds when they got in.

They'd only been playing jacks this evening, but Connie had organised a knock-out tournament, and there'd been seven teams of four so it had turned into quite an epic battle. Connie had been the adjudicator and Jessie the scorekeeper, keeping his tally with a pencil-end scrounged from the dairy foreman who'd also then given Jessie a piece of paper to log the teams as Jessie had thanked him so nicely for the inch-long stub of pencil.

The reason the jacks tournament had turned into a hotly contested knock-out affair was that Connie had managed to cadge a bag of end-of-day broken biscuits from a kindly warehouseman at the Peek Freans biscuit factory over on Clements Road – the warehouseman being a regular at The Jolly Shoreman and therefore on nodding acquaintance with Ted and Big Jessie – as a prize for the winning team. These Connie had saved in their brown paper bag so that

Jessie could present them to the winning four, who turned out to be the self-named Thames Tinkers German Bashers.

As the game of jacks had gone on, every time Jessie had peeked over at the paper bag containing the biscuits that his sister had squirrelled close to her side (once, he fancied that he even caught a whiff of the enticing sugary aroma), his mouth had watered even though he knew the warehouseman had only given them to Connie as they were going a bit stale and had missed the day's run of broken biscuits being delivered to local shops so that thrifty, headscarved housewives would later be able to buy them at a knock-down rate.

Jessie knew that Connie had wanted him to present the biscuits to the winning team as a way of subtly ingratiating himself with the jacks players, without her having to say anything in support of her brother. She was a wonderful sister to have on one's side, Jessie knew, and he would have felt even more lost and put upon if he didn't have her in his corner.

Still, it had only been a couple of days since he had begged Connie to keep quiet on his behalf from now on, following an exceptionally unpleasant few minutes in the boys' lavatories at school when he had been taunted mercilessly by Larry, one of the biggest pupils in his class, who'd called Jessie a scaredy-cat and then some much worse names for letting his sister speak out for him.

Larry had then started to push Jessie about a bit, although Jessie had quite literally been saved by the bell. It had rung to signal the end of morning playtime and so with a final, well-aimed shove, Larry had screwed his face into a silent snarl to show his reluctance to stop his torment just at that moment, and at last he let Jessie go.

Jessie was left panting softly as he watched an indignant Larry leave, his dull-blond cowlick sticking up just as crossly as Larry was stomping away.

To comfort himself Jessie had remembered for a moment the time his father had spoken to him quietly but with a tremendous sense of purpose, looking deep into Jessie's eyes and speaking to him with the earnest tone that suggested he could almost be a grown-up. 'Son, you're a great lad, and I really mean it. Yer mam an' Connie know that too, and all three o' us can't be wrong, now, can we? And so all you's got to do now is believe it yerself, and those lads'll then quit their blatherin'. An' I promise you – I absolutely promise you – that'll be all it takes.'

Jessie had peered back at his father with a serious expression. He wanted to believe him, really he did. But it was very difficult and he couldn't ever seem able to work out quite what he should do or say to make things better.

Back at number five Jubilee Street following the jacks tournament, the twins wolfed down their second tea, egg-in-a-cup with buttered bread this time, and then Barbara told them to have a strip wash to deal with their filthy knees and grime-embedded knuckles.

Although she made sure their ablutions were up to scratch, Barbara was nowhere near as bright and breezy as she usually was.

Even Connie, not as a matter of course massively

observant of what her parents were up to, noticed that their mother seemed preoccupied and not as chatty as usual, and so more than once the twins caught the other's eye and shrugged or nodded almost imperceptibly at one another.

An hour later Connie's deep breathing from her bed on the other side of the small bedroom the twins shared let Jessie know that his sister had fallen asleep, and Jessie tried to allow his tense muscles to relax enough so that he could rest too, but the scary and dark feeling that was currently softly snarling deep down beneath his ribcage wouldn't quite be quelled.

He had this feeling a lot of the time, and sometimes it was so bad that he wouldn't be able to eat his breakfast or his dinner.

However, this particular bedtime Jessie wasn't quite sure why he felt so strongly like this, as actually he'd had a good day, with none of the lads cornering him or seeming to notice him much (which was fine with Jessie), and the game of jacks ended up being quite fun as he'd been able to make the odd pun that had made everyone laugh when he had come to read out the team names.

As he tried willing himself to sleep – counting sheep never having worked for him – Jessie could hear Ted and Barbara talking downstairs in low voices, and they sounded unusually serious even though Jessie could only hear the hum of their conversation rather than what they were actually saying.

Try as he might, Jessie couldn't pick out any mention of his own name, and so he guessed that for once his parents weren't talking about him and how useless he had turned out to be at standing up for himself. He supposed that this was all to the good, and after what seemed like an age he was able to let go of his usual worries so that at long last he could drift off.

Chapter Two

When the children had been smaller, Ted and Big Jessie had met a charismatic firebrand of a left-wing rabble-rouser called David, and eventually he had talked the brothers into going to several political meetings in the East End aimed at convincing the audience of the need for working-class men to band together to form a socialist uprising. A lot of the talk had been of fascists, and the political situation in Spain and Germany.

It wasn't long before Ted and Big Jessie had been persuaded to go with members of the group to protest against Oswald Mosley's Blackshirts' march through Cable Street in Whitechapel, although the brothers had retreated when the mood turned nasty and rocks were pelted about and there were running battles between the left- and right-wing supporters and the police.

Ted, naturally an easy-going sort, hadn't gone to another meeting of the socialists, and within a few months David had left to go to Spain to fight on the side of the Republicans.

Still, his tolerant nature didn't mean that Ted would always nod along down at The Jolly Shoreman whenever (and this had been happening quite often in recent months) a patron seven sheets to wind would suggest that any fascist supporters should be strung up high. He didn't like what fascists believed in but, deep down, Ted believed they were people too, and who really had the right to insist how other people thought?

But in recent weeks Ted had had to think more seriously about what he believed in, and how far he might be prepared to go to protect his beliefs, and his family.

As he was a docker, working alongside Big Jessie on the riverboats that spent a lot of their time moving cargo locally between the various docks and warehouses on either side of the Thames, Ted had witnessed first-hand that the Government had been preparing for war for a while.

He'd seen an obvious stockpiling of munitions and other things a country going to war might need, such as medical supplies and various sorts of tinned or non-perishable foodstuffs that were now stacked waiting in warehouses. There'd also been a steady increase in new or reconditioned ships that were arriving at the docks and leaving soon afterwards with a variety of cargo.

And recently Prime Minister Neville Chamberlain had taken to the BBC radio to announce hostilities against Germany had been declared following their attack on Poland. His words had been followed within minutes by air-raid sirens sounding across London, causing an involuntary bolt of panic to shoot through ordinary Londoners. It was a false alarm but a timely suggestion of what was to come.

Understandably, the dark mood of desperation and foreboding as to what might be going to happen was hard to shake off, and during the evening of the day of Chamberlain's broadcast Ted and Barbara had knelt on the floor and clasped hands as they prayed together.

Scandalously, in these days when most people counted themselves as Church of England believers (or, as London was increasingly cosmopolitan, possibly of Jewish or Roman Catholic faiths), neither Ted nor Barbara, despite marrying in church and having had the twins christened when they were only a few months old, were regular churchgoers, and they had never done anything like this in their lives before.

But these were desperate times, and desperate measures were called for.

As they clambered up from their knees feeling as if the sound of the air-raid siren was still ringing in their ears, they took the decision not, just yet, to be wholly honest if either Connie or Jessie asked them a direct question about why all the grown-ups around them were looking so worried. They wouldn't yet disturb the children with talk of war and what that might mean.

The next day, when Connie mentioned the air-raid siren, Barbara explained away the sound of it by saying she wasn't absolutely certain but she thought it was almost definitely a dummy run for practising how to warn other boats to be careful if a large cargo ship ran aground on the tidal banks of the Thames, to which Connie nodded as if that was indeed very likely the case. Jessie didn't look so easily convinced but Barbara distracted him quickly by saying she wanted his help with a difficult crossword clue she'd not been able to fathom.

Although naturally both Ted and Barbara were very honest people, they could remember the Great War all too clearly, even though they had only been children when that war had been declared in 1914, and they could still recall vividly the terrible toll that had exacted on everyone, both those who had gone to fight and those who had remained at home.

This meant they felt that even though it would only be a matter of days, or maybe mere hours, before the twins had to be made aware of what was going on, the longer the innocence of childhood could be preserved for Connie and Jessie, as far as their parents were concerned, the kinder this would be.

Once Ted and Barbara started to speak with the children about Britain being at war, they knew there would be no going back.

Now that time was here.

Just before the children had arrived home from school, things had come to a head.

For schoolteacher Miss Pinkly had called at number five to deliver a typewritten note to Barbara and Ted from the headmaster at St Mark's Primary School.

When Barbara saw Susanne Pinkly at her door, immediately she felt an overpowering sense of despair.

Without the young woman having to say a word, Barbara knew precisely what was about to happen.

By the time that Ted came in after the twins had gone

to bed – Barbara not bringing up the topic of evacuation with Connie and Jessie beforehand as she wanted the children to be told only when Ted was present – Barbara was almost beside herself, having worked herself up into a real state.

Ted had just left a group of dockers carousing at The Jolly Shoreman. Ted wasn't much of a drinker, but he had gone over with Big Jessie for their usual two pints of best, which was a Thursday night ritual at 'the Jolly' for the brothers and their fellow dockers as the end of their hard-working week drew near.

Now that Ted saw Barbara standing lost and forlorn, looking whey-faced and somehow strangely pinched around the mouth, he felt sorry he hadn't headed home straight after he'd moored the last boat. No beer was worth more than being with his wife in a time of crisis, and to look at Barbara's tight shoulders, a crisis there was.

Barbara was standing in front of the kitchen sink slowly wrapping and unwrapping a damp tea towel around her left fist as she stared unseeing out of the window.

The debris of a half-prepared meal for her husband was strewn around the kitchen table, and it was the very first time in their married lives that Ted could ever remember Barbara not having cleared the table from the children's tea and then cooking him the proverbial meat and two veg that would be waiting ready for her to dish up the moment he got home. Normally Barbara would shuffle whatever she'd prepared onto a plate for him as he soaped and dried his hands, so that exactly as he came to sit down at the kitchen table she'd be placing his plate before him in a routine that had become well choreographed over the years since they had married.

'Barbara, love, whatever is the matter?' Ted said as he swiftly crossed the kitchen to stand by his wife. He tried to sound strong and calm, and very much as if he were the reliable backbone of the family, the sort of man that Barbara and the twins could depend on, no matter what.

Barbara's voice dissolved in pieces as she turned to look at her husband with quickly brimming eyes, and she croaked, 'Ted, read this,' as she waved in his direction the piece of paper that Miss Pinkly had left.

At least, that was what Ted thought she had said to him but Barbara's voice had been so faint and croaky that he wasn't completely sure.

Ted stared at it for a while before he was able to take in all that it said.

Dear Parent(s),

Please have your child(s) luggage ready Monday morning, fully labelled. If you live more than 15 minutes from the school, <u>(s)he must bring his case with him/her</u> on Monday morning.

<u>EQUIPMENT</u> (apart from clothes worn)
- Washing things – soap, towel
- Older clothes – trousers/skirt or dress
- Gym vest, shorts/skirt and plimsolls
- 6 stamped postcards

- Socks or stockings
- Card games
- Gas mask
- School hymn book
- Shirts/blouse
- Pyjamas, nightdress or nightshirt
- Pullover/cardigan
- Strong walking shoes
- Story or reading book
- Blanket

<u>ALL TO BE PROPERLY MARKED</u>

<u>FOOD</u> (for 1 or 2 days)
- ¼lb cooked meat
- 2 hard-boiled eggs
- ¼lb biscuits (wholemeal)
- Butter (in container)
- Knife, fork, spoon
- ¼lb chocolate
- ¼lb raisins
- 12 prunes
- Apples, oranges
- Mug (unbreakable)

Yours sincerely,
DAVID W. JONES
Headmaster, St Mark's Primary School,
Bermondsey

The whole of Connie and Jessie's school was to be evacuated, and this looked set to happen in only four days' time.

Her voice stronger, Barbara added glumly, 'I see they've forgotten to put toothbrush on the list.'

After a pause, she said, 'Susanne Pinkly told me that not even the headmaster knows where they will all be going yet, although it looks as if the school will be kept together as much as possible. Some of the teachers are going – those with no relatives anyway – but Mr Jones isn't, apparently, as St Mark's will have to share a school and it's unlikely they'll want two headmasters, and Miss Pinkly's not going to go with them either as her mother is in hospital with some sort of hernia and so Susanne needs to look after the family bakery in her mother's absence now that her brother Reece has already been given his papers.

'But the dratted woman kept saying again and again that all the parents are strongly advised to evacuate their children, and I couldn't think of anything to say back to her. I know she's probably right, but I don't want to be parted from our Connie and Jessie. Susanne Pinkly had with her a bundle of posters she's to put up in the windows of the local shops saying MOTHERS – SEND THEM OUT OF LONDON, and she waved them at me, and so I had to take a couple to give to Mrs Truelove for her to put up in the window and on the shop door. While the talk in the shop a couple of days ago made me realise that a mass evacuation was likely, now that it's here it feels bad, and I don't like it at all.'

Ted drew Barbara close to him, and with his mouth

close to her ear said gently, 'I think we 'ave to let 'em go. The talk in the Jolly was that it's not goin' to be a picnic 'ere, and we 'ave to remember that we're right where those Germans are likely to want to bomb because the docks will be – as our Big Jessie says – "strategic".'

They were quiet for a few moments while they thought about the implications of 'strategic'.

'I know,' said Barbara eventually in a very small voice. 'You're right.'

Ted grasped her to him more tightly.

They listened to the tick-tocking of the old wooden kitchen clock on the mantelpiece for an age, each lost in their own thoughts.

And then Ted said resolutely, 'We'll tell our Connie and Jessie at breakfast in the mornin'. They need to hear it from us an' not from their classmates, an' so we'll need to get 'em up a bit earlier. We must look on the bright side – to let them go will keep them safe, and with a bit of luck it'll all be over by Christmas and we can 'ave them 'ome with us again. 'Ome in Jubilee Street, right beside us, where they belong.'

Barbara hugged Ted back and then pulled the top half of her body away a little so that she could look at her husband's dear and familiar face. 'There is one good thing, which is that as you work on the river, you're not going to have to go away and leave me, although I daresay they'll move you to working on the tugs seeing how much you know about the tides.'

There was another pause, and then Barbara leant against his chest once more, adding in a voice so faint that it was little more than the merest of murmurs, 'I'm scared, Ted, I'm really scared.'

'We all are, Barbara love, an' anyone who says they ain't is a damned liar,' Ted said with conviction, as he drew her more tightly against him.

ONE PLACE. MANY STORIES

Bold, Innovative and
empowering publishing.

FOLLOW US ON:

@HQStories